She walked away from him, paused by the rambler in full bloom and turned to wave goodbye. A frightening lump came into his throat at the sight of her looking so lovely against the flowers but he managed to smile and wave in return. God! Was he turning into a romantic too? Heaven forbid. He'd the tour to lead. Money to make. Things to do. Things to do. Mr Fitch to get on side when he returned from the Far East. Sir Ralph to persuade. A campaign to organise. A whole new career to tend. But as he listened to Georgie crossing the gravel drive the other side of the gate he pondered the might-have been, which had now become the never-will-be.

Educated at a co-educational Quaker boarding school, Rebecca Shaw went on to qualify as a teacher of deaf children. After her marriage, she spent the ensuing years enjoying bringing up her family. The departure of the last of her four children to university has given her the time and opportunity to write. Her latest novel in paperback in the highly popular Tales from Turnham Malpas series is *Whispers in the Village*. Her latest hardback novel, *A Village Feud*, is also available from Orion. Visit her website at www.rebeccashaw.co.uk.

By Rebecca Shaw

A Village Dilemma

Rebecca Shaw

An Orion paperback

First published in Great Britain in 2002
by Orion
This paperback edition published in 2002
by Orion Books Ltd,
Orion House, 5 Upper St Martin's Lane,
London WC2H 9EA

Reissued 2005

A CIP catalogue record for this book is available
from the British Library.

Typeset by Deltatype Ltd, Birkenhead, Merseyside
Printed and bound in Great Britain by
Clays Ltd, St Ives plc

The Orion Publishing Group's policy is to use papers that
are natural, renewable and recyclable products and
made from wood grown in sustainable forests. The logging
and manufacturing processes are expected to conform to
the environmental regulations of the country of origin.

www.orionbooks.co.uk

INHABITANTS OF TURNHAM MALPAS

Nick Barnes	Veterinary surgeon
Roz Barnes	Nurse
Willie Biggs	Verger at St Thomas à Becket
Sylvia Biggs	His wife and housekeeper at the Rectory
Sir Ronald Bissett	Retired Trade Union leader
Lady Sheila Bissett	His wife
James (Jimbo) Charter-Plackett	Owner of the Village Store
Harriet Charter-Plackett	His wife
Fergus, Finlay, Flick and Fran	Their children
Katherine Charter-Plackett	Jimbo's mother
Alan Crimble	Barman at the Royal Oak
Linda Crimble	Runs the post office at the Village Store
Georgie Fields	Licensee at the Royal Oak
H. Craddock Fitch	Owner of Turnham House
Jimmy Glover	Taxi driver
Mrs Jones	A village gossip
Vince Jones	Her husband
Barry Jones	Her son and estate carpenter
Pat Jones	Barry's wife
Dean and Michelle	Barry and Pat's children

Revd Peter Harris MA (Oxon)	Rector of the parish
Dr Caroline Harris	His wife
Alex and Beth	Their children
Jeremy Mayer	Manager at Turnham House
Venetia Mayer	His wife
Neville Neal	Accountant and church treasurer
Liz Neal	His wife
Guy and Hugh	Their children
Tom Nicholls	Retired businessman
Evie Nicholls	His wife
Anne Parkin	Retired secretary
Kate Pascoe	Village school head teacher
Sir Ralph Templeton	Retired from the diplomatic service
Lady Muriel Templeton	His wife
Dicky Tutt	Scout leader and bar-manager at The Royal Oak
Bel Tutt	School caretaker and assistant in the Village Store
Don Wright	Maintenance engineer (now retired)
Vera Wright	Cleaner at the nursing home in Penny Fawcett
Rhett Wright	Their grandson

A Village Dilemma

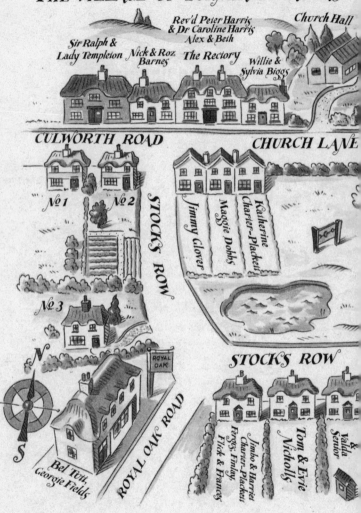

THE VILLAGE OF TURNHAM MALPAS

Church Hall

Rev'd Peter Harris
& Dr Caroline Harris
Alex & Beth

Sir Ralph &
Lady Templeton
Nick & Roz
Barnes
The Rectory
Willie &
Sylvia Biggs

CULWORTH ROAD

CHURCH LANE

No 1
No 2

STOCKS ROW

Jimmy Glover
Maggie Dobbs
Katherine
Charter-Plackett

No 3

ROYAL
OAK

STOCKS ROW

N
S

ROYAL OAK ROAD

Bel Tutt,
Georgie Fields

Jimbo & Harriet
Charter-Plackett
Fergus, Finlay,
Flick & Frances
Tom & Evie
Nicholls
Valda
Senior
&

Chapter 1

Jimbo, observing the growing crowd collecting in Church Lane, said, 'Harriet! What am I doing dressed like this?'

'Enjoying participating in village life.'

'I'm not, though. I feel an absolute idiot.'

Harriet appraised his appearance, taking in the dishevelled wig she'd insisted he wore, the old leather sandals long abandoned by him at the back of his wardrobe and, most genuine-looking of all, the scratchy, brown, muddied shift affair she'd crafted out of a length of hessian she'd found at a sale. 'Actually, you look very peasantlike. I'm quite proud of you. Especially your tights.'

Jimbo inspected the thick brown tights he wore. 'Proud?' He turned to look at her and, noting the twinkle in her eyes, couldn't help himself laughing. 'OK. OK. Point taken. Why I ever allowed myself to be dressed up I'll never know.'

'Because you're a darling and a sucker for country ways.'

'No, it's because you can twist me round your little finger, that's why.'

'Never once have you joined in the parade, you always find an excuse for being busy, busy, busy behind the counter and not participating; well, this year you are, so

1

cheer up. Oh, look! There's the twins. Suddenly they look so grown-up.' Harriet waved to Beth and Alex. 'Come and walk with us, or the girls are up at the front if you prefer.'

Alex spoke for both of them. 'We'll join the girls, thanks.' Instead of leading Beth by the hand as he'd done since the day they could both walk, Alex gave her a push in the direction of the head of the procession, and she willingly accepted his decision and followed him.

Harriet watched the two of them press their way forwards. 'Strange how Beth is really the more outgoing of the two and yet she accepts Alex's lead without a murmur. Can't believe the two of them will be leaving the village school next year. Doesn't seem two minutes since they were born.'

'The piper's tuning up. Am I ready for this? No, I am not.'

'Yes, you are.' Harriet grinned at Jimbo's discomfort. 'Right! Here we go. I get all primeval and go like jelly inside when I'm doing this. Maintaining a six-hundred-year tradition really makes me feel as though I *belong*. Doesn't it you?'

Jimbo considered how he felt. 'I suppose. But I do feel a complete idiot.'

Movement began at the head of the procession, the piper, at the very front, began to play a melancholy tune on his ancient silver flute and they all started to move off towards the village green with Jimbo still feeling all kinds of an idiot.

Into view, as they reached the green, came the stocks covered to the very top with dead flowers. Standing beside it was the Rector dressed in his devil's costume, the horns

2

on his headgear glinting in the bright June sun. There came an eager mumble as soon as the dozens of sightseers gathered in front of the houses surrounding the green caught sight of them. The press were there in force, as always, and Jimbo desperately hoped that they wouldn't recognise the urbane, stylish, man-of-the-world Store owner, seeing as he wasn't wearing his striped apron and his straw boater. The wig was beginning to itch his bald head. Surreptitiously he scratched as best he could without disturbing the damn thing. God! It irritated him. Why had he ever allowed himself . . . but now, having walked all the way round the green, it was his turn to beat the dead flowers off the stocks. He surprised himself by beating the living daylights out of them and suddenly he was a village peasant angered by the vagrant who had brought the plague to the village and thus killed all his children, or his wife, or his mother. He looked up at the Rector as he straightened himself and saw one of his bright-blue eyes close swiftly in a wink. Jimbo grinned back. So at least, maybe, Peter was participating with his tongue in his cheek, as indeed any sane member of a twenty-first-century village must. Although . . .

Harriet thrust his bunch of fresh flowers into his hand. He glanced at her and saw with surprise how distressed she was. 'Darling!'

'It all seems so real, Jimbo. So real. God! Just think how you would feel if you really had lost . . .' Tears sprang into her eyes.

'I know, I know . . .' And he did. But his two girls were up at the front with the other village children, his two sons at Cambridge and beside him was his beloved Harriet, and his mother was somewhere in the procession, no doubt

3

beating the dead flowers from the stocks with her usual gusto as though her ancestors had been born and bred here for centuries. Thankful that he'd had the foresight to move his family from London and that blasted rat race, Jimbo stepped smartly round the green for the second time, his flowers clutched tightly in his hand. When he reached the stocks he saw Peter was divesting himself of his devil's costume and was revealing the white cassock he wore only today, Stocks Day, and when conducting weddings. Jimbo placed his fresh flowers on the stocks to symbolise a new beginning, a laying aside of death and destruction. The plague had finally gone. Death had been beaten.

Peter's prayer of thanksgiving for the survival of the village and his blessing of everyone taking part rang out across the green, the long, mournful dirge of the piper subtly changed to a lively, bouncing tune, signalling that the villagers could feel safe from disaster for yet another year.

Cameras flashed, voices called out, 'Look this way.'

'That's right.'

'One more! You two stand together. That's it.'

'One more! One more!'

Jimbo obliged, his wig askew, his hessian costume now also itching like fury, but a bright, relieved smile on his face brought on by doing his bit like everyone else.

'Your name? Your name?' Looking more closely when he didn't get an immediate reply the photographer said, 'Oh! It's you, Mr Charter-Plackett, didn't recognise you.'

Inwardly Jimbo groaned; his reputation had just bitten the dust well and truly. Grumpily he said to Harriet, 'I'm not wearing this for the rest of the afternoon, you know. I'm going home to change.'

'Spoilsport.'

'This wig is flea-ridden.'

'It never is.'

'It is. It itches.'

But Harriet's attention was elsewhere. 'Jimbo, look! I could swear that's Bryn Fields over there.'

'Where?'

'Over there by the oak. His back's to us, but I'm sure it's him. Well, that's a turn-up for the books. How many years is it since he did his moonlight flit?'

'You're imagining things. He'd never dare come back, not after what happened.'

Harriet stood on tiptoe. 'I'm sure it is. He's turned round. Look, there! There! Talking to Willie Biggs.'

'Nonsense! That chap hasn't a flying officer's moustache like Bryn had.'

'It's very like him even so. He's very tanned, which he would be, wouldn't he, if what they say is true.'

'Maybe he has a brother. I'm going home to change.'

'I'm not. I never do. I'm going to the fair with our children and then having my tea on the green like all self-respecting villagers.'

'I'll check the Store, give a hand and come along for tea when I see the tables out.'

Harriet, still agog at the prospect she might be right about Bryn Fields, didn't notice that Jimbo was looking at her. She ignored the jostling by the crowds too as they pushed past to get to the spare land where the annual joys of the fair awaited them, and tried to keep her eye on that tall, distant figure. She was certain it was him. It must be. She became aware of Jimbo and glanced at him to see why he was still there. Raising her eyebrows she said, 'What is it?'

'This Stocks Day thing must be getting at me. I'm so grateful I still have you.' Despite the hustle and bustle of the crowd he kissed her.

'Oh! It has got to you, hasn't it? It always does to me. Glad you joined in?'

Jimbo nodded, smiled and went home, feeling gratified deep down that he'd done his bit for the village. He shook his head. What was he thinking of? How could beating dead flowers from the churchyard off the stocks and then heralding a new beginning by laying fresh flowers there possibly have any effect on anything at all, especially when the plague had died out years ago? How could a rational, educated man, an entrepreneur, a man of means, a man getting ahead in the world believe in such a thing? No, not *getting*, he *was* ahead. His chest swelled at the thought. He pushed his key into the front door with pride. Nothing, but nothing would stop further successes this year. He'd just seen to that by doing what he'd done.

He took the precaution of standing in the bath while he undressed and left his clothes and his wig soaking in it in hot water and disinfectant, just in case. The Store was extremely busy when he got there and he had to stay to help. They were selling everything from rolls of film to fresh fruit, from sweets to sticking plasters. Mentally Jimbo rubbed his hands with glee; this was how it should be, the till whirring itself silly and his special bell jingling joyfully each time the door opened. He became lost in the clamour and forgot to look out on to the green for when the open-air tea was ready, but he wasn't allowed to forget for Flick and Fran came bursting through the door shouting, 'Daddy! We're saving you a seat! Come on!'

They were so alike, these two. Seven years between them and Fran looked like a miniature of Flick, but even so he had to admit in his heart that Fran was by far the most beautiful of the two. But Flick! So grown-up now. A woman, no less, at just fifteen.

'Coming! OK, Bel? Back in half an hour. Right.'

Bel, at the till, smiled her beautiful relaxed smile, which lit up the whole of her face. 'Fine. See you. Next! That'll be two pounds twenty-nine. Thank you. Have a nice day. Next!'

Jimbo spared a thought for her as he crossed Stocks Row to take his place beside Harriet and the girls on the wooden benches borrowed from the church hall. Dear Bel. So willing but he always felt that at the heart of her she was very lonely. Some people got dealt rotten cards where life was concerned.

A large area of the green had been covered with trestle tables and benches, and every place was taken. The tables, half an hour ago laden with plates of food, were being rapidly cleared. One could almost have thought that the villagers had purposely not eaten anything all week. The simple old wooden benches they all sat on added to the illusion that it was the day six hundred years ago when the entire village had sat down to celebrate their victory over the plague, but then there would have been far fewer people for they had been decimated by the disease. Some families were entirely wiped out, in others only the most robust were left to tell the tale.

He sat between Flick and Fran, and ate a hearty tea. He sank his strong white teeth into a sausage roll, ate a slice of

7

quiche – the cheese and broccoli one which was the most popular on his delicatessen counter – he munched his way through a ham sandwich, the flavour of which he definitely recognised, and finished it all off with a hefty slice of Harriet's special mail order fruit cake. Jimbo washed it down with a mug of cider, then sat back to survey the scene.

It never ceased to amaze him that this quiet backwater could galvanise itself into such incredible activity on special days. They might have television and mobile phones and e-mail but they were still a centuries-old village at heart. Even the ones the villagers disparagingly called the 'weekenders' made sure they were down for the weekend when anything special was on. He looked across at the old oak tree, still coming into full leaf each spring as though five hundred years of doing it were a mere nothing in the span of time. Jimbo had to admit to himself he loved the old place.

'Daddy!'

Jimbo roused himself to answer Fran. 'Mm?'

'Daddy,' she whispered. 'Is Mummy my mummy?'

'Of course she is. Why do you ask that?'

'Beth asked me if she was. I said she was but I wanted to be sure.'

Realising he was on delicate ground, Jimbo answered cautiously but positively, 'Well, you are, definitely.'

'I'm not borrowed, then?'

'No. You are not.'

'She's my real mummy, then. I grew in her tummy?'

'Yes, darling, you did.'

'Good.' Fran picked up her drink, finished it right to

the bottom and said with a nod of her head towards the fair, 'Right, then. Come on, Flick, you promised.'

Flick raised her eyes to the heavens. 'All right, then. But this is the last time. I never get a chance to be with *my* friends, I'm always looking after you. One ride, that's all, because we've spent almost all the money Mum gave us.'

Jimbo winked at her and gave her a five-pound note.

Fran's bottom lip trembled. 'You've got to look after me, haven't you? You are my sister, aren't you?'

'And don't I know it. Thanks, Dad.' With a sigh Flick swung her legs over the bench and dashed to catch up with Fran already zigzagging her way through the crowds to the roundabout.

Harriet waited until they were out of hearing and then said quietly to Jimbo, 'Whoops! That sounds like one ten-year-old girl we know is asking about her parentage and desperately wants to know. Must be those sex lessons they've been having at the school.'

'Poor Beth.'

'And poor Alex, too. One might be tempted to quote "Be sure your sins will find you out".'

'Harriet!'

'Well, let's hope Peter comes up with something to explain it all.'

'Have they never been told, then?'

'Not the whole truth. I understand they know Caroline couldn't have children so she's not their real mother, but as for the rest . . .'

'Well, watch out, you may be getting some questions too.'

'I can't tell our girls the truth before Peter and Caroline have told the twins, can I?'

Jimbo accepted another glass of cider from the vast earthenware jug one of the helpers was hoping to empty before clearing up and said, 'No, definitely not. I'm going, Bel will be at the end of her tether.' He sank his cider at one go and squeezed his thickset frame off the bench.

'So am I. I feel quite queasy after going on the roundabout and then eating a big tea. I'll come and help in the Store, but I'd better go home to change first. I'll catch up with you.'

As they made their way to the Store, Harriet glanced up Stocks Row before they crossed and was sure she saw Bryn Fields again, walking down Church Lane. But it couldn't be him now, could it? Still open to a charge of attempted murder, he wouldn't dare show his face, would he?

Always hectic on a normal summer Saturday evening, Stocks Night usually beat all the records in the bar of the Royal Oak. There weren't enough chairs to seat everybody inside, so many of the customers were sprawled on the green or luxuriating on the garden furniture that Georgie in her wisdom had placed in a new outside garden made from a section of the car park. Hedged about as they were on the new fashionable green chairs by the excess of cars, her customers still managed to enjoy the late evening sun.

Willie Biggs wrinkled his nose at the smell of fumes from the exhaust of a car, which had just sidled into a vacant space too close to his table for comfort. 'This new idea of Georgie's would be all right if we didn't have these 'ere cars so close.'

Sylvia knew he liked nothing better than a good

grumble but decided the day had been too good to be spoiled by one of Willie's grumbling sessions. 'Come on, Willie! Don't grouse. It's been a great day, the sun's shining and we're breathing God's good air.'

'No, we're not, we're breathing His air made foul by man.'

'Oh, dear! We are in a mood.'

Willie looked into her laughing grey eyes and gave her half a smile. 'I am. I'm worried sick.'

Sylvia studied his thin, lined face and noted the stern set of his lantern jaw, and wondered what petty irritation had brought on such gloom. 'Tell me. I expect it's all something and nothing.'

'You wouldn't say that if you'd spoken to who I spoke to this afternoon.'

Sylvia, alerted by his tantalising statement, sat up and leaned towards him saying, 'Who?'

Willie took another sip of his ale before he replied. 'Someone who I thought we would never see again.'

'Well, who, then? Not Kenny Jones come back?'

Willie shook his head.

'Terry Jones?'

'No. Someone closer to where we are now.'

'Not Betty MacDonald?'

'You're getting close. You're on the right lines.'

'I can't think of anyone else who might . . . not poor old henpecked Mac?'

'Close.'

Finally Sylvia grew tired of the guessing game and gave him a shove on his shoulder. 'Tell me, then.'

Willie glanced around to check no one was within hearing and whispered in her ear, 'Bryn Fields.'

Sylvia's mouth dropped open with shock. 'Get on. You're pulling my leg.'

Willie flatly denied any such thing.

When finally she got her voice back Sylvia said loudly, '*Bryn Fields!*'

'Sh! They'll hear.'

'But . . . you couldn't have. He wouldn't dare.'

'Well, he has. Large as life.'

'I didn't see him.'

'You didn't see a lot of folk, seeing as you were in the church hall helping with the catering. But I did. I spoke to 'im.' He leaned back again in his chair enjoying taking centre stage with his piece of hot news.

'What had he to say for himself, then?'

'He was miffed, he hadn't realised it was Stocks Day.'

'I'd have liked to see him. So what's he like after . . . what . . . four – or is it five years since he disappeared? Did he say why he'd come back?'

Willie shook his head. 'Tanned, he is, and you'll never guess what!' He sipped his ale again to prolong his moment.

'What?'

'He's shaved his moustache off.'

'Never. Well, I don't know, he won't be the same without it. Anyway, I don't suppose he'll hang around long. No one will want him.'

'Oh, he will. He's staying at Neville Neal's.'

'Neville Neal's! That figures. They're both trouble-makers. They make a pair. Well, we don't get far but we do see life as they say. Bryn Fields! Well I never.'

'So now you can see why I'm worried.'

Sylvia thought over the possibilities for trouble. Counting them off on her fingers she said, 'Georgie, for a start, though at least she might get a divorce at last, and then Dicky can make an honest woman of her. Dicky! My good heavens! He'll be frightened to death. Poor Dicky. The Rector won't take kindly to it either, considering the problems Bryn caused.'

'With his temper, we'd better all look out. I never look up the church tower without thinking about poor Dicky coming close to being pushed off the top. It's a bloody long way down.'

Sylvia shuddered. 'Oo! Don't remind me.' She shuddered again. 'I can't think why he's here. Maybe it's to make things straight for Georgie. He did love her, you know. He really did. I expect that Elektra was more fun to run away with but only for the moment. But she'd never stay . . . She's not with him, is she?'

'Not so far as I know. I don't think even Neville Neal would want a tart staying, not with his two lusty boys.'

'Willie! What a thing to say. Anyway, there's one thing for certain. He won't dare show his face in here.'

Willie stood up, holding his empty glass. ''Nother one?'

'Yes, please. See if there's a table free inside, it's starting to get cold out here.'

'OK.'

Well, Bryn Fields. Of all people. She remembered the madness in his eyes when they finally got him down from the church tower and the rage in every shaking limb. Like something out of a film on telly, that was. What a mess there'd have been if he really had pushed Dicky over. Smashed to smithereens he'd have been, even though he was only the size of a jockey. Sylvia didn't like the idea of never hearing Dicky's cheerful voice again or not seeing his jolly laughing face; nothing ever fazed him . . . Well, except when he was white as a sheet and sweating buckets being helped down the spiral stairs. How he ever got down . . .

Willie caught her eye, signalling to her to come in. She picked up his jacket and went in, to find him already seated at their favourite table. 'Dicky's giving one of his comic turns in five minutes.'

'Oh, good! I could do with a bit of cheering up.'

Dicky Tutt, a sprightly little man, pillar of the Church Scout Troop and the light of Georgie's heart, stepped from behind the bar at precisely ten p.m., pushed a couple of tables closer together to make a space, clapped his hands and started his Saturday night comic turn.

'Good evening, ladies and gentlemen. I won't say anything at all about what a wonderful day we've had, the sun in the right place and a happy, busy day for all of us. Nor will I mention how wonderful the tea was, provided as usual by the ladies of the village and made possible by the great generosity of our esteemed Village Store owner, namely Jimbo Charter-Plackett, nor will I talk about the wonderful performance our Scout Band gave prior to the start of the procession. Whoever is in charge of those Scouts deserves . . .'

'Give it up, Dicky!'

'We've heard it all before . . .'

'Get a move on!'

Dicky laughed and began a story about the Royal Navy being billeted in a girls' school during World War Two. He had reached the climax with the line '. . . so this notice on the dormitory wall said "Please ring this bell if you need a mistress during the night . . ."' The roars of appreciation drowned the sound of the outside door opening. In fact, there was such a crowd standing by the door listening to Dicky that for a moment no one could see who'd come quietly through the open door as Dicky had begun his comic turn. It was only when the newcomer had pushed his way through the crowd to get to the bar and they saw Dicky's face had gone drip white that they all turned to see what was up.

He was a good six feet in height with dark hair going white at the temples and a well-tanned face with strong, severe features. He was wearing a smart tropical suit and sandals, which marked him out as someone from abroad.

Georgie looked across to see what had stopped the laughter so abruptly.

Someone coughed.

Someone gasped.

Someone said, 'Never.'

The man said jovially, 'Good evening, everyone' and, squeezing between the tables, went straight to the bar. 'Now, Georgie, busy as ever! I'll have a whisky on the rocks.'

Georgie out of habit automatically poured his drink and pushed it across the bar to him.

He tossed it back in one gulp, slid the glass back to her and asked for a refill. He didn't take his eyes from her but after the first recognition Georgie never once caught his eye.

'As lovely as ever.' Bryn shot the second whisky down and then, leaning his forearm nonchalantly on the bar top, surveyed the customers. 'Same old faces, too. Nothing changes. That's what's so good about this place, nothing changes. That's what I like.' He nodded to a few faces he recognised, then turned back to look at Georgie. 'Nothing to say to your dear husband come back to make things right?'

Georgie's face was no longer pretty; it was twisted and distorted by venom. In a voice totally unlike her own she snarled, 'How dare you! How dare you come back here, you nasty, thieving, no-good, cheating, lying womaniser. You're a thief! A no-good thief! Get out and get back under that stone you've just crawled out from under. Out! Out! Out!' To emphasise her point she banged her clenched fist on the counter and leant towards him.

The customers reacted as though she were about to spit in each of their faces. They recoiled as one.

But Bryn never flinched. 'My, you're lovely when you're in a temper.'

'You've seen nothing yet. Just go. I don't want you in here.'

'I see that obnoxious little tiddler is still sniffing around. I would have thought you'd have sent him off with a flea in his ear long ago.'

The little tiddler in question was keeping such a tight grip on his fear that he seemed to have reduced in size, if that were possible.

'Still telling his pathetic jokes and you're all still laughing at them I see.'

At this insult to his theatrical abilities Dicky flushed, the first sign of life in him since Bryn had walked in. All eyes were on him. He saw they were and it gave him strength.

He stalked stiffly across to stand in front of Bryn, and despite the cost to him and the terrible fear he felt at facing this monster who had come so close to killing him, drawing on reserves he didn't know he possessed he looked up at Bryn and said quietly, 'The licensee has asked you to leave. Git!'

'Oh! So now the little bantam cock has fluffed up his feathers, has he? Going to turn me out, eh? I don't think so.'

Keeping his eye on Bryn, Dicky said, 'Shall we ring for the police, Georgie?'

'No, no, that won't be necessary. We don't want them here. No. I'll leave the bar to you and Alan for half an hour. You come with me.' She beckoned Bryn, then disappeared without a backward glance through the door marked 'Private'. Bryn followed.

A collective sigh of disappointment flowed after them. But the door was shut firmly behind Bryn.

Georgie took him into their sitting room, which in Bryn's day had always had boxes of crisps and the like stacked in corners because it was used as an overflow from the stockroom. Now it was as elegant as it was possible to make a room at the back of a public house.

Georgie waited until he'd chosen a chair to sit in, then stood facing him. 'Well, what does all this mean? Not a word all this time and now you turn up. She's left you, has she?'

'Elektra's done very well for herself. Married a rich American self-made man. All money and no style. But he's besotted . . . for now. She'll get plenty of alimony; she'll be set up for life.'

'Bully for her.'

Bryn studied her face. 'The years don't show.'

'I'm happy, that's why.'

17

'Happy? Come on, Georgie! Happy! With that little squirt.'

'He has more love and consideration in his little finger than you have in all your great hulk. I've brought you in here, not because I wanted you here, but because I didn't want you showing him up with some sort of macho behaviour. He's been my strength, has Dicky, and I won't have him done down.'

Bryn stood up. 'I'll use the toilet if I may.'

She stood aside, knowing full well he was going to take the opportunity to take a look around the bedrooms. Georgie waited and smiled to herself as she heard his footsteps above her head. Outwardly she hoped she looked calm and in control, inwardly she was shaken to the core. He looked so different, so outgoing, so *positive*. She could hear him coming down the stairs and took the premier chair in the room to give her the upper hand when he returned. 'Satisfied?'

'Surprised.'

'He doesn't sleep here, you see.'

'Who does, then?'

'Bel Tutt.'

'You've had our bedroom done up and a single bed.'

Georgie nodded. 'Why not? Life doesn't stop because you've done a bunk. Anyway, since Dicky joined me as manager, profits have soared.'

'Right.'

'He does the books, orders the stock, serves behind the bar, keeps Alan under control, all with the lightest of touches. Such a pleasing man to work with, you see.'

'I see. And you two . . .' He jerked his elbow as though nudging someone and winked.

18

'That's my business. Nothing to do with you. What have you been up to?'

'Bar work on cruise liners. Then Elektra met this passenger and before I knew where I was she'd gone off with him.'

'That's why you've come home, is it?'

'No, it isn't. It's two years since she went. I have to confess she hadn't your style. Common, you know.'

Georgie burst out laughing. 'Surprised you didn't know that first off.'

Bryn enjoyed her delight even if she was laughing at him. He was doing better than he'd hoped. 'Devastated, I was, by that dwarf . . .'

Georgie wagged a stern finger at him. 'I've warned you. There'd have been no business to come back to if it wasn't for him.'

Bryn saw he was doing much much better than he'd hoped, but he wouldn't take her up on that for the moment, mustn't push his luck. 'I'm glad you had help. I didn't want you to go down.'

'You *shot* me down, taking all our money with you.'

Bryn looked suitably contrite. 'I didn't want to. Elektra saw a bank statement and argued that seeing as I was leaving you with a viable business I had a right to the money.'

'She's not just an ugly face, then.'

He had to smile at that. 'You're right. Without her warpaint she was damn ugly. Come to think of it, she was ugly *with* her warpaint on. God, what a sight.' He brooded for a moment on the image that had been Elektra, then looked at Georgie. She might be older, but she still had

19

that something special for him. 'I'm staying with Neville and Liz.'

'I see.'

'They invited me. I didn't realise it was Stocks Day. It still pulls the old heartstrings, doesn't it?'

'Didn't realise you still had a heart. Be frank. Why are you here?'

Too early yet to spill the beans.

Georgie wondered why he took so long to answer. 'Height of the cruise season so have they thrown you out for fiddling the till or something?'

'Got sick of it, to be honest.'

Georgie doubted that word honest, there was something behind this reappearance and she couldn't fathom what. He'd changed a lot since he'd left, become more of a man of the world, more . . . she couldn't put her finger on it. She stood up. 'I can't leave those two much longer and it's almost closing. Go out the back way.'

Bryn put his hand in his pocket and brought out the key to the back door. 'I've always kept it. Sentimental reasons, you know.'

He looked wistful, but Georgie didn't fall for it. 'That was a complete waste of time.'

'You mean you don't want me here.'

'In a nutshell. Out now, if you please, or I really will get the police.'

'All right, all right. You look good enough to eat.'

'Maybe, and it's flattering, but for now, hop it.'

As she was closing the back door after him she said, 'By the way, you might as well throw that key away, I've had all the locks changed.' After she'd bolted the door she stood leaning against it for support. Georgie's heart was racing. Thud. Thud. Thud. Why had that thieving, lying toad made her heart beat like this? He meant nothing to her at all. Nothing. But . . . there was something there which hadn't been in him before; a certain suaveness, a kind of polish. Shaving off his stupid greying moustache had definitely taken years from his age. She heard the door to the bar being opened cautiously. 'All right, Dicky, he's gone. I'm just coming.' It really was too cruel of Bryn to call Dicky a dwarf, he was a love and, more important, *her* love.

When 'time' was called the customers made a concerted rush to get out and spread the news. By Sunday morning the story of Bryn's surprising return had spread like wildfire through the village and to friends and relatives in the adjoining villages. Ancient rivalries between Turnham Malpas and Little Derehams surfaced, and there were scathing remarks passed about the notoriety of Turnham Malpas and an underlying envy that nothing of such a spectacular nature ever happened in Little Derehams. In Penny Fawcett the inhabitants made a note definitely to attend the Monday morning farmers' market in their village hall to hear the latest scandal direct from the lips of any of the Turnham Malpas people who regularly deserted Jimbo's Village Store on Mondays in search of home-grown food bargains.

The return of Bryn Fields kept everyone talking for more than a week. Wherever he went, whatever he did was the big talking point; the car he bought, the people he visited, the outrageous clothes he wore. But by the end of the week they were no wiser as to his reasons for being there than they had been when he'd first arrived.

21

Chapter 2

They all knew Bryn had been to see Willie Biggs on several occasions but no amount of treating him to a pint of his favourite ale in the Royal Oak, or confiding in him bits of news of their own to draw him forth, would make Willie tell what Bryn had been seeing him about. Some had even resorted to trying to get Sylvia to spill the beans but to no avail; she was as tight-lipped as he. More than one said, 'That's what comes of working at the Rectory. She's sworn to secrecy about who comes and goes, and now she can't let it out not even for a winning lottery ticket.'

A week to the day of Bryn's surprise arrival he appeared once more in the bar at the busiest time. Willie, gathered with his cronies at his favourite table, gave Sylvia a wink to warn her. Jimmy, downing his last pint before going out to do his Saturday stint with his taxi outside Culworth station, caught the wink midstream as it were and said slyly to no one in particular, 'Bryn keeps himself busy.'

Willie deliberately ignored his remark and said, 'Cricket team's doing well this season. Should be the top of the league if they keep it up.'

'Never mind about the blinking cricket team. What's going on?'

Willie took his time to answer. 'How should I know, he doesn't confide in me.'

'Oh, doesn't he? Well, why does he keep calling? Is he fancying Sylvia?'

Sylvia blushed right to the roots of her hair.

Willie made a fist and threatened Jimmy. 'One more word and that's what you'll be getting right between the eyes, make a right mess of that hawk nose of yours. Can no one do anything in this village without someone casting aspersions?'

'Aspersions! What have you done, swallowed a dictionary?'

'No, Jimmy Glover, I have not. Just let it drop.'

Sylvia muttered, 'Oh Lord, he's coming across.'

Bryn made his way over to them, carrying a loaded tray. 'Been some time since I had the pleasure of buying you all a drink. I hope after all this time I've remembered your favourite tipple. He put down the tray and the five of them inspected it. 'Orange juice for Don, gin and tonic for Vera, ale for Jimmy and Willie, and for you, Sylvia, a Martini and lemonade.'

'Martini, oh no! That's not me. I like a snowball; you know, advocaat and lemonade.'

Bryn groaned. 'Of course. Sorry. I'll have this and I'll get you a snowball. Does the dwarf know how to make one I ask myself?'

'That's cruel, Bryn. Don't call him that. We all like him,' Sylvia protested.

Jimmy interrupted by stoutly defending Dicky. 'He stood by Georgie and kept this pub going for her in the first few weeks after you hopped it. Thanks for the drink, I won't be so churlish as to refuse it but don't buy me another. I can buy my own.' He half turned his back to Bryn, clinked his glass with the others and sat brooding about whether he should be friendly with Bryn.

When he came back with Sylvia's snowball, Vera and Don thanked him graciously and, after a nudge from Don's knee under the table, Vera started up a conversation with Bryn with the positive intention of finding out why he'd come back. 'It's no good, I've got to come right out with it. We're all wondering why you've come back, Bryn.'

Bryn tapped the side of his nose with his forefinger. 'Ah! That would be telling and I'm not ready to say anything until my plans are all in place.'

'Plans! What kind of plans could you be having for this sleepy old place?'

'You all need waking up, there's no doubt about that. And I'm the man to do it. You wouldn't be averse to earning an extra bob or two, would you, Jimmy?'

'Might.'

'I'll call round then.'

'I might listen – then again, I might not.'

Bryn twisted round in his chair and shouted, 'Dicky! Same again over here, and don't hang about.'

'Don't order any more for me, I'm driving tonight.'

'One more won't harm, I'm sure.'

Jimmy's heavy-lidded eyes rested on Bryn's face. 'You won't soften me up, not even with a whole gallon of ale. I can't forget your behaviour before you left. It was only the Rector being so strong that prevented you from murdering Dicky. I don't know how the poor chap can bear you in the same room as him. Why you haven't gone to prison for it I'll never know. Anyway, time I was off.' Jimmy strode out, leaving behind him an uncomfortable silence.

Sylvia pretended to check her watch, cleared her throat and said, 'I've a programme to watch on TV, if you'll excuse me.' She picked up her bag from the settle and squeezed out. 'Goodnight.'

Willie followed, glad of an excuse, leaving a half-finished pint on the table. Vera and Don felt uneasy. If he wasn't going to tell them why he was there, what was there to talk about? They were saved any further embarrassment by Georgie coming to the table with the tray of drinks Bryn had ordered.

Georgie looked at Vera and Don but avoided Bryn's eyes. 'Oh, dear! What a surprise,' she said, 'your guests are disappearing one by one. What do you want me to do with this lot, Bryn?'

'Oh! We'll drink it, won't we, Vera?'

Vera blushed. Don grunted and made to take his orange juice from the tray, but Georgie stepped back so the tray was out of his reach. 'I've a better idea.' Without any warning she tipped the drinks over Bryn's head. Ale and orange juice and gin and tonic ran all over him and the glasses crashed to the floor around him. All he could do was to sit there gasping, soaked to the skin, wiping away drink from his eyes with his well-tanned hand.

Between clenched teeth Georgie snarled, 'Another time don't you ever dare shout for Dicky to bring you drinks in that nasty way. I run a well-mannered pub here and I won't stand for it. You'd speak to a dog better than that.'

Bryn stood up and came as close as he had ever done to striking Georgie. He brought his arm back to do that very thing, but the savage glint in her eye and the thought that he wouldn't get what he wanted from her by alienating her stopped him just in time. It was difficult to be taken seriously when wet through and smelling like a brewery, though, but he tried. 'I'm very sorry, Georgie, love, I shouldn't have asked like that. Forgetting my manners.' He paused to wipe the trickles of drink running off the end of his nose. 'Won't happen again.'

'In future remember what I've said. I won't have you speaking like that in here. And you can pay me for that lot before you go.'

Bryn spread his hands wide in a placatory gesture. 'I'd better get changed first. I'll be back.' He threaded his way between the tables, causing customers to snatch at their coats to avoid getting them wet. A long wet trail was all that was left of Bryn when the door closed behind him.

'Vera, let's be off. I don't want any more of him embarrassing me. Don't know what's got into him. He's not the same man at all. Come on.' Don took her elbow to assist her to rise, and in a gentlemanly fashion picked up her bag from the floor and tucked it under his arm.

'Thanks. 'Ere let me carry that.' They stepped around Dicky who was mopping the floor after Bryn. 'Don't know how you put up with it, Dicky, 'im coming in here. Just don't do anything daft, mind.'

Dicky looked up. 'I won't. If we knew why he'd come back it would help.'

'There's a reason, but none of us can fathom it yet. But believe me, we're all on your side.'

'Thanks.' Dicky stopped mopping to watch them leave. He leant on his mop handle and silently cursed Bryn. When he thought about it the worst scenario would be that this newly revitalised Bryn might take Georgie away from him – after all, they were still married, it was no problem. Then Bel would be back in Glebe Cottages with him and he'd be back to that old boring job. A sister wasn't quite the same as a lover, still less was a lover as good as a wife and a wife, namely Georgie, was what he wanted most of all. He finished the mopping, emptied the bucket in the grate outside and was storing them away in the cleaning cupboard when Georgie appeared.

'Dicky!' Georgie put her hands on his shoulders and, looking into his eyes, said, 'Don't be afraid. I won't go back to him, no matter what. I'm asking him for a divorce tonight. That's God's truth.' She gave him a peck on his lips, gently placed her finger on his mouth for him to kiss and then went back into the bar to help deal with the rush.

Uncanny, that, thought Dicky, she even knows what I'm thinking. But then Georgie always knew what he was thinking, it was typical Georgie, it was. His insides ached with the pain of loving her. A terrible paralysis crept over him when he considered perhaps having to face the rest of his life without her. The thought made him shudder deep inside; it didn't bear thinking about. It wasn't at all what he wanted, having snatched moments, sneaking off for weekends away, all because tongues wagged too freely in this close community. It had its advantages, though: they'd welcomed him and Bel with open arms and when they'd found out their secret – that he and Bel were brother and sister – no one really minded. But the Rector had made his opinion absolutely clear on the matter of him and Georgie: 'While you are the leader of our Church Scouts I will not tolerate you openly living with Georgie. I know it's not in line with current thinking, but there you are. Added to which, in the eyes of the boys you would become the object of unseemly mirth and sniggering, and with it all the hard work you've put into establishing the largest and most successful Scout group in the county would be gone, never to be regained. You are brilliant as leader, I could challenge anyone to find a Scout leader better than you. Don't lose all that, for your sake or the boys'.'

Dicky pottered about in the cleaning cupboard tidying this, reorganising that, until he could find nothing more to tidy. He gave a great sigh. Peter always saw the greater good, the long term, what was best for all concerned and after all he did have to be grateful to him for his very life. If it hadn't been for Peter being so very fit, Bryn would have had him over the top of the tower and he, Dicky Tutt, would have been strawberry jam. It struck him in a flash. Of course, that was it! Insist on prosecution. Of course! That would get rid of him sharpish. Bryn would be discredited for ever, Georgie could get a divorce, no sweat, and they could marry and he could live at the pub . . . Why had he allowed Peter to persuade him not to prosecute?

He perched on a case of carpet shampoo in the dark and his heart sank. He knew full well why. It was as Peter had said at the time, the whole story of Bryn, and Georgie and Bel would be open to public view and to distortion by the press. Let's face it, thought Dicky, I did torment Bryn with all the tricks I got up to. Anyway, Peter was right. It really wasn't in his nature to want revenge. He'd got Georgie's love and that counted for a lot. But hiding behind her skirts by leaving her to deal with Bryn . . . he had to laugh, though – pouring the drinks over him; what a woman!

28

'Dicky! Can you come?'

That was Alan wanting more help. He got up, shut the cupboard door and marched into the bar with a grin plastered on his face. 'Who's next?'

It was Bryn, a very smart Bryn. Dressed more suitably for the Caribbean than Turnham Malpas, he certainly made heads turn, no doubt about that. Dicky steeled himself not to go white at the implied threat of Bryn's presence. 'What can I get you, Bryn?'

'Whisky on the rocks . . . please.' He dug out his wallet crammed with notes, peeled off a twenty and said, 'Take for that tray of drinks that got spilled as well.'

'Thanks.'

Bryn threw the whisky down his throat and asked for another. He took that to a table and sat down to wait. It unnerved Dicky having to work with Bryn's eyes on him all the time. He felt like a goldfish swimming round and round its bowl, with a cat poised for whisking him out with its paw if he swam too close to the top of the water.

Bryn sat there until closing time, then went to the bar and asked Georgie if he could have a word.

'I can't leave all this mess. Wait ten minutes.'

'I'll give you a hand.'

'No, thanks.' But he did. He collected the empties and put them in the wheelie bin. He found a cloth and wiped a few tables, he collected some crisp bags off the floor and finally got out the cloth bag, which they'd always used to put the takings in the safe until the morning.

Georgie snatched it from him. 'That's my job. Go in the back, the door's unlocked.'

She and Dicky said a quiet goodnight to each other by

the outside door. 'I won't let him persuade me, honestly, Dicky. I will not have him back. Believe me.'

'Are you sure?'

'Yes, I'm sure. I'll let you know tomorrow.'

'Right. I'll come straight after communion. Right.'

Georgie smiled at him. Their eyes were on a level and she could look straight into his and loved him so. She said, 'Right. I'm sorry about all this, but at least we might get a chance to sort things out. Goodnight, love.'

'Goodnight.'

Georgie turned out the lights and made her way across the bar and upstairs to Bryn.

She found him seated in a comfortable chair in the sitting room waiting for her. He stood up as she entered and it gave her heart a turn. He hadn't done that for years. 'I'm going to have a cup of tea.'

'Like you always did after a busy day. Can I make it for you?'

'Bel will be in the kitchen making herself a drink, so I'd better do it.'

'Very well.' He relaxed back into the chair and shuffled his shoulders about as though making himself comfortable for a long time.

'You want one?'

'No, thanks. Tea's not my tipple any more.'

When she came back with her tea she had the odd feeling that he'd been out of the chair poking through her belongings. The desk drawers were closed, the papers on top apparently undisturbed, all the same . . .

Georgie sat down and sipped her tea, expecting that Bryn would be the one to open the conversation. But he didn't. She heard Bel unlock the bathroom door, listened to a car roaring up the Culworth Road. Then the deep silence of the countryside descended. Eventually she said, 'I thought you wanted to talk.'

'I've a proposition to make.'

'Spill the beans, then.'

'While I've been managing bars on the cruise liners I've come into contact with a lot – and I mean a lot – of Americans, Americans who travel a great deal. Many of them want to come to Europe but haven't the know-how to make a successful job of it. They want to see the real England, what makes us tick, what makes us what we are, to get the feel of our heritage. I've an address book crammed with names and telephone numbers, and I've planned a tour, an off-the-beaten-track kind of tour. When they come to London they'll have two or three days there doing the Tower, Buckingham Palace, a performance at the Globe Theatre et cetera, then we'll travel to Bath, on the way . . .'

'You're not thinking of bringing them here, are you?'

'I'm coming to that. I shan't have them staying in the kind of hotel that can be found all over the world and they could be waking up in Hong Kong or Sydney or New York. No, that's not for me. They'll be staying in typically English country house hotels, hotels with ambience, ones just that bit different from the usual tourist dumps, so I thought . . .'

'Yes?'

'I thought that on their way to Bath and Stratford they could call here for lunch.'

'Here meaning here?' Georgie pointed to the floor to emphasise her point.

Bryn nodded. 'That's right, lunch here at the Royal

31

Oak. They could have a tour of the church, call in at the Store for souvenirs, feed Jimmy's geese, finish off here for lunch: typical old pub, talk up the history a bit, you know the kind of thing. Perhaps even visit a cottage for some more atmosphere. What do you think? It could be a real money spinner for everyone. Us included.'

'Us? Who's "us"?'

'Well, you, I mean.'

'How many?'

'Groups of twenty, no more than twenty-five or the exclusiveness would be lost.'

'How often?'

'Well, this summer I've got one planned for August, one for September. That's all. But it could mushroom. They'd be here Thursday, which is never a good day for lunches in our dining room, is it?'

'You keep making the mistake of saying "us" and "our". It isn't yours, Bryn. You took the money, remember, and I got the business and my name is over the door.'

'Sorry.' Hastily Bryn spread his hands in a placatory gesture. 'Habit, you know, you and me, a team for years, it's hard to drop the habit.'

Georgie sat sipping her tea, thinking about his plans. Twenty-five people for lunch on a Thursday would certainly be a boost. 'If I decided to do it, I'd have to consult Dicky first. It would have to be the same menu for everyone, I don't think the kitchen could cope with twenty-five people all wanting serving at once with different dishes.'

'Absolutely. Typical old English menu. Windsor soup,

steak and ale pie with home-grown vegetables, spotted dick steamed pudding with custard, coffee and liqueurs.'

'What's Windsor soup when it's at home?'

'Anything you like, just sounds impressive. Drinks, of course, would be up to them, wine, beer, whisky, whatever they wanted. These people are rich, Georgie, real rich. I'll have them eating out of my hand. Two hours we have here, that's all. Should be enough. What do you think?'

'I'm too tired, Bryn, to get my mind round it, but it's definitely an idea. The problem I see is will you have a full load each week to make it worthwhile? That will be hard, making up the groups.'

'No sweat. I've got contacts you wouldn't believe. I cultivated them, you see. Didn't know why, then the whole idea burst into my mind and I realised the possibilities. I'll come back in a day or two when you've had time to think.'

'OK. Make it Tuesday. But you must understand' – into Georgie's eyes came a hard look – 'it is strictly a business venture. I want paying before the group leaves. They'll be escorted of course?'

'That goes without saying. You'll be paid on the dot and I shall be escorting for the first couple of seasons till we get the ball rolling. This tour scheme of mine could be a money spinner, personal touch and all that, and I shan't stop at just this one tour. I intend expanding as fast as possible. Visiting prime English gardens, castle tours, you name it.' Bryn rubbed his hands together in anticipation. 'You and me, together we'll show 'em.'

Georgie became caught up in his enthusiasm and allowed herself to smile. 'Sounds good; in fact, very good.

Personal contact as you say. Now, I've got to get to bed. I'll let you out.'

'Thanks.' They both stood up at the same time and Bryn very lightly took her arm. 'Good to see you. I've lived to regret my treatment of you. I really have. Should have had more sense, not neglected you.'

Georgie stiffened and drew away from him. 'Too late now.' She led the way to the back door and let him out.

Bryn stepped outside and turned back to say, 'We could still make a good team, Georgie, I can feel that old something between us. Can you not feel it?'

'No. Goodnight. See you Tuesday.'

Bryn smiled to himself as he turned into Church Lane. He called out a cheerful friendly 'Goodnight' to Jimbo who was just leaving his mother's cottage. He'd be calling at the Store tomorrow. Jimbo'd be as easy as pie to influence, him being always ready to make money, so long as it was legal.

Bryn was at the Store as soon as the morning rush of mothers from the school had finished their shopping. He gauged that around half past nine would be about the best time.

He couldn't believe that Linda was still at the post office counter. 'Good morning, Linda. How are you? Still here I see. Thought you'd have gone long ago.'

'Why, Mr Fields. I wondered how long it would be before you called. How are you? My, I hardly recognise you, you're so ... brown and, well, years younger without that moustache. No need to ask how *you* are!' She grinned ruefully from behind the grille and finally answered his question quietly. 'I think I've been sacked a total of four times now, but he always comes crawling back asking me to return, because he can't find anyone who can do it as well as me.'

'Watch it! The next time might be the last.'

'Oh, don't say that! It's so handy being able to drop Lewis off at the childminder and come straight here. Are you wanting something?'

'Just to see Jimbo. Is he in?'

'I'll give him a shout. Hold on.' Linda unlocked the door of her cage, as she called it, and carefully locked it after her. She excused her caution by saying apologetically, 'Can't be too careful!' She slipped into the back of the Store to find Jimbo.

Bryn looked round as a preliminary to his conversation with Jimbo. He preferred to be well armed before a business discussion. He noted the picture postcards of the area, especially the ones of the church and the village green, then he progressed to the jams and marmalades, remembering Jimbo had a line called 'Harriet's Country Cousins' whatever. Now that would be a good line for souvenirs. The title was perfectly splendid for his needs. Of course, he'd want a percentage when the sales grew. Which they would. He picked up a beautifully evocative jar, a six-sided pot with a red-and-white gingham cover on the top and an elaborate label saying 'Harriet's Country Cousins' thick-sliced Grapefruit Marmalade, made to a recipe from an old notebook found . . .'

'Yes!' Jimbo stood beside him resplendent in his striped apron and with his bow tie matching the ribbon around the crown of his straw boater. 'What can I do for you this bright morning? You wanted to see me?'

Bryn was instantly aware of the belligerent tone of

Jimbo's voice, so he set himself out to charm and by the time he'd finished his spiel about his rich tourists and the money that could be made, he had Jimbo eating out of his hand.

At least he thought he had, until Jimbo suddenly said, 'And what is there in it for you, if I'm selling doodahs to your tourists?'

Bryn hesitated in order to demonstrate delicacy of feeling. 'Well, perhaps when we get things really going you could see your way . . .' He tapped the side of his nose and winked.

Jimbo said, 'I make no promises. I'm not here to make you a rich man, you know, Bryn. Margins are tight in a set-up like this, I've to watch every penny.'

'Oh, I can see that.' Bryn gazed around Jimbo's well-equipped, stylish set-up. 'Margins are very tight.' His right cheek bulged with the pressure of the tip of his tongue.

Jimbo was forced to smile. 'I'm still not promising you a percentage of my profits on anything I sell as souvenirs. Accounting for it would be difficult.'

Bryn nodded gravely. 'Of course, of course it would. You need to expand what you have on offer, though. Little framed pictures of the village houses. A small model of the church and perhaps the school, and of course a model of the Royal Oak. Now they would sell. Oh, yes. They would sell. Tasteful, of course.'

Stung by the implied lack of good taste on his part, Jimbo answered, 'Absolutely.'

'Think about what else you could sell. Once the old brains get going, who knows what we might come up with. I specially like Harriet's jams et cetera, they would go down a bomb with the tourists.'

'Are we to expect tourists every week?'

Bryn laughed. 'Not to start with, but I've every intention of directing as much business as I can to this village.'

'Let's hope they thank you for it.' Jimbo touched the brim of his boater. 'Must get on. Be in touch. When's the first lot?'

'August.'

'Right. I'll be in touch as I said.'

Bryn extended his hand. 'Thanks for your attention, I'm going to make sure it works. I've got quite a few ideas which, if they come to fruition, will put Turnham Malpas on the map. Ye olde yokel sitting by the pond, et cetera, you know the sort of thing. It's those little touches that really make a tour.'

Jimbo shook his hand and Bryn left with a satisfied smile on his face.

Chapter 3

After their evening meal Jimbo explained to Harriet the purpose of Bryn's stay in Turnham Malpas. 'In addition he's going to have what he describes as an olde yokel sitting by the pond.'

'That's you, is it?' Harriet asked.

The two girls shrieked with laughter. Fran asked what a yokel was and Flick told her between gasps of laughter. 'I can just see you, Dad! Have you still got that old smocked thing, Mum, you bought in that sale? You know, the Victorian farmer's thingy?'

'I have. He could wear it, couldn't he? Very authentic.'

Jimbo said, 'Less of the mirth. What he wants us to do is expand our range of souvenirs.'

'We haven't got any souvenirs.'

'We've got your jams and marmalades.'

'Of course, I never thought of them in that light.'

'We've got postcards.'

Harriet thought for a moment and suggested, 'Turnham Malpas pencils with those dear little rubbers on the end.'

Flick said, 'Framed pictures of the village.'

Fran proffered the idea of sweets in Turnham Malpas tins.

Flick scoffed at her idea. 'Trust you to think of sweets, you'd eat all the profits.'

'I wouldn't, would I, Mummy?'

'No, darling, in fact you've come up with a good notion there. We could also put our Belgian chocolates in Turnham Malpas tins.'

Flick was appalled at such duplicity. 'That is outrageous. Dad, don't let her. She mustn't. That's cheating.'

'Definitely cheating.' But he winked at Harriet, which further outraged Flick.

Fran, being too young to understand what they were meaning, asked, 'Is there anything Flick and I could do? We'll be off school in August. I'd like to dress up.'

'We'll see.'

Harriet checked her watch. 'Come along, Fran, time you were off to bed.'

'I really want to talk business with Daddy.'

'You've talked enough. You had one of the best ideas so far, so that's sufficient to be going on with. Move!'

Tucked up in bed, the curtains drawn against the light, Fran said, 'Sit down to talk.'

Sensing there was something on Fran's mind, Harriet did as she asked. 'Two minutes, that's all.'

'Mummy.'

'Yes?'

'How can you be someone's little girl if she's not your tummy-mummy?'

'First, you're not worrying about yourself, are you? Because, let it be clearly understood, I am your tummy-mummy.'

'I know that because Flick remembers me being born in the hospital car park.'

'And you've been in a hurry ever since. However, there are some ladies who would love to be a mummy but they've got an illness or something and the doctors say they won't be able to have a baby growing in their tummy, so-o-o they can make a solemn promise to care for a baby who has no mummy or has a mummy who can't look after it and that's called adoption, and it's just as if the baby is theirs, except it hasn't grown in their tummy.'

'They look after someone else's baby.'

'That's right.'

'So is that what happened to Beth and Alex?'

'Yes, because Caroline isn't able to have babies.'

'So whose tummy did they grow in, then?'

'Someone's who couldn't look after them and gave them away to Caroline and Peter when they were tiny, tiny babies, because they thought it was for the best.'

'Did you know them?'

'I knew them when they were tiny.'

'No. I mean did you know their real mummy? I wonder who she is. Beth wants to know. I thought you might be able to tell her.'

'Fran, it's something very personal for Caroline and Peter, and I honestly think you shouldn't get involved. It's for them to tell her, believe me.'

'Beth keeps on and on about it. Every time I see her. She's asked loads of girls.'

'It really isn't any of our business.'

Fran turned over on to her side, closed her eyes and said, 'I think you know, but you won't tell me. It's not fair. Goodnight.'

'It's not my secret.'

'I shall tell Beth to ask Caroline.'

'You'll do no such thing. You'll mind your own business. Goodnight. I mean what I say. It's all too private.'

'Mm.'

Just as Harriet left her bedroom Fran called out, 'Teaspoons with a tiny church on the end. How about that for an idea? Or doorstops made out of wood with one of Jimmy's geese painted on.'

'Fran! I'll tell Daddy, but switch off now, please.'

Harriet found Jimbo in his study doing rapid sums on his calculator. 'I wish you'd never mentioned this idea just before Fran went to bed. Her head's full of souvenirs. She'll never settle and you know how much she needs her sleep.'

Jimbo looked up, lost in thought. 'I know this idea of Bryn's is only a possibility. It may or may not work depending, but we do get lots of other visitors from all over the place so whatever we decide on could be a year-round line. Why on earth I haven't thought of it before I don't know.'

'Teaspoons and doorstops she's come up with now. Heaven alone knows what she'll have thought of by morning.'

'She's a true daughter of mine, is Fran. I'll put those on the list. In the scheme of things this is only a small matter, but every penny counts. I tell you who'd be good for the doorstops: Vince Jones. He's a wizard with wood, remember?'

'And for framing the pictures. But has it occurred to you that you haven't spoken to the Jones family since Mrs

41

Jones went steaming through the Store casting all before her?'

Jimbo laid down the calculator and leaned back in his chair. 'Ah! I'm getting carried away here.'

'I also remember all the cursing you did about the Jones family when their Terry and Kenny had to disappear quick sharp before the police caught up with them, or worse, those gangsters. Think of the outlay for all these things! The returns could be quite slow and we've no guarantee that Bryn's idea of tourists would work.'

'Agreed, but . . . the idea grips me and if an idea grips me then most often it turns out to be a good one. I'm going to play around with it, see what comes up. Doesn't cost much to have two hundred pencils embossed with Turnham Malpas Store, does it? You're not listening to me.'

'No, you're right, I'm not. I'm off to see Peter and Caroline.'

'Why?'

'Because Beth is obssessed with where she came from. They've always known, the two of them, that Caroline isn't their mother but that Peter is their father, but now apparently she wants to know the rest and those two should do something about it.'

'They'll deal with it when the time is ripe.'

'It's ripe now, believe me. Fran says Beth's asking everyone at school and before long some child is going to spill the beans.'

'Harriet, is this wise?'

'I'm going. Won't be long.'

Jimbo stood up. 'Please, think about it.'

'I'm *going*. I won't have Fran getting all upset, it's not

right. What's more, the whole situation means I can't tell my own daughter the truth and that's certainly not right.'

'Very well, but tread very carefully, please.'

Hand on heart Harriet answered, 'I am the soul of discretion.'

Peter came to the door when she knocked at the Rectory. 'Hello, Harriet, come in. If it's Caroline you want to see she's out, I'm afraid.'

'Well, it was both of you, but maybe on second thoughts I'm quite glad it's you on your own.'

'Had we better go into my study?'

'All right, then, yes.'

Peter opened the door for her and she went in and flopped down in an easy chair. Peter sat at his desk and waited for her to speak. She was struck as always by his commanding presence – his height, the breadth of his shoulders, his fresh complexion and thick reddish-blond hair – he was very handsome in any woman's eyes. But his penetrating blue eyes made him intimidating, for they seemed to see straight through you, and it felt as though all your smallest and most unworthy thoughts were exposed to his scrutiny.

'Peter, I have a problem. Well, at least it's not my problem, it's yours and I don't quite know how to phrase it.'

'Mine? What are we talking about?'

'Your Beth and Alex.'

'Have they been misbehaving?'

'No. Never. They're always well-mannered and never any trouble. No, it's not that.'

Peter waited a moment, then said, 'Well?'

'You know they've been having sex lessons this term . . . well, it has caused them both, I think, but mainly Beth to . . . to be honest, it's time you and Caroline came clean about . . . well, not clean exactly, that's not what I meant to say, but it's time you and she spoke to the twins about their origins before someone else does and makes a balls of it. Because if that happens the twins could be irreparably hurt.'

Harriet thought it must have been at least a whole minute before Peter replied but of course it wasn't, it was seconds. 'I see. She's never said anything to us about it.'

'Well, it will be difficult for her, very difficult for them both, won't it? They won't want to hurt Caroline for they love her so, but they ought to be told, because it's causing Beth such anguish. Fran tells me she's asking everyone if their mother is their real one, hoping, I expect, to find someone else who's been adopted so she can compare notes or something. But what's made me come tonight is the fact that Fran asked me who their real mother is. And I don't like not being able to tell the truth to my children.'

'We shouldn't have made it so you can't be straight with your children. I'm deeply sorry about that. Obviously the moment we've avoided thinking about has come at last.'

'I know they know Caroline isn't their real mother, but I think if you told them the whole truth they'd be able to face it at their age. It doesn't mean they will want to go charging off to find . . . Suzy . . . does it?'

Peter got up and went to stand at the window. 'She longs to see them.'

Harriet was glad they weren't face to face or he would

44

have seen the shock written there. She'd no idea they'd been in touch since Suzy left the village.

'That was long ago when she came to visit Michael while she thought we were on holiday. I told her, no, I couldn't allow it both for Caroline's sake and for her own. Her conceiving my children was one moment of shame, my shame, which I shall carry with me to the grave. Yet from it Caroline and I were blessed with the children we both needed.' Peter gave a huge sigh. 'It was Caroline who asked Suzy if we could have the children, you know. And when she told me what she'd done I said no. Caroline said, "I see. So we can adopt children we know nothing of but you won't let me adopt your own flesh and blood." She told me Suzy wanted us to have the twins as soon as they arrived, because Suzy wouldn't allow herself to see the children as they were being born in case she weakened. Such courage.'

Peter turned from the window, his eyes full of tears. 'I saw her immediately after the birth, you know; her pain at relinquishing them to Caroline and me was terrible to witness. But she knew she couldn't keep them, a widow with three little girls already, it would have been impossible for her. Yet she was so brave . . . she even asked me for my blessing. Can you believe that?'

Harriet shook her head, too emotional to speak, grateful he was looking anywhere but at her.

'When Caroline told me that Suzy wanted us to have the children and I'd said no, I told her I couldn't face looking at them every day and being reminded of my shame. I considered only myself with never a thought for what I'd done to *her*. I threw all her love and self-sacrifice

45

back in her face. I have never met such forgiveness in a human being either before or since.'

'Peter! Should you be telling me all this?'

He shook his head but carried on to say, 'How Caroline coped with what I did, I shall never know.'

'So Suzy wasn't the only one to be brave.'

'Indeed not.' He paused for a moment, then his head came up and he looked her straight in the face. 'Thank you for telling me, Harriet, I appreciate it. I've always been intensely grateful for the way the village has kept our secret. Deeply appreciative.'

Harriet stood up, crying inside herself, longing to get away. 'I'll go now I've said my piece. It was only in your best interests and the children's. I hope you'll forgive me for speaking out.'

'There's nothing to forgive. God bless you, Harriet.'

'If anyone mentions anything to you from this conversation it won't be me who's told them.'

She left Peter to his heartbreak, made her escape, and went home to Jimbo and the no-nonsense world in which the two of them lived.

But stupidly the first thing she did when she saw Jimbo still working at his desk was to fling her arms round him and weep. 'Darling! Oh, God! You wouldn't believe.'

'Harriet! Were they angry with you? Tell me. Here, sit on my knee.' He gripped her tightly and let the tears run their course. 'Here, look! A clean handkerchief. Wipe your face and tell your Jimbo.' He wiped it for her and hugged her tight. 'I did say don't go.'

'I know but I'm glad I did.'

'Doesn't sound like it.'

'I think I'm not nearly as brave as I believe myself to be. Those two over at the Rectory, well . . .'

'Go on.'

'They're an example to us all.' Harriet told him everything she'd learned and finished by begging him not to say a word to anyone.

'Cross my heart and hope to die.'

'Promise?'

'Promise.'

'I never think about how lucky we are to have had four children as easily as we have done, and nothing wrong with any of them, but tonight I am. Peter and Caroline are in such a mess about this. If only they'd been able to have children of their own . . .'

'It's their problem, Harriet. I do feel very sorry for them but there's nothing either you or I can do anything about, except be good friends to them both.'

'I know, but what a predicament. I wish I could wave a magic wand and make it all right for the four of them. Heaven alone knows what the children's reactions are going to be.'

'I'm not often given to fanciful thoughts but I always think their love is something quite different from ours. Theirs is like a skittish, highly strung horse, all temperament and searing passion. It must be hell to live with a love like theirs, all up and down and sensitive and touchy. We're like a couple of shire-horses, confident and strong.'

'You make it sound damned boring, Jimbo.'

'Boring! No, not boring, more beautifully comfortable, kind of. However, as I said none of it is our fault. It's Peter's.' He slid her off his knee and turned to his desk. 'Look, I've made a list of souvenirs I fancy selling. I've decided to be magnanimous and restore the Jones family to the bosom of our enterprise.'

Harriet was astounded. 'After all you've said about them? I can't believe this.'

Jimbo gave her a conspiratorial smile. 'I know, I know, but business is business. Mrs Jones can come back to do the mail order business, because none of her replacements has measured up to her and Vince can do the doorstops et cetera and the picture framing. Now he's retired they need a helping hand and I'm in a position to give them it, so I must.'

'So that's how you justify it. Well, you can ask them because I shan't, it's all too embarrassing.' Harriet gave a huge sigh as she finished speaking.

He heard her sigh and said, 'Harriet! Don't worry about the twins; you've done your bit, just leave it to them. I can't bear for you to be unhappy. I love you, you see, and what hurts you hurts me.' Jimbo caressed her hand and twisted round to look at her standing behind him.

She smiled down at him and bent to kiss him. 'And I love you, even if I am a shire-horse.' They both laughed, Harriet picked up his sheet of notes from the desk and they began discussing Jimbo's souvenir scheme. But for Harriet it didn't entirely block out her worry about Peter and Caroline.

Peter was sitting in his study brooding on the problem when Caroline came home. She put her head round the study door and knew even before he spoke that Peter was troubled. 'Darling! What's the matter?'

'Harriet's been to see me.'

'Yes?'

'Apparently Beth is asking all round the school about . . .' Peter hesitated, unsure how to phrase Harriet's news. 'Well, to be blunt, about her real mother. She wants to know who she is.'

'Oh, God!' Caroline sat down abruptly on the sofa.

'Caroline! We knew it would come some time and it's come *now*, so we have to face it.'

'Not yet, not now. Please. I need time.'

'We've had ten years of time to think and all we've done is amble along from day to day, putting it off, thankful for their ignorance.'

'I won't face it. I just won't. I'm not ready for it.'

Peter's answer to Caroline's anguish was not the sympathetic one she'd hoped for. 'I'm sorry, darling, but they *are*, even if we're not, and something must be done about it.'

'No, we don't need to. We can just amble along as you say, and wait and see. They haven't asked *us*, so it can't be that serious.'

'That's probably because they don't want to hurt us, especially you. Harriet pointed out to me the strong possibility that others might tell her and that could be catastrophic.' Peter paused for a moment while he searched for the right words. 'You see, other people might be . . . cruel . . . you know, and Beth and Alex can't fight that kind of cruelty without having a strong bond with us about the whole matter. I know it's painful, my darling, but we're the grown-ups in this and we've to smooth their pathway.'

Caroline shook her head vehemently. 'I know they need to know, but not yet, they're so little. So innocent.' As she said 'innocent' she gave a great agonised sigh.

Peter went to sit beside her on the sofa. He put his arm round her shoulders and held her close. 'I know, I know. We don't need to tell them today or even tomorrow, but we must very, very soon. Deep down, you know I'm right. If they have a need to know then now's the time, isn't it? Otherwise it puts us on the wrong foot and makes us appear deceitful, and . . . Suzy herself didn't want that. She begged me to be truthful and we both know she was right.' Peter gave her a gentle shake. 'Eh? Don't we?'

'But what will they think of you?'

'That's my burden, not theirs.'

Caroline shrugged his arm from her shoulders and turned to face him. 'My absolute dread is if they want to see her.'

'I don't think they will, not yet anyway, but we can't blame them if they do, can we? It's only natural. Think it over, seriously, please.'

'I will. But how shall we . . . kind of . . . do it?'

'Heaven knows. We'll think of something. We're not entirely bereft of brains, are we?'

'I wasn't thinking of brains, it was heart and feelings and . . . things I'm most concerned about.'

'Ah! Yes.'

Never one to allow the grass to grow under his feet, Jimbo had Mrs Jones installed in the mail order office and Vince doing practice runs with doorstop designs in less time than it takes to tell. Mrs Jones glowed with satisfaction the first morning she was allowed back in the Store.

Linda waved cheerfully from behind her post office grille. 'Hello, Mrs Jones. Quite like old times. I expect you'll be glad to be back, just like me.'

Mrs Jones's normally grim face was creased with smiles. 'You've no idea! Things have been very tight since Vince retired, but now the sun is out as you might say and I'm back doing what I was cut out to do.' She looked around the Store, glad to know she'd be able to shop in here again instead of trailing to Culworth for everything she needed.

She bounced into the back of the shop and went straight to the mail order office, closed the door behind her and breathed a sigh of delight. There was a pile of orders waiting for her so she flung off her coat and hat, dug in her bag for her reading glasses and waded in. She reached out and took down a jar of 'Harriet's Country Cousins' Seville Orange Marmalade' but, before she parcelled it up for the post she ran her finger round the label, stroked the red gingham cover, teased the neatly tied bow of the gold cord encircling it and read out the description of the contents, then held the jar up to the light and enjoyed the golden orangey glow of it. There wasn't a single jar of home-made marmalade on the market to compare. She felt a surge of contentment run through her veins, decided the jar was the most beautiful thing in her life at that moment and set to work as though she'd never been away.

Jimbo, with an ear to her office door, listened to her banging away with the stapler and rejoiced at the old familiar sound. He really would have to stop sacking staff the moment they displeased him because it always meant him eating humble pie and he was growing tired of the taste.

Harriet caught him listening to the ripping sound of parcel tape being dragged off the reel and poked him in the ribs whispering, 'Satisfied?'

51

'I am. Music to my ears, that is.' With a smug smile on his face he went on. 'She's promised not to lose her rag ever again and she says I can call her Greta now.'

'Oh! Who's a lucky boy, then?' Harriet, grinning from ear to ear, went towards the kitchen to face a day of making puddings and cakes to fill the freezers. Halfway through the morning she remembered about the twins and Peter's distress, and it took the edge off her pleasure.

Dicky Tutt had the edge taken off his pleasure in the Store that same morning but not because of the problem at the Rectory. He had called in for a copy of the *Culworth Gazette* for Georgie on his way to the pub for his morning stint and found himself facing Bryn right by Jimbo's newsstand. The hairs on the back of Dicky's neck stood up and his scalp prickled.

'Good morning, Dicky! Nice day.'

Dicky picked up on the mocking tone in Bryn's voice. Remembering how he'd hidden behind Georgie's skirts the night she'd poured the drinks over Bryn's head, Dicky decided to stand his ground. 'The morning would be a lot nicer if you weren't here.'

'Don't be like that, I mean no harm.'

'Don't you? Just go back where you came from and leave us all alone. Georgie's had enough of you and so have I.'

Bryn took hold of the lapels of Dicky's jacket. 'See here, you stunted little specimen, you miserable little dwarf. I'm still Georgie's husband and it's staying that way. She and I are business partners, right? I'm going to bring big business to the pub and that's what she wants. See? So your Georgie this and Georgie that means nothing.' Bryn snapped his fingers in Dicky's face and disdainfully dusted off his hands as though he'd been touching something unseemly.

Linda rang her panic button.

Dicky snapped. He grabbed hold of Bryn's shirt at chest level and jerked his face down towards his own. 'See here, matey, Georgie is mine and I'll move heaven and earth to keep it that way. So you can take your miserable pathetic business elsewhere. Find another pub and use that for your pie-in-the-sky plans. Any more of you aggravating me I'll go straight to the police, and talk about church towers and such. They'll listen to me. After all, I had plenty of witnesses and they've all got long memories.' Dicky relaxed his hold on Bryn. 'So git before I do my worst.'

Jimbo appeared by the news-stand.

Dicky saw by Bryn's eyes that he was alarmed, but only for an instant. Then they changed and Bryn sneered, 'You! A little squirt like you? Ha!'

'Yes, a little squirt like me. Any more sniffing around Georgie and I will, God help me, I will.'

Something in the sparky way Dicky defied him triggered the idea that Dicky was intending to marry Georgie. 'I do believe you're thinking of marrying her, aren't you?' Bryn roared with laughter, holding his sides, his mouth wide open, his eyes screwed tight, his head thrown back. The sound of his amusement bounced from wall to wall. He got out a handkerchief and wiped his eyes. 'Oh, God! What a laugh. You and Georgie! Oh, my word!'

One customer crept round to the front of the meat counter to get a better view, another put down her basket and abandoned all pretence of shopping to stare, and

Jimbo prepared to roll up his sleeves and break up a fight. But they were all disappointed because Dicky, red in the face with rage, drew himself up to his full height, all five feet four of it, and said, while prodding Bryn's chest with a forefinger, 'That's my intention. I want Georgie as my wife and she wants me. And by God, we will be together one day if I have to *kill* you to get her.'

Dicky stalked out of the door with such dignity that the observers almost clapped their approval, but then they looked at Bryn and saw a frightening mixture of hate and fear in his face which boded ill for Dicky. Poor chap.

Linda had stopped her pretence of counting her stock of stamp books. Mrs Jones, having come out to see the fun, scuttled back to her office in panic. Jimbo heaved a sigh of relief and the customers got on with their own affairs, mindful as they did so to give Bryn a wide berth.

He was rooted to the spot, apparently unaware of his surroundings. Jimbo watched Bryn almost shake himself and focus his eyes on Jimbo himself. Bryn laughed. 'Did I imagine that or did the little dwarf actually threaten to murder me?'

'He did.'

'My God! I'd like to see him try.' Bryn smoothed the front of his shirt and said, 'Right, Jimbo. Have you had any more thoughts about what we talked of yesterday?'

'Come into my office.' Jimbo jerked his head towards the back of the Store and strode off in front of Bryn.

Jimbo took off his boater and, carefully placing it on a shelf, slowly turned and said in measured tones, 'The next time you want to have a fight don't choose my Store as the venue.'

'Get on with you! You know full well it's good for

trade and that's what matters to you, isn't it? They'll all be in here tomorrow hoping for a further instalment and what does that mean? More money in your tills. It's your Achilles heel, isn't it, Jimbo? Profit and more profit. You don't fool me. This morning's little episode will do this place no end of good.'

'Bluster doesn't impress me. So listen and get the message. I'm going along with the idea of souvenirs because I want to do it. Not because you've persuaded me but because it makes sound commercial sense. It'll be a long time before I see fit to give you a slice of the action. Right. Got that straight. If there is a repetition of this morning you'll never get a percentage no matter how big it is. That man has a right to threaten you and I'd back him one hundred per cent. Not as far as murder, but certainly where his ambitions for Georgie are concerned. So . . . watch your step.' This time it was Jimbo's forefinger prodding Bryn's chest.

Bryn looked seriously disconcerted and backed off. 'OK. OK. I get the message. That's the trouble with this damned village: everyone thinks they have a right to take sides.'

Jimbo ignored him and moved on. 'Mm. This is a list of the ideas we've come up with and I'm getting organised.'

Bryn studied Jimbo's list and felt heartened by his enthusiasm. 'Excellent. Excellent. I like the idea of sweets in Turnham Malpas tins. And the pencils. And the doorstops.'

'Must press on. Be seeing you.'

'Can I keep this list?'

'You can.'

Jimbo watched him walk out of his office and shook his

head in amazement. How could the chap dare to return? Attempted murder was the least of the charges the police could get him for. Yet here he was, throwing his weight about and expecting them all to be on his side. Scoffing at Dicky was idiotic and bound to cause bad blood. Only Harriet could settle his ruffled feathers, so he went in search of her.

Chapter 4

The next morning was idyllic. It had been a wonderful spring and now the summer was living up to its name. Each morning dawned bright and warm, so much so that there were constant threats of reservoirs in danger of running dry and the possibility of hosepipe bans, but everyone was determined to enjoy the weather and ignore the warnings. Jimmy Glover went out early to inspect the pond and found it now only half full at the most.

His geese clustered round him, honking for food. He had ten fully grown ones and nine goslings, and they were a picture. Jimmy knew that there was some opposition to him keeping them, but there'd been geese belonging to the Glover family on the green for one hundred and fifty years and more. It said so in some old parish records and, though there were no more Glovers left to keep them after he'd gone, he'd every intention of finding someone who would take them on. Made a mess indeed. Threatened visitors indeed. Fouled the road. Huh! Grazed on the blooms in the tubs outside the cottages. Wandered into Neville Neal's garden and ate his ornamental flowers. So what if they did?

He sat himself down on the seat kindly provided by the

council, opened up his plastic bag, and began pulling out pieces of bread and tossing them on the grass.

'Mr Glover! Mr Glover! Wait!'

Across the green came Beth Harris. A bonnier sight he couldn't hope to see. Her lovely ash-blonde hair in plaits today, her bright-blue eyes, so like the Rector's, sparkled with anticipation, and those lovely rounded cheeks of hers, rosy with the heat of the day, reminded him so much of . . . She was wearing her white shorts with the cornflower-blue shirt that matched her eyes. What a treasure! 'All right, Beth, there's plenty left for you.'

'I thought I was too late. Isn't it a lovely day? Mummy's taking us into Culworth today, and we're going boating on the lake and taking a picnic. Do you like boating on the lake?'

'Not much. Can't swim.'

'I can. Daddy taught us both years ago. Alex is better than me, he swims like a fish, Mummy says, and he can dive. I can't.'

'You will one day. Here's another piece.'

Beth concentrated on feeding the geese. She liked the goslings best, their parents were so huge and got so angry if something didn't suit. When she was little she used to stand on the seat to feed them she was so afraid. 'Don't you think geese on the green is a lovely idea?'

Jimmy nodded.

'I do too. It's like an old-fashioned picture of a village, isn't it?'

'It is an old-fashioned village, that's why.'

'You're right. I hope the geese will always be here, for ever and ever, don't you?'

'I do that.'

'Have you got any children who can look after them when you are too old?'

'No.'

'I didn't think you had. I could look after them for you. That is, if you wouldn't mind.'

'That would be a grand idea.'

'You've no wife either, have you, Mr Glover?'

'Well, I don't talk about it much, but I did have a wife and I did have a baby but they both died when the baby was newborn.'

'I'm so sorry. I shouldn't have pried.'

Jimmy looked at her contrite face. 'That's all right. It happened a long time ago.' And somehow, talking to her, it didn't matter as much as it used to do. In fact, no one had mentioned it to him for donkey's years; perhaps no one except him remembered. He stared across the green thinking about the old pain and how time healed.

Beth sat on the seat beside him admiring her new trainers. She stuck up a foot and asked, 'Do you like these? As soon as I saw them I loved them. They were expensive but Daddy said I should have them.'

'He's a good chap, is your dad. We're all glad he came here.'

'He can get cross sometimes, you know, specially if we're mean. I hate when he's cross, he makes me feel so bad.'

'Quite right. You shouldn't be mean.'

'No.' Beth sat silent for a moment, then she said, 'Mummy's lovely too.'

Jimmy nodded his approval. 'She is that. Always got time to listen, she has, even though she's busy with church and the practice and your dad and you two.'

'She's not actually my real, real mummy, you know.'

'I know.'

'She couldn't have babies so she adopted us.'

'That was a lucky day for you. You couldn't have a better mother, not anywhere in the whole wide world.'

Beth, still admiring her trainers with half her mind, banged her feet together to hear again the delicious clumping sound they made, and startled the geese. The goslings fled to the pond for safety, while the older geese stood their ground. 'We did have a mother, but she couldn't keep us.'

'I see.'

'Did you know our proper mummy?'

Jimmy unexpectedly found himself at the sharp end and terribly exposed. He'd walked right into that one and not seen it coming. He shooed away a goose trying to sneak off with his plastic bag, then made a pretence of fastening a bootlace to give himself time to think. 'I never lie, but I'm giving you fair warning that I am about to. No, I didn't know her.'

Beth studied Jimmy's statement. So he must mean he did know her but he wouldn't tell. Was she some dreadful person, then, whom no one wanted her to know about? Pictures of witches took form in her mind, dreadful people with chins that almost met their noses and wicked, cold grey eyes and blackened teeth. She shuddered. 'I'm going home; it's cold.'

'That's right. You go home and give that mummy of yours a kiss and hug her tight. She's worth it, she is. I wish she was mine.'

With eyes wide open with surprise Beth looked at Jimmy saying, 'You do?'

'I most certainly do. If I'd had a mother like yours I could have conquered the world.'

'You could?'

'Oh, yes. Mine, you see, didn't want me, so I was always a nuisance. Always telling me I was no good, and look where that got me? Long-time poacher and now part-time taxi driver. But I'd always fancied sailing the world, exploring and that, and writing books about it when I got back.'

'Really!'

'Oh, yes. The thing I would have liked to do most was to find an island no one else had ever seen and tell everyone about it, and they'd have to alter their maps to make room for it. Paradise Island I'd have called it.'

'Would you have lived there?'

'Possibly.' Jimmy stood up. 'Remember, with a mother like yours you can do anything in the world. She's a treasure, think on. And don't forget what I said about giving that mum of yours a hug as soon as you get in. It's time I took Sykes for a walk. Now I'm going to stand out here in the lane and watch you to your door. See you safe home.'

Beth said, 'I can take myself home now I'm ten.'

'I know that, but there's always cars come unexpected and I'd never look your mum in the face again if anything happened to you, you being so precious.'

''Bye, then, Mr Glover. Why do you never bring Sykes with you when you feed the geese?'

''Cos he's a bad lad and chases them, and they hate him for it and try to peck his tail.'

'Why does he chase them?'

'Jealous, that's what. Plain jealous, because he thinks I might just love the geese better than 'im.'

'But you don't, do you?'

Jimmy rubbed his chin and thought for a moment. 'All in all, I think Sykes might just have the edge.' He grinned down at her. 'I can talk to him and he understands, but these geese don't understand a blasted word I say.'

When Beth got to the Rectory door she turned to wave to him. He touched his cap to her as if she were a proper lady and shouted, 'Have a good day on the lake.'

'I will. The geese must be silly, Sykes hasn't got a tail.'

Jimmy had to smile. He went indoors hoping his mother would forgive him his outrageous fib about her. Still, it was in a good cause. Though the part about exploring and writing a book had been true; he'd just been too idle to get round to it.

He was about to set off with Sykes when there came a knock at the door. He heard it open and it was Bryn Fields, bright and breezy, dressed to kill. 'Come to see you about this scheme of mine. Have you a minute?'

Sykes ran at him, not knowing who he was and fancying he was a burglar at the very least. 'Sykes! That will do. He's a friend. I think.'

Sykes stopped barking and went to sniff Bryn's trouser leg.

'Five minutes, that's all, I'm just off out with Sykes.' He drew up a chair at the table for Bryn and sat himself down on the other one. 'Sit here, seeing as it's business.'

Jimmy listened open-mouthed to Bryn's plans, not letting on that he'd already overheard the drift of them in the Store one morning.

'And you want me to dress up and have a basket of bread to feed the geese and let them have a go.'

Bryn nodded. 'That's right, but not only that. I want you to tell them about your geese having been there for centuries and that yours are the descendants of geese the village had at the time of the plague . . . well, your family had, unbroken for fifteen generations, that kind of thing. I'm going to make a thing about it on the way here on the coach microphone you know, tell them how devastated the village was and about Stocks Day. "Same as that tree," you say and point to the old oak, and tell them that if the tree dies so will the village and how old it is.'

'Sounds a bit dodgy to me.'

'Not at all, they'll lap it up. Willie's going to mug up on the church history, and put on his old verger outfit and take them on a guided tour of the church.'

'Willie is?'

'He is. No doubt there'll be something in it for him.'

Jimmy thought over what he meant. 'Tips, yer mean?' He rubbed his thumb and forefinger together as though handling money.

'Exactly.'

'I see. Dress up, you said, you mean in my funeral suit?'

'Certainly not. No, I mean in some kind of old smock thing like old farmers used to wear.'

'I haven't got one of those. I'm sorry.'

'Pity. I'll have to apply my brains to that, then.'

'In a basket yer say.'

'Well, you can't have it in a plastic bag or something, can you. It wouldn't be in character.'

'You're not making me out to be the village idiot, are you? I'm not having that.'

63

'Certainly not. Simply a chap who's a real villager, a genuine memory they can take back with them to the States. I'm determined this is going to work. We'll all be making money at it, believe me.'

Jimmy stroked his chin, a habit he had when he was going to come out with some remark which would set the cat among the pigeons, as his old mother used to say. 'How about if I don't get any tips? I'm not doing it for nothing, not for no one.'

'I tell you what. You tell me what tips you get and if they don't add up to enough I'll add some to make it right.'

'And what if they add up to more than we expect? I'm not having you ripping me off.'

'Jimmy! I wouldn't do a thing like that. You know I'm as straight as a die.' Bryn looked affronted.

But Jimmy ignored that. 'Straight as a die. Oh, yes! That's why you took all Georgie's money, is it, when you flitted with that tart. That was very straight as a die. Don't take me for a fool.' Jimmy tapped the table sharply with his knuckles to emphasise his point.

'That was a big mistake on my part and has nothing to do with what we're talking about now. I'll think about it and come up with a sum of money I think will be fair.'

Jimmy frowned. 'It's all off if you don't play fair and square with me. I'm not having it. Come back when you've had another think.' He stood up, tucked his chair under the table, and indicated his intention by taking his old poaching coat from the peg on the back of the door and putting it on ready for walking Sykes.

'That's it! Poaching! You could tell some of your poaching tales. I never thought about that.'

'How long have they got here, then?'

'Ah! Two hours and they've to eat lunch, go in the Store for souvenirs, look around the church, listen to you.'

'Heck! They'll have it all to do at a run.'

'Leave it to me. I might squeeze in another half-hour. I'll look into that. But I take it I have your co-operation, then? You'd like to do it?'

'I think so. Twice this summer you say?'

Bryn nodded. 'That's right, more next year when I really get the ball rolling. It's going to be a money spinner I can tell you. This village is amazing, you know. No road signs, no street lights, no house numbers, a real genuine backwater it is. They'll love it. We live here and don't value it enough. It's normal to us, you see. To people who live in New York it's a piece of living history.'

'*It is.*'

'I know, we need to remind ourselves, though, just how left behind we are. Wonderful.' Bryn went to stand at Jimmy's front door. 'I mean, just look at it. Where in the world would you see houses still looking like they did the day they were built? Not a single house out of character. The only eyesore is the bus stop outside the Store. There's nothing else to spoil it, is there?'

'That's right, if yer don't look at Neville Neal's house. Or at Sir Ralph's Hipkin Gardens.'

'I know, but even those have been sensitively designed.'

'I'll give you that. Right, I'm off.' Wryly Jimmy added, 'I've no doubt you'll be back.'

Bryn found himself being turned out, but he didn't mind. He'd won his case, so another piece of his jigsaw was falling into place. He paused for a moment, watching Jimmy and Sykes wandering off down Stocks Row towards the spare land. No need for a lead for Sykes, just the right kind of freedom for a dog, but only this village could provide it. Imagine that, no zebra crossings, no one-way signs, nothing to mar the beauty of it. Bryn closed his eyes and felt himself to be back centuries, then the peace was disturbed by the sound of a car. When he opened his eyes he saw it was Sylvia Biggs, driving past the Royal Oak and on to heaven knew where. He glanced at his watch, half past nine, Georgie wouldn't be downstairs yet, give her another half-hour and she'd be having her morning coffee and he'd join her, with a bit of luck, and they could discuss their plans in more detail. Frankly, at the moment he found her presence enjoyable in a way he'd never found Elektra's. What a fool he'd been not to have seen the signs earlier and done something about winning Georgie back before it was all too late. Well, in his book it was never too late.

He found himself outside the Store where Jimbo was standing gazing at his new window display. 'Good morning, Jimbo.'

'Oh, right, good morning. What do you think then? Give me your opinion.'

'Absolutely excellent. If that doesn't empty your freezers of ready meals I don't know what will.'

Jimbo stepped further back and looked up to assess the impact the headquarters of his empire was making.

Bryn, in order to ingratiate himself, said, 'It's so good, I'm surprised you don't open another one in a similar situation.'

'With mail order and catering and this, I've enough on my plate. Another outlet would spread me too thinly and I'd spend too much time running back and forth, till in the end I'd finish up doing nothing well. No, we do better with just this. I've a couple of sample souvenirs to show you.' He strode off into the Store without bothering to see if Bryn was following, but he was right behind him, glad Jimbo was so enthusiastic.

When he emerged again into the front of the Store he found Georgie paying for some groceries. Bel had them packed into two bulging bags. Bryn said, 'Allow me. I was just coming across to see you.'

'Only to talk business.'

'Yes, and a coffee. I know there'll be one going about now. You see, I haven't forgotten your little ways, have I?' He heaved the bags from the counter, Georgie opened the door and the two of them went off down Stocks Row.

At that moment Dicky was outside at the front of the pub watering the window boxes with the hosepipe. He bent down to test the compost in the tubs and as he straightened up he caught sight of Georgie's bright-orange top. He made to wave but saw that Bryn was with her. They were both absorbed in conversation and hadn't noticed him. Damn him. The two of them had a togetherness he didn't like. A kind of companionableness which even four years of separation hadn't dented. Dicky snapped off the hosepipe and began winding it up on to his forearm. He disconnected it from the tap on the wall and carried it into the bar, leaving the door propped open, thinking Georgie and Bryn would follow.

He only had to see Bryn and the few doubts he had about Georgie's love surged to the front of his consciousness. She'd promised to ask Bryn for a divorce but he knew full well she hadn't. Dicky went to put the hosepipe away by the back door and found himself an unwitting eavesdropper. The two of them were standing just outside the back entrance talking.

'It's no good, Bryn, I don't object to doing business with you but as for anything else, well, it's Dicky you see, we want to marry.'

He heard Bryn gasp. 'So it's true, then. What are you thinking of, Georgie? For heaven's sake. The man is a twat. A runt. He's got no business acumen, nothing. And what about my share of the business? Eh? What about that? Our partnership has never been dissolved and I know he couldn't buy me out in a month of Sundays. Come to your senses, woman.'

'Don't you "woman" me. The money is no problem, he has the promise of whatever's needed for buying into the partnership and that's what I want him to do. Buy you out! Not that you deserve it considering how much money you took with you when you went off with that tart. You can try your best, Bryn, but I am marrying Dicky and I want a divorce *now*, or the lunch business is off.'

Dicky considered coughing in order to let them know he was there but the chance to hear the outcome of this conversation was not to be missed and he stayed where he was.

Bryn began laughing, that head-thrown-back, loud, mocking laugh he'd used before. When he calmed down he said, 'You wouldn't do that to me. Not to me! We mean too much to each other.'

'Now I know where you are I shall instruct my solicitor. I've plenty of evidence. I want a divorce immediately. Then Dicky and I can marry. He'll move in here and Bel will go to her house, which she longs to get back to. I can't wait to get my life straight. OK?'

'I don't want a divorce.'

'Well, you're getting one.'

'So where's he getting the money from to buy my share?'

Quickly Dicky dropped the hosepipe on the stone floor, swore loudly, picked it up and meandered through the door as though he'd just that moment arrived. He'd always known he was cut out to be an actor. He smiled at Georgie and said, 'Alan's made the coffee, when you're ready' and brushed past Bryn as though he didn't exist, hung the hosepipe on the bracket ready for another time and calmly went back into the bar. So she did want him. She did. He punched the air, triumphant. A triumph tinged with a bitter hatred of Bryn.

But Bryn wasn't aware of the rage burning in Dicky and after he'd had an enjoyable chat with Alan and a quiet word with Georgie he set off back to Neville's to use his computer for writing some business letters. On the way he noticed the church door was open so he decided to go in and have a look around to value its potential for a conducted tour. As he went up the church path he felt goosepimples coming up on his skin and didn't look up at the church tower. He must have been mad at the time, absolutely mad. He went in and began walking about. There appeared to be no one around so he assumed he must have the church to himself.

Some long forgotten memory surfaced as he looked at one of the tombs. Surely tombs were supposed to lie from east to west in a church, but this one lay north to south; how odd. He'd get Willie to look it up, there was definitely some history attached to it. He studied the carved screen, stood for a moment in the war memorial chapel looking at the names on the roll of honour. My God! Biggses and Joneses and Neals and Parkins, and *four* Glover brothers, and that was the list for the First World War. Sobering thought. He made a note in his little book to remind Willie to point out to the tourists about the four Glovers and then they'd meet one of their descendants on the green. What a touch. They'd be eating out of his hand in no time. Brilliant! On a special plaque of its own he read of the Templetons of Turnham House who'd also given their all for their country; in the American War of Independence, the Crimea, the Boer War and the two World Wars. What a history! What a sacrifice! For one brief moment Bryn wondered if he really should be making money from such tragedy, but quickly comforted himself with the thought that as they were all dead, and had been for years, they wouldn't be any the wiser.

The lights were on, but it was gloomy in the church because the storm clouds, which had been gathering over and beyond the bypass all morning, had finally arrived. The rain began clattering against the windows above the altar, beating a strange rhythmic tattoo on the stained glass, then lightning filled the church with a blaze of startling blue-white light, followed by the most enormous clap of thunder Bryn had ever heard in his life. Directly overhead, it appeared to make even the foundations of the building shudder. It was closely followed by another flash of lightning, which illuminated the whole of the window behind the altar and made the figure of Christ appear to move. In horror, Bryn sucked in his breath through clenched teeth. Thunder followed immediately, just as

70

loud and close as the first clap. Bryn, who couldn't remember having been as frightened ever before, not even as a kid watching a horror film, grasped the end of the nearest pew for support. For the first time in years he prayed. For the first time in years he felt a need to cower and hide. However, in the nick of time the man in him resisted. But the storm didn't abate for ten whole minutes by which time he was a wreck. The thunder and lightning passed over, the glowering skies lightened, gradually the rain reduced to a gentle pattering and the church once more became the friendly, secure place it always was. He sat down in a pew, wiped the sweat from his face and hands, and pulled himself together.

'All right, Bryn?'

Bryn almost shot out of his skin at the sound of the voice so kindly enquiring after his health. He turned, dreading whom he might see. It was Peter. Relief. What a relief. That was odd, Peter was completely dry so if he'd only just come in how could he be . . . ?

Bryn held out his hand. 'My, what a storm! Never known the like, not even a tropical storm.'

Peter shook hands saying, 'How are you? I've been going to call.'

'I'm well and you?'

Peter nodded. 'Fine, thanks. You've come back to make things right for Georgie then?'

Bryn was about to say yes but as always Peter's blue eyes saw right through him and he couldn't tell a lie – well, not a serious one anyway. 'I've come back to help make amends, yes.'

'Good! May I sit down? Have you time to talk?'

'Oh, yes.' He moved down the pew a little and Peter sat beside him.

'What do you propose?' Peter rested his elbow on the back of the pew and waited for a reply.

Bryn knew all about Peter's ability to leave a silence, which one felt compelled to fill immediately and which often made one fall right into a trap of one's own making, but he thought for a while before answering. 'I'm bringing some business to Georgie and the pub, and the rest of the village if they want it.'

'This American tourist business.'

'That's right.' Bryn got carried away explaining his plans, embroidering his spiel here and there to make it more appealing, mentioning the tour of the church and his hope that the tourists might contribute to church funds. He'd thought about a collection plate or something . . .

'I'm not sure I like the idea of people paying to enter a house of God.'

'There wouldn't be a fixed charge, just . . .' He searched for the word. 'Donations.'

'I'll think about that. Sounds an excellent idea, but I wasn't meaning your business plans at all. I meant making things right so Dicky can marry Georgie.'

Again that dratted silence of his.

This time Bryn had no defence against it and, fumbling in his mind for a reply, said the first idiotic thing that came into his head. 'Let's be honest here, padre, she won't do herself any good at all marrying that little squirt. What does he know about business? He's a non-starter, he is. No, I'm doing her a favour by *not* divorcing her.'

'I don't believe in divorce, Bryn, but I have come to realise that if life is hell then something has to be done

72

about it. I can think of not one single thing in your favour that could persuade me you are not under a moral obligation to release Georgie.'

After he sorted out what Peter meant, Bryn's jaw dropped open.

Peter got to his feet. 'I mean it. In my view the cards are all stacked against you. Give it some thought. If you need someone to talk it over with, my door is always open.'

Bryn watched Peter walk towards the choir vestry and hardened his heart to his advice. Divorce? Not likely. Perhaps things wouldn't get back entirely to what they were – after all, he'd be travelling to the States drumming up business and then he'd be going round England escorting his tours – but divorce was out. Bryn stood up and decided to go into the churchyard for a breath of air now the rain had virtually stopped.

He stood under a tree and looked over the wall towards Turnham House. Magnificent building, that. One day, you never knew, he might be living in such a house. He mused on the subject for a while, realising that it would be no fun without Georgie.

The moral dilemma Peter had presented to him niggled away at the back of his mind. What the hell, she was still his legal wife and he would resist divorce with every fibre of his body. Her marrying that ... he cringed at the prospect of Dicky being Georgie's husband. It was like something out of one of Dicky's joke books. He focused his eyes on the figure crossing the field between him and Turnham House. It was Jimmy returning from his walk. Way behind him came a flash of white and black: Sykes hurrying to catch up. Bryn thought, he's going to get back into the village by crossing Rector's Meadow and then climbing the gate into Pipe and Nook.

But Jimmy changed direction and appeared to be heading for the little gate in the churchyard wall. Well, he couldn't be bothered with Jimmy at the moment, he'd too much on his mind, so Bryn set off down the church path, into Church Lane and turned through the gates of Glebe House.

Jimmy had changed his intended route because he'd seen some people emerge from the little copse which backed up to the churchyard wall and wondered what they were up to. There'd been gypsies about for a while and he thought maybe they were them, making a reconnaissance of the church with a view to theft. But as he drew closer he recognised Gilbert Johns. Jimmy waved. Gilbert called out, 'Hi!' The three young people who were with Gilbert also waved. They were carrying papers and clipboards and measuring tapes and, despite sheltering in the copse, were soaking wet.

'What you up to, Gilbert? Thinking of buying this place, are you?' He jerked his head in the direction of the Big House.

Gilbert laughed. 'No. No. These three are archaeology students; they're working in my department for a few weeks. We're looking for the possible site of a plague pit somewhere close to the church wall. We know there is one and we think it might be in this copse.'

Jimmy stood stock still. Sykes, who by now had caught up with him, bristled and growled and, when he saw Jimmy looking as though he intended to walk forward towards Gilbert, he flattened himself to the ground showing his teeth in a nasty snarl and then, apparently overcome by terror, fled under the gate into the church-yard and disappeared.

'You're not thinking of digging?'

'We might, if we decide it's the right place.'

'You'd better not, all hell'll be let loose.'

Gilbert smiled and the students sniggered, hiding their laughter behind their clipboards.

'You can laugh. No one goes in that copse. See my dog? He gives that copse a wide berth every time we come past. I couldn't *drag* 'im in there even if I wanted to, which I don't. Take my advice and leave well alone. We all do, that's why it's so overgrown. The groundsmen never touch it.'

'Come on, you know more than you're saying. Tell all.'

It was the long pause before Jimmy answered that made the students want to laugh out loud. Gilbert repeated, 'Tell all.'

'Old people around here, *if* they mention it at all, call it . . . Deadman's Dell.'

The students shouted, 'We're right, that'll be it.' They almost danced a jig at the prospect.

Gilbert raised an eyebrow. 'Deadman's Dell? Really? That sounds hopeful.'

Jimmy backed off. 'You're not thinking of . . . like . . . digging there, are you?'

'We very well might.'

'It's not right, it's irreverent, that is, digging for bones. Didn't them poor devils suffer enough before they died, never mind digging 'em up now? Them could be ancestors of folk who still live hereabouts. It's not right. No, grave robbing's not right.'

The students looked scornful. Gilbert said quietly, 'As county archaeologist I can guarantee that whatever we do – if, in fact, we do anything at all – would be done with the greatest respect.'

Jimmy backed off a little further. 'It'll be safer if you do nothing at all. We don't want that copse digging up; tempting fate, that is, tempting fate.' Jimmy wagged his finger at them. 'It's already started. What do yer think that storm was about? It was a warning, that's what. Leave well alone, do you hear me? Serve yer bloody right if you all get the plague yerselves.' He walked off towards the little gate, put his hand on it, briefly turned back to look at them, wagged his finger again, and shouted, 'Take heed! You'll be cursed!' Then he went through and disappeared from sight.

The students at first doubled up with laughter and then fell silent, suddenly feeling concerned.

'Cursed?'

'Where have we come? I mean, don't they know in this village that it's the twenty-first century. We haven't gone into a time warp, have we?'

Gilbert assured them that no, they hadn't, and that Jimmy was being incredibly naïve and of course they weren't cursed; there was no such thing as being cursed and with Mr Fitch's permission they'd investigate. Mr Fitch, he knew, would give the go-ahead without hesitation, because he was a practical, down-to-earth man who would love nothing better than . . .

'But should we be disturbing ancient bones? After all, they've been buried there more than six hundred years. What would we gain when all's said and done?'

Gilbert placed a finger on his temple. 'Knowledge. A paper published. Progress.'

'And afterwards?'

'To appease everyone we'd have the bones interred in the churchyard with a headstone or a plaque, and we'll have a funeral service, which they wouldn't have had at the time of the plague. No priest, no time.'

'Gilbert, be honest, you must be feeling a bit of concern because you used the word "appease".'

'Only because these people are superstitious beyond belief. They'll imagine all kinds of terrible things will happen, which could have happened anyway even without us opening up that pit. Right? I'll see the Rector, too, on Sunday and make it right with him.'

Jimmy had expected to find Sykes waiting for him outside his cottage door, but he wasn't there. Eventually he went looking for him in the church, it being Sykes's second home, and found him shivering and afraid, hiding under a pew in the very darkest corner. Jimmy knelt down and peered under the seat. 'Come on, Sykes, old chap. Jimmy'll take you home. Come on, now.' But Sykes wouldn't come and had to be dragged out by his scruff, and carried home because he refused to walk. Sykes cowered in his bed for the rest of the morning and only came out when Jimmy, in desperation, offered him a saucer of warm milk sweetened with a spoonful of honey which, in Sykes's opinion, came a very close second to Dicky's home-brewed ale.

Chapter 5

Jimmy didn't go to Culworth station to work his taxi that night; he went to the pub instead and hoped to find as many local people as he could to whom he could relate his experience of the morning. With Sykes tucked under the settle, he had a small crowd gathered round him listening avidly in no time at all. 'So-o-o, it has to be stopped.' Jimmy took a pull at his ale, banged the tankard down and waited for some reaction.

Vince Jones, now doorstop manufacturer and picture framer to Charter-Plackett Enterprises, scratched his head and said a little scornfully, 'I reckon you're making too much of this thunderstorm business. It wasn't that bad.'

'You should have been out in it. I was. I know.'

'It was pure coincidence, that's what. Wasn't it, Willie?'

Willie, who had experienced funny coincidences in the past with a tomb in the church, didn't dismiss Jimmy's argument quite so decisively. 'He could have a point. There's some funny things happen because of the past. But what's the use of digging up old bones, what would they do with 'em when they'd got 'em? Nothing. Rector won't agree anyway, believe me.'

Jimmy looked towards Sylvia and asked her what she thought.

'Well, that would be for the Rector to say, he knows best. But I think they should be dug up and buried right.'

'It's not on holy ground, though, so it's got nothing to do with 'im. If anyone can protest it's old Fitch, it's on his land.'

Mrs Jones piped up, 'I reckon Willie is right, what does it matter anyway? There's more important things than a few old bones, Jimmy.'

'Not much more important if it brings destruction down on the village. It doesn't do to interfere with the past. Just think, Vince, they might be ancestors of yours.' Certain he'd thought up a reason which would bring Vince out in support, Jimmy had another long drink of his ale and waited for Vince's reaction.

'You've backed the wrong horse there, Jimmy. My great-grandfather came from the Rhondda Valley way back, but definitely not as far back as them bones. So they're not my relatives.'

'No, Vince, but they could be mine.' Mrs Jones suddenly discovered a deep empathy with those bones in Deadman's Dell. 'There's been Flatmans in the parish records for years. I think I might have a right to a say what happens to 'em.'

Vince snorted his disdain at her fanciful idea. 'Get on, yer daft beggar, what the hell does it matter?'

Willie, brought abruptly to life by Sylvia's championing of the bones burial question, demanded, 'You mean you'd go against me?'

'Well, yes, I think I would. They've a right to Christian burial, they have.' Sylvia shuddered as though she were being asked to be buried in unholy ground. Sensing a row brewing, however, she said, 'Anyways, they could dig and

79

find nothing at all, so I'm not going to worry myself about it till it happens, if it ever does. Willie, go get the drinks in. Will you join us Mrs Jones, Vince?'

They'd just got themselves nicely settled with their drinks at Jimmy's table when in came Bryn Fields. Jimmy debated as to whether or not Bryn would support him and decided that he didn't want him on his side anyway, so he'd keep quiet. But he hadn't bargained for Alan Crimble having overheard their conversation while he'd been going round collecting empty glasses.

Alan served Bryn his drink and then, leaning confidentially on the bar counter while Bryn downed his first whisky of the day, he confided what he'd heard.

Bryn listened with great concentration, wondering how he could turn this to his advantage. Of course! Willie could show the tourists the site of the plague pit and make the point about bones interred there being those of ancestors of people still living in the village. It all fitted in beautifully. Maybe they could put up a plaque, 'Here lie victims of the Black Death', in old-fashioned writing. My word! Things were coming together better than he could ever have hoped. 'Thanks, Alan. That might come in useful.'

'O' course, Jimmy's convinced that storm was caused by them students poking about in the Dell. Reckons we'll be in right trouble.'

Bryn pushed his glass across the counter and intimated he wanted a refill. That storm. He still felt distinctly iffy about it. Could Jimmy be right? God! This place was getting to him. He'd got a turnip for a head if he thought like that. By the time he'd drunk his second whisky he'd got things under control. This was a real gift, oh, yes! An absolute gift. Well, he'd bide his time and play the long game. Talk about a stroke of luck. By Jove! Things couldn't be better.

The question of Deadman's Dell became the main topic of conversation in the bar. It spread to the dining room to people wholly unconnected with the village, people who only saw it as a quaint place to eat on a summer's evening, but they also had opinions on the matter. Roughly, had there been a head count, they were divided fifty-fifty as to whether or not the Dell should be the subject of an archaeological dig.

Gilbert Johns, in the choir vestry the following morning organising his collection of choirboys into an angelic chorus, remembered that he had to speak to Peter after the service about the Dell, as he chastised one boy for his crumpled surplice, another for his unruly hair, held out a tissue to a third, demanding he remove his chewing gum, reminded the youngest member not to rustle sweet papers during prayers and asked for silence.

Twenty pairs of eyes looked up at him and Gilbert said, as he always did, 'Good morning, chaps. We'll run through our exercises, get ourselves in trim. Ready?' He raised his hand, gave them their note and started them off on a pattern of chords and scales they could have done in their sleep. They'd sung in cathedrals and won choir competitions under his tutelage, and next to archaeology the choir was his passion. Gilbert was so proud of them all, and they in their turn worshipped him. He had the knack of treating them as equals, yet keeping control, of bringing out the best in them but not demanding more than they had to give. This September two of them would be going to cathedral choir schools, and there weren't many village church church choirs could boast of that. All in all they were a brilliant bunch and what was so encouraging was the list of boys waiting their turn to join. They came from Turnham Malpas, Penny Fawcett and Little Derehams, and even from as far away as Culworth.

Gilbert checked his watch: nine fifty-nine precisely. He cocked an ear for Mrs Peel's final trill before . . . there it was. 'Ready. Quiet now. Here we go.' He snapped a thumb and finger twice, his signal for them to adopt what he called their 'church face', and opened the door. Whether it was the ruffs around their necks or the glowing red of the choirboys' cassocks or their shining morning faces, the hearts of the congregation always lifted when the choir appeared and quite a few female hearts fluttered at the sight of Gilbert processing down the aisle. He had his choirmaster face on and didn't even see his Louise, freed from their three little ones by the crèche to sit for an hour in comparative peace.

Once the service was over and he had dismissed the choir he went in search of Peter. He found him in his vestry removing his surplice. 'There you are.'

Peter said, 'I am. I expect you've come to see me about the Dell?'

'You know, then.'

'I do. They're all talking about it and expecting me to stop you doing it. Shall I?'

'Do you want to?'

Peter sat on the edge of the table, folded his arms and asked 'Do you want me to?'

'In fact, you can't, because if we're right it isn't on church land.'

'Somehow, though, overnight, bones have become my responsibility.' With a wry smile on his face Peter asked, 'You tell me what is really happening.'

'As opposed to rumours and counter-rumours.'

'That's right.'

'We think there's a pit, dug at the time of the plague, where they buried people because they had no priest to hold services and they were dying so fast they'd no one to dig proper graves so they did the next best thing: dug a big hole outside church land and bunged them all in. If we are proved right, which we can only do by digging, we shall examine the remains, find out what we can. Then what I propose, with your approval, obviously, is to hold a service and bury them in the churchyard. That way they'll have had a funeral service and be buried on consecrated ground even though it's ... what? ... six hundred and more years late.'

Peter sat thinking for a moment, head down, staring at a worn patch in the vestry carpet. 'No doubt I shall be harangued from Little Derehams to Penny Fawcett for agreeing but yes, I think you should, mainly because I prefer the idea of them being buried in consecrated ground and only for that reason, and you can tell everyone I shall conduct the funeral service.'

'Thanks. You know we'll deal with everything with the greatest respect.'

'Of course. I wouldn't expect anything other. Mr Fitch will be delighted, he loves anything like this. I hope you'll make sure for his sake that it gets into the papers.' He grinned at Gilbert who raised a finger in acknowledgement of Peter's understanding of the workings of Mr Fitch's mind.

'I shall be seeing him tomorrow. He'll be glad of your approval, likes to be seen nowadays "doing what's right by the village". Must go. Louise will be champing at the bit to be off.'

'Your brood OK?'

'Fine, thanks.'

'Good. Doesn't get easier the older they get.'

'Thanks for the warning. Talking of warnings, there's going to be a lot of opposition. Apparently that storm we had was solely a warning to me for poking about in the Dell and worse is about to fall if we continue. Just thought I'd say.'

'I can see what they mean, though.'

They both laughed.

Gilbert left, then came back and, putting his head round the vestry door, said, 'By the way, thanks. Grateful for your support.'

As he went to gather up Louise and the children he met Bryn who had paid one of his rare visits to church that morning. He was lurking by the lych-gate clumsily clutching the baby, while Louise was playing a complicated chasing game between the gravestones with the two older ones. Bryn handed the baby to him saying, 'Here, this is yours. I was waiting for a word.'

'Be my guest.'

'I want you to know you have my full support over the Dell. I've been thinking, if you find what you think you'll find, how about a plaque, say, on the church wall by the little gate explaining all about it?'

'Where my hunches are concerned, I've learned to wait and see until I'm proved right. Everything points to us being right but one never knows. However, it would be Peter who would have to give permission for that.'

'Well, I just wanted you to know that at least you have *my* full support. We should know about these things, it's important to the village's history.'

Rather sourly, for him, Gilbert replied, 'To say nothing of your tourist scheme, eh?' The baby began to stir fretfully. 'This baby is about to scream for his food and my mother-in-law will be frothing at the mouth; she's expecting us for lunch. Will you excuse us?'

Bryn opened his mouth to protest that he was only thinking of the good of the village, but Gilbert shouted, 'Louise! Come!' and she did, scooping up the two gravestone chasers as she came, so before he could explain himself properly to Gilbert they were already crossing the green.

By Saturday a fire was burning near Deadman's Dell. The students had arrived that morning in a dilapidated old car equipped with rakes, billhooks and thick gloves to clear the undergrowth before commencing their dig.

A small group of onlookers had gathered, among them Alex and Beth from the Rectory, having spied the activity from the attic window, Bryn who tried to pretend he hadn't a vested interest in their success but seriously failing to do so, going so far as to offer to supervise the bonfire, Willie leaning on the church wall, Fran and Flick who'd had a phone call from Beth in case they were at a loose end, and Mrs Jones who'd walked up to the village to go to a coffee morning in the church hall but couldn't resist taking a peek, having no doubts that numerous Flatman ancestors were about to see the light of day.

Willie, concerned that the children were getting far too close to the fire, called out, 'Beth! Alex! You'll have a better view if you sit on the wall.' He patted the top of the wall and hoped they'd come; the two of them could come up with some devilish arguments for doing exactly as they wished, arguments which defeated his powers of reasoning. Fortunately for him they saw the merits of his idea and came running. Beth, to her fury, couldn't get up onto the wall and he had to lean over and help her, but Alex had sprung up without assistance. Beth put out her tongue at Alex, then settled herself after she'd found a smooth piece of coping stone on which to sit. The two of them talked non-stop to Willie and he had to admit to a sigh of relief when he spotted Sylvia arriving with a bag of sweets.

Beth spied the bag immediately. 'Sylvia! Are those sweets for Willie?'

'They were, but I dare say he's kind enough to share.'

They were assorted sweets from the pick'n'mix in Tesco's, and Beth loved the Turkish delights. With her mouth full of chocolate and Turkish delight, Beth asked Sylvia if she thought she might have ancestors in the pit.

'I doubt it. My great-grandmother came from far, far away.'

'How far?'

'Scotland.'

'That's a long way. What about your great-grandfather?'

'Same. Came to work on Nightingale Farm.'

Beth considered this for a while, watching the great piles of brushwood the students were heaping on the fire, and helping herself to another sweet from Sylvia's bag. 'Just think, if we'd got seven children in our house like the Nightingales . . .'

'Thank heavens you haven't, I don't think I'd have coped. Think of the ironing.'

It was almost possible to hear the workings of Beth's mind. 'Did you work at the Rectory *before* we were born?'

There was a cautious note in Sylvia's voice when she replied, 'No, I started when you were about four weeks old.'

'So you remember us being born, then?'

'No. I've just said you were about four weeks old.'

'Does Willie remember?'

'They'll be needing a saw for them thick branches. I'll go and get one for 'em.' Willie beat a quick retreat, and Alex in his absence dropped down off the wall and went to help Bryn with the fire.

Beth turned her guns on Sylvia again. 'Did you know my mummy isn't my mummy?'

'Yes, but if you're going to ask me if I knew your real mummy, I didn't. It's like I said, you were four weeks old when I came to live in. Now watch the fire, it's getting bigger and bigger, isn't it?'

Beth agreed. She felt the urge to know about her mother much more than Alex did. They'd discussed it a lot these last few weeks when no one was about and he'd refused to try to find out. But she couldn't help herself. Something kept rising in her chest, something she couldn't make go away, a need to *know*, a need to feel, a need to talk about her real mother. Daddy was Daddy and Alex was like him, so much like him it was unbelievable and the bigger he grew the more like Daddy he looked. But Beth Harris didn't look like anyone she knew. It certainly wasn't Harriet or Miss Pascoe at school, or any of the mothers who gathered at the school gate or taught in the

Sunday School or helped with the Brownies or walked the streets of Culworth. She was always on the lookout and had not yet seen anyone with her rounded cheeks, her fair skin, or her thick ash-blonde hair, or her sturdy legs, no one at all. So where was she, this mother of hers and Alex? Maybe she'd died when they were born. That could be it! Having twins must be hard work. As Miss Pascoe had said in those lessons they'd had, mothers had to push their babies out and she'd had it to do twice!

Willie came back with the saw but took care not to stand anywhere close to Beth. She knew why. He didn't want to tell her anything if he could avoid it. Nobody did. She wasn't a logical person at all, she left all that to Alex, but like a flash of light she realised that the only, only person she could ask who really would know and would give her a truthful answer was her daddy.

So one day she would take her chance. He didn't bath her any more now she was grown-up. In the past that had always been a good time to talk, so she'd . . . the fire was out of control, smoke was billowing and blowing straight at her, Sylvia was coughing and waving her arms, shouting, 'Children! Come with me. Alex! Where's Alex?' It caught the lower twigs of a tree growing inside the churchyard wall, the breeze aiding and abetting its spread. 'Alex! Where are you?'

Beth stood up on the wall and screamed, 'Alex! Alex!'

Sylvia pulled her down and hurried her away, insisting she stood by a gravestone well away from the fire and didn't move. Then Beth saw flames leaping, smoke rising in great clouds, voices shouting; that was Willie, that was Bryn, that was Sylvia. Flick and Fran joined her and they stood huddled together, horrified; the tree which had given up its lower branches to the scorching heat now took on a fire all of its own and the flames crackled and licked up the branches.

Willie raced by calling, 'Go home, out of the way.'

Flick tried to move her away but Beth refused to go. 'Alex! Alex!' she kept shouting. 'Alex!' Great sobs exploded in her chest. 'Alex!'

With her eyes squeezed tight with fear she didn't see him come running through the little gate. 'Isn't it a great fire? It's caught two trees in the churchyard now.' His face was aglow with excitement. 'Willie's gone for the hose.'

Beth opened her eyes, truly saw him standing there in front of her, unharmed and ready to burst with excitement and, fuelled by relief, all the fear balled up inside her went into the beating she gave him. Her fists flying, her feet kicking, her voice hoarse with shouting, she charged him time and again, and it wasn't until Caroline came running and took hold of her that she stopped.

Willie fastened the hose to the tap in the wall, Bryn and one of the students heaved the reel over into the field and unwound it as fast as they could, Willie turned on the tap but the flow from one hose made little impression at first. Gradually it began to get the fire under control. By then, though, everyone from the coffee morning and most of the villagers living around the green were in the churchyard watching.

Caroline was sitting apart on a flat gravestone, hugging Beth, with Alex standing beside them, puzzled by her onslaught. 'I didn't do anything, Mum, honestly I didn't. It was her.'

'I know you didn't. She was frightened, that's all.'

'It's a brilliant fire, isn't it? It happened whoosh! Just

like that. I was throwing twigs and things on and then whoosh! Up it went. I was there right in the middle of it all. Did you see the flames?'

'All right, Alex, that will do. Yes, I did, that's why I'm here.'

Beth wriggled free of her mother's arms and looked at Alex through her tears. 'I thought you'd been burned up.'

'No-o-o. Not me. I was too quick.'

'I shouted and shouted.'

Brimming with excitement, Alex told her he couldn't hear her shout for the crackling of the flames. 'You should have seen it.'

'I did!' Fresh tears rolled down her cheeks. She put her arms round Caroline's neck and buried her face in her shoulder. 'Go away, you *stupid* boy.'

Caroline began to laugh, as much with relief as anything else. 'Oh, darling, I do love you. I'd have wanted to do just the same.'

'Hit him?'

'Well, perhaps not quite so hard as you did, but yes. It's being glad they're all right, isn't it? After being so frightened.'

'I thought he'd b-b-burned up like a guy.'

'Here, let's wipe your face.' Caroline took out a tissue and dabbed Beth's face for her, smiling with love while she did. 'There we are, you're all presentable now. Better?'

Beth nodded. There was nothing quite like a good hug when you're frightened and Caroline knew just how to hug her to make her better. Perhaps she'd leave finding out about her own mother till she was bigger. Then, looking over Caroline's shoulder, she saw her daddy striding between the graves towards them, looking both relieved and angry at the same time. He'd given her his blue eyes, she could see that. She squeezed Caroline's neck more tightly. There was no doubt that he was their daddy. He came over and gave them both a hug and a kiss. 'I couldn't get off the phone. Thank heavens you're all right. Where's Alex?'

Beth answered him, 'The stupid boy is in the field.'

'Whose fault is this?'

Caroline, her hand cradling his as it gripped her shoulder, said, 'No one's. I think it just happened.'

'I'll go and see. Coming, Beth?'

She shook her head in reply and held tight to Caroline, content to wallow in security and love for a while longer. 'You're the best mummy ever.' Gradually the excitement of the fire got to her and, filled with curiosity, she disentangled herself and stood up. 'I'll just go and see what he's up to, the stupid boy.'

He was standing by, listening to his father tearing a strip off the students and Bryn.

'Didn't it occur to you that the fire should have been made much further away from the wall. I am surprised at you. Where is Gilbert?'

'Coming.'

'Is he indeed. Well, I suppose we have to be thankful it didn't spread to the church hall. There's one thing about it, you won't have to clear the Dell any more, the fire's done it for you.'

Deadman's Dell was now a charred mess. The trees were only blackened and scarred on their trunks, leaving the twigs and leaves more or less untouched and would soon recover, but the undergrowth was totally burned away exposing rich-looking soil undisturbed for centuries and, once the sun had done its job and dried the blackened grass and weeds, digging would be easy.

Peter stood gazing down at the soil wondering what secrets it might or might not reveal. He turned his attention to Alex. 'You've learned a lesson this morning. Tell me what it is.'

'Fire's dangerous?'

'And unpredictable.'

'And *strong*. Whooosh!' Alex imitated the flames with his hands, swooping them here and there in wild, excitable gestures.

'Powerful's the word. Never to be tampered with. Never to be regarded lightly.'

'I see that.'

'Good. So long as you've learned to treat it with respect. Like the sea, when it's out of your control it's your master not your friend.'

'Fire's a friend when it keeps you warm. Fire's a friend when it cooks your dinner. It's a friend for a blacksmith . . . and a glass blower.'

'Because they don't let it get out of hand, do they? Life's precious and you're precious. I wouldn't want to make you afraid of life, but if you take risks, Alex, then make sure they're calculated risks.' Peter put a protective arm round Alex's shoulders.

Taken off his guard by finding himself unexpectedly in the midst of a confidential talk, Alex took a step he never intended to. 'Man to man, Dad, are you my dad?'

'I am.'

'Then who's my mother? It's not Mum, is it? I remember she said so years ago.'

'No. As she told you, she can't have children, so someone else had you for us. You'll have to be content with that for now.'

'All right. But . . .'

Seeing Beth skipping towards them, Peter answered sharply, 'Enough, Alex.'

'But . . .'

'Enough.' He despised himself for not being truthful, he who valued truth so highly in all his relationships. 'If you want to see the start of that film, we'd better go home for lunch right now. Has Mummy gone home, Beth?'

Beth nodded. 'Will they really find bones, Daddy?'

'Gilbert hopes so.'

'I shan't be a bone person.'

'Neither shall I. I'm going to be a fighter pilot.' Alex zoomed off, arms outstretched whirring about Rector's Meadow lost in thought.

Beth shouted, 'Come back, you stupid boy.' Staring scornfully at him as he wheeled about she said, 'You wouldn't think he was ten, would you, Daddy?'

Peter looked down at her and thought, she's older than we realise. She'll have to be told. They'll both have to be told and the innocence of childhood, which he and Caroline had striven so hard to preserve for them, will be gone for ever. And worse, what would their opinion be of him? As he'd said to Caroline that night when they'd discussed what Harriet had told him, their opinion of him was a burden he had to bear.

Alex came back to join them and they made their way home, along with the people who'd rushed out of the coffee morning to see the fun.

One said, 'That was a fire and a half, wasn't it, Rector? You didn't see the worst of it.'

Another said, 'Wouldn't mind, but they haven't even lifted a trowel yet and it's caused trouble. They shouldn't be doing it.'

And yet another, 'Don't be daft. It wasn't them bones that caused the fire.'

'I'm surprised at you, Rector, encouraging 'em with promises of a service and burial and that.'

'So am I. Downright asking for trouble.'

'Downright irresponsible of you, Rector, if you ask me.'

Peter stopped to confront his accusers. 'When they died they were deprived of the services of a priest and of burial in consecrated ground, so I shall see they get it, just as I shall make sure, if I am still here, that when you enter eternal life you too will have a service in this church and be buried here as is your right.'

Gasps of astonishment at his forthrightness could be heard, but Peter ignored them and continued home through the lych-gate.

Alex muttered, 'Good for you, Dad.'

But they weren't to escape because just as Peter put his key in the door of the Rectory Bryn hailed him.

Peter said, 'Go in, children, I won't be a moment. Yes, Bryn, what can I do for you?'

'Just want to say thanks for standing up to them, and for promising to support the dig. I'm all for it. Important for the village and all that.'

'No, Bryn, be honest, important for *you* and your tourist scam. My motives have nothing whatsoever to do with that. It would be a whole lot better if you paid attention to the matter I discussed with you the last time we spoke. If you'll forgive me, my lunch is ready.' Peter went inside leaving Bryn angry and upset.

Jimmy called across from his front door, 'Put that in your pipe and smoke it, Bryn Fields. Serves yer right.' He went into his cottage, hooting with laughter.

Bryn made a rude gesture at him and went back to Glebe House to lick his wounds.

Chapter 6

One of the best places for catching up on the latest gossip was by the tinned soups in the Store. There was something comfortable and private about that small area and many were the tales told in the confines of that secluded spot which proved totally untrue, but also there were many which proved startlingly and unbelievably accurate.

Mrs Jones, getting her shopping after finishing her stint in the mail order office, had decided to treat Vince, now he was working, to a nice tin of cream of chicken soup. She browsed along the shelves debating whether or not to pay over the odds and get a really tasty one with white wine in it, or whether his doorstops and picture frames really did merit such madness. Behind her she heard footsteps and turned to see who it was.

Linda Crimble was doing her shopping.

'Who's looking after the post office, then?'

Linda sprang indignantly to her own defence. 'Mr Charter-Plackett. It is my lunch hour you know.'

'Who's rattled your cage?'

'Nobody.'

'Somebody must have, snapping at me like that. I only asked a civil question.'

Linda put her wire basket down on the floor. 'Sorry, it's Alan, he's all at sixes and sevens.'

Mrs Jones raised an eyebrow and waited.

Linda drew closer. 'Heaven alone knows what's going on at the pub; Alan can't make it out. Every night when he comes home he goes on and on about it.'

Mrs Jones's eyebrow rose a little further.

'Bryn's . . .'

Someone brushed past in a hurry, snatching a Scotch Broth as they went.

'Bryn's causing such ructions, you wouldn't believe.'

'With Dicky you mean.'

Linda nodded. 'Well, Bryn's like . . . courting Georgie.'

'Courting?' Both Mrs Jones's eyebrows went the highest they ever could.

'Sh! He's making up to her like nobody's business; there every night, flirting and that. Dicky's fit to boil.'

'No!'

'He is. Bryn never gives him a chance to talk with Georgie, private like.'

'But I thought Georgie was wanting a divorce.'

'She is. But he's so charming to her, is Bryn, you wouldn't believe.'

'Well I never.'

'Alan says you could cut the atmosphere with a knife some nights and Georgie's been quite sharp with Dicky a time or two.'

'Well . . .'

'Alan says one night there's going to be a bust-up, and you can't quite forget, you know, that Bryn did try to . . .' Linda drew a finger across her throat.

'Exactly. Well, you never know, do you?'

'You don't. Dicky's always so pleasant, it's not fair to 'im. He's not been so good with his comic turns as he usually is, bit quiet like, but there's no wonder, is there? Bryn was so against him doing it when his name was over the door. My Alan says sometimes Georgie really falls for Bryn flattering her.'

Mrs Jones folded her arms across her chest, her big brown eyes agog with interest. 'Really! Yes, well, I dare say he can be a charmer when he wants, though I've never noticed it. It must be difficult for your Alan, being in the middle of it all so to speak.'

'It is. Alan reckons there'll be murder done there before long.'

'Does he really?' Hoping to learn more, Mrs Jones bent her head a little closer to Linda and prompted her with a question. 'Bryn doesn't stay the night, does he, by any chance?'

They both heard Jimbo clearing his throat and Linda looked at her watch. 'Whoops, that's me. Time's up.'

'Keep me posted.'

Linda winked. 'I will.'

That same night Dicky was at Scouts so Bryn saw his chance. He'd been working up to it for days and now was his moment to take steps. He didn't know where they would lead him but he knew where he wanted them to lead: straight into Georgie's bedroom. He debated the choice of cravat or bow tie and decided that the cravat in Turnham Malpas would look out of place, but would give a more relaxed impression. He smoothed the grey hairs above his ears, wondered if he should dye them, but decided the grey added a touch of dignity and authority, checked his trousers were pin neat, notched his belt a little tighter, thrust back his shoulders and decided that, yes, how could she possibly resist him. He'd noticed a definite softening in her attitude over the last few days and . . .

When he'd tossed back his second whisky he leaned confidentially across the bar counter and said to Alan, 'Georgie?'

'Broken a nail. Won't be a minute.'

'New girl working out OK?'

Alan's habitual deadpan face broke into a slight grin. 'Trish is great. Thumbs up, as you might say.'

'Like that, is it?' Bryn looked across and watched her weaving between the tables, wiping spills and collecting glasses. Trim bottom she had, no sagging there. Mm . . . he could see what Alan meant. Bright as a button she looked, so they weren't all dunderheads in Penny Fawcett, then. He ordered a third whisky while he waited for his prey to return to the bar.

When she did, Bryn was overcome with genuine admiration for her. Tonight Georgie wore a black suit, with a white shirt in a fine material which had a soft, frilly, waterfall sort of collar. Her blonde hair, mercifully still not needing assistance from a bottle, was kind of bubbly and frothy around her still pretty face and he felt a gut-wenching he hadn't felt in years. The cold, scheming plan he'd had back at Glebe House fell apart; just as he had when he'd very first met her, he fancied her like hell. A lump came into his throat at the memory.

He held up his half-empty glass and toasted her, calling out, 'Pretty as ever, Georgie, I don't know how you do it.'

Georgie, who'd thought she had the problem of Bryn

well sorted in her mind, noticed the jaunty cravat below the well-tanned face and thought how handsome he looked. Such presence he has tonight. I'll have to watch my step. She answered, 'Less of your cheek, Bryn Fields. How many of those have you had?' She nodded towards the whisky he held in his hand.

'My third.'

'Didn't know you drank at this pace. Nothing to do?'

'Plenty, but I try not to work in the evenings. Too much work makes Jack a dull boy.'

'We can't have that, can we?'

Bryn smiled at her, sensing again the softening of her attitude. 'Quiet in here tonight.'

'Often is, Mondays.'

'I see Georgie's little helper isn't about.'

'No. Scouts.'

'You're looking very attractive tonight. Haven't seen that outfit before.'

Surprised to find that the mild flirting they were doing was exceedingly welcome, Georgie said, flicking a finger at the waterfall collar of her shirt, 'It's new, glad you like it.'

'Oh, I do. That collar softens the severity of the suit.'

'Just what I thought.'

'A feminine touch, so to speak.'

'Exactly.'

Georgie realised that the few customers at the tables had gone very quiet and were avidly listening to them. She flushed at the thought that they were giving their audience such entertainment.

Bryn noticed her blush and felt elated. 'I'll give you a hand at closing, I know how much there is to do.'

A week ago she would have refused him point blank but not tonight. 'Thanks.'

'My pleasure, I assure you.'

Georgie served a lone customer who'd strayed in and as she slotted the money into the drawers of the till said, 'Alan! You and Trish can manage for half an hour, can you?'

'Of course.'

'Just need to talk business with Bryn about the tourists.'

Alan gave her a wink, which Georgie didn't find amusing. She unlocked the door marked 'Private' and nodded to Bryn to follow her.

Bryn carried his whisky through into the sitting room but didn't sit down. He waited for Georgie to invite him to, feeling it looked more gentlemanly, which was the approach he'd planned before he came but which now came naturally because of the sudden eruption of his feelings for her. More than he ever had, he regretted neglecting Georgie to the point where she fell out of love with him. 'Georgie, I . . .'

She gave him the full treatment of those large blue eyes of hers and his insides melted. 'Yes . . . you were saying . . . ?'

Bryn cleared his throat. 'I was going to say that I hope for your sake as well as mine I pull off this tourist business.'

'So do I.'

'Did you know they've found what they were looking for in Deadman's Dell? Bones and bits and pieces. I've been to have a look. A bit gruesome, but I'm thrilled. Really thrilled. It'll make all the difference for my groups. These idiots who say we shouldn't do it, the worst will happen et cetera, they're mad. Completely mad.'

Georgie had to smile at his enthusiasm. 'We could do with some nice steady lunch trade on Thursdays. If it comes off it will be brilliant. Clever of you to have thought of it.'

Bryn somehow, but he didn't know how, began to tell her about life on board a cruise liner and before he knew it they were both laughing their heads off, pouring another drink, wiping tears of laughter from their eyes and enjoying themselves so much they didn't notice the time. Georgie crossed those elegant, slender legs of hers and Bryn caught a glimpse of a lacy petticoat.

'My God, Georgie, you still have that something that makes a man's insides turn to liquid gold.'

'Bryn!' She sat up straight and uncrossed her legs.

'I mean it. How about it? We're still man and wife you know.' He bent forward and gently caressed her right knee with his thumb.

She pushed his hand off her leg but understood what he meant by liquid gold. At the same time her brain said no. No! No! 'This won't do, Bryn.'

'Why not? Both you and I still have rights. There's no one to say we shouldn't, now is there?' The persuasive tone of his voice was almost her undoing.

Georgie hesitated and then remembered Dicky. 'There's Dicky.'

Bryn sat up. 'Dicky!' He only just managed to keep the scorn out of his voice. 'Come on, Georgie. He'll never know if you don't tell him and I certainly shan't.'

Georgie smiled. 'You wouldn't be able to resist! A feather in your cap you'd see it as.'

Bryn saw he might be in with a chance. 'No, not a feather in my cap, not a conquest, just the need of a man for his lovely wife. It's been a very long time, Georgie, love.' He placed his hand on her leg just under her skirt hem and found she didn't resist. While he talked he rubbed her leg with his thumb. 'You have to admit to a certain feeling for me tonight. I'm no longer the thieving blackguard you saw me as at first, am I?'

'There's Dicky,' Georgie protested and found herself weighing up how she'd feel about Dicky if she did fall for Bryn's charms just this once. As he rubbed her leg she knew he was a very different man from the one who'd left her four years ago. Very different, and she seriously fancied a taste of this very different man. She leaned towards him meaning to kiss him but somewhere a door banged and a voice called out, and she drew back.

Bryn's hand stayed on her knee, though, caressing and enticing, his eyes never leaving her face. 'Come on. Upstairs. Eh?' Georgie half rose as though intending to lead the way, Bryn leaned over and kissed her lips and she returned the kiss in full measure.

Georgie murmured, 'This is not on.' And kissed him again. 'We mustn't.' He stopped her protests with another kiss, gentle and yet urgent. He took her elbow, helped her up and held her close, enjoying the smell of her hair and the feel of her body pressed so willingly against his. 'Oh, Georgie, I've been such a fool. Such a fool.'

Like the crack of gunfire the door burst open and there stood Dicky, his face flushed with anger. In his hand was the cricket bat Georgie kept for emergencies. He held it with both hands as though about to hit a six, and silently lunged towards Bryn. Georgie screamed, 'No!' She sought to release herself from Bryn's arms, he began to lose his balance and, as he tried desperately to regain it, Dicky swung the cricket bat at Bryn's head and felled him like an ox.

Georgie didn't know she was still screaming 'No! No! No!'

Dicky let go of the bat and it thudded to the floor.

Bryn lay in a tangled heap between the cupboard and an easy chair, the whisky decanter and two glasses splattered across the carpet around him.

The only sound was that of Georgie's breath racing in and out of her lungs in great noisy, hysterical gulps. Dicky was carved from stone. Alan and Jimmy stood in the doorway also carved from stone.

It was Jimmy who broke the spell. 'What the hell's going on here?'

'I said I'd do for 'im and I have.' Dicky's voice was grotesquely unlike his own.

Georgie knelt down, her breath rasping in her throat, and felt for Bryn's pulse.

'Is he dead?' Alan asked.

Georgie shook her head.

'I'll go for Dr Harris.' Jimmy fled on winged feet.

Georgie nodded.

Dicky dropped into a chair, all the fight gone out of him.

The three of them remained speechless, frozen in their positions, staring mutely at Bryn until they heard a woman's swift footsteps.

Georgie sat down, Dicky stood up and Alan moved away from the door so Caroline could get in. She knelt down beside Bryn and as she did so Bryn began to stir. 'Bloody hell! Ah! My head!'

Caroline rested a firm hand on his shoulder. 'Lie still for

a moment, Bryn, till you come round properly. You're going to have an almighty bruise and a lump. Could we have an ice pack or frozen peas or something, Georgie, to keep the swelling down. Don't worry, Bryn, you're going to be all right. You must have cracked your head on the corner of the cupboard as you tripped.'

Dicky looked at Georgie and saw a warning in her eyes.

'Too many whiskies, that's the trouble with him. I did tell him.' She somehow got up from the chair and walked as quickly as she could out of the room. Jimmy caught her eye as she passed him and winked. She squeezed his fingers in thanks.

Alan, remembering that he'd left Trish to manage in the bar on her own, disappeared. Bryn sat up. Dicky still didn't speak, but he did see the bat lying just where he'd dropped it.

'I'm sure you should go to hospital. You could have it X-rayed. I can't tell whether or not you've cracked your skull.' Caroline helped Bryn into a chair.

Dicky moved closer to the bat.

Georgie came back with some ice cubes in a plastic bag. 'Will this do?'

'Splendid.' Caroline applied the ice bag to the side of Bryn's head and he winced.

'That's painful!' He tried to jerk his head away but even that hurt.

Dicky got the toe of his shoe to the bat and edged it under the coffee table. 'Got to get back to Scouts.' He sidled out of the room, leaving Georgie with Jimmy and Caroline and her patient.

Jimmy said he'd better be going, or he wouldn't get another pint in before closing time.

Caroline felt puzzled by the secretive atmosphere and decided to remain out of it until she'd worked out what had really happened. If Dicky thought she hadn't noticed him pushing the cricket bat under the coffee table he was sadly mistaken. 'Bryn, you should go to hospital.'

'I'm not. I'm going back to Glebe House as soon as maybe. A night's sleep is all I need. Feel better in the morning. In fact, I feel better already. This ice is doing the trick.' He took it off his head to rearrange it and winced. 'Wow! Some cupboard. I don't remember falling.'

'Perhaps you will tomorrow when your head's settled down. I'll walk with you to Glebe House. Tell me when you're ready. I still think you should go to hospital, though.'

Bryn said no and tried standing up. 'There you are, you see, you're too cautious, Dr Harris, too cautious. Sorry to have bothered you.'

'That's OK.'

Georgie said nothing at all except, 'Thanks.'

But she had plenty to say when she walked round to Dicky's house after she'd closed up and she knew he'd be home from Scouts. She let herself in with her key and found him standing with one foot on the bottom step of his spiral staircase, as though making up his mind to go to bed.

'Dicky, love!' Georgie, arms wide, intended kissing him but Dicky was having none of it.

He backed away from her. 'No, Georgie. No.'

'It was all nothing what you saw, it was the whisky talking.'

'I'm not a fool.'

'I know you're not.'

'If that's how you feel you'd better go back to him and have done with it.' His face crumpled and she thought he was going to weep.

'Don't, Dicky, please don't.'

'Don't be upset by what I saw? What else can I be? Eh? What else? You stood there in *his arms*, the man who tried to murder me. Or had you forgotten? I've watched him this last few days trying to get closer and closer to you, and he has, Georgie, he *has*. You've let him.'

She knew she was guilty of that. 'You shouldn't have hit him like that, though, you know. You could have killed him, then where would the two of us be? Thank God you didn't. I couldn't bear the thought of you being in prison after all we've been through.' Then a thought occurred to her. 'How did you know to come right then?'

Dicky looked away. He fiddled with an ornament on the mantelpiece. Then he said quietly, 'Alan doesn't like Bryn, you see, but he and me, we're mates, so he rang me on my mobile, on a thought-I-ought-to-know basis. He was damn right too, I did want to know. I'd do the same all over again. I've threatened to kill him and I will because he's not having you. I had thought you loved me.' He turned to face her to see her reaction.

She did love him. She did. She must have been crazy this last week. Hang what the village thinks, I'm staying the night with him. 'Dicky! Love!' She held wide her arms and this time he came into them and hugged her tight.

She was ready for off before seven the next morning but hadn't bargained for Peter's early-morning run. She stepped out of Dicky's door, shut it quietly behind her, went down the garden path and set off down Church Lane to find herself facing Peter as he turned out of the lych-gate after saying his early-morning prayers in the church. He made a handsome figure in his old college rugby shirt and shorts. She could have sworn that briefly there appeared to be a halo of light round his fair hair.

'Good morning, Georgie, another beautiful day.'

'It is indeed, Rector.' Not a word or a hint of criticism but Georgie felt shabby. She knew those penetrating blue eyes of his had seen how she felt. He might not have said anything but, after all he'd done to preserve her standing in the village, she'd let him down and no mistake. Well, there'd have to be an ending to all this hole-in-the-corner sneaking about. She'd have that divorce from Bryn and she and Dicky would have things put right by a register office wedding, though she'd have loved Peter to marry them in the church. At the flick of a net curtain to her left she knew Grandmama Charter-Plackett had watched Peter greeting her. Damn and blast!

Linda, of course, knew the whole story, having listened to it until after midnight, with Alan describing in full his part in the night's happenings. She couldn't wait for Mrs Jones to come to work. Straight up on nine she was there, unaware of the gossip Linda was about to impart. Linda opened the steel door to the post office section and beckoned her for a word.

'What's up? I'm in a hurry.'

'You'll never guess what happened in the Royal Oak last night.'

Mrs Jones's eyebrows worked overtime. 'What?'

They were so absorbed in their gossip that neither of them noticed Jimbo had returned to the front of the Store

108

and was busy rearranging the cards on the Village Voice notice board.

'Your Alan *rang* him?'

'On his mobile.'

'The miracles of modern science.'

'Exactly. So he arrived . . .'

Neither of them noticed that Jimbo had found some writing pads on the stationery counter in need of straightening.

'Without saying a word he went behind the counter, picked up the cricket bat Georgie keeps there in case of trouble and went straight through to the lounge and fetched Bryn one.'

Mrs Jones almost fell from her perch with shock. 'Dicky hit Bryn with a cricket bat! I don't believe it, wait till I tell Vince, he won't half laugh.'

'Well, he did, as true as I'm here. Course Alan wasn't right behind him so he didn't know what they were up to when Dicky burst in, but it must have been something serious, mustn't it, otherwise why hit him with it? Out for the count he was. They got Dr Harris to see to him and she wanted him to go to hospital but he wouldn't.'

'He should've.'

By now Jimbo was openly listening.

'He should, but he didn't and Dr Harris saw him home.'

Reluctantly they had to put an end to their conversation as the rush of mothers from the school had begun. Jimbo went to the till, Mrs Jones to the mail order office and Linda to opening up the post office and sorting out her cash for the morning's business.

Gradually the story of Dicky's foolhardy bravery

infiltrated the village houses and spread via the milkman and the postman as far as the outlying districts. If Georgie had hoped that Caroline's idea of Bryn having hit his head on a cupboard as he slipped would carry the day she was to be sadly disillusioned. What was worse, Grandmama Charter-Plackett, making her early morning call at the Store before departing for Culworth, let out by mistake what she'd seen at seven that morning.

Her nose pressed to the grille, Linda said, 'So the Rector knows they've been . . . you know . . .'

'I didn't say that. I said the Rector spoke to her just as she left Dicky's cottage, that's all. Nothing more. For all I know they could have sat up talking all night.'

Linda stared into the distance, lost in thought. 'Given the choice, I know who I'd prefer.'

'Linda! Really. What would your Alan think to that.'

At this precise moment Alan was doing a lot of thinking as, out of Dicky's hearing, he was getting his come-uppance from Georgie. 'I may have known you a long time but you have nothing to do with my private life and I won't stand for you putting your pennyworth in. Do you hear me? If he'd killed Bryn last night how would you have felt? Tell me that.'

'I didn't know he was going to do that, did I? It's not right, you and Bryn, he'll be . . .'

'What's right and what's wrong is my business, so you keep your long nose out of it in future and leave me to sort things out for myself. Right. Or else you'll be out on your ear.'

Alan blenched. Lose his job. Get thrown out. He knew nothing else but bar work with Bryn and Georgie.

Nothing at all. Briefly he saw destitution looming, little Lewis homeless, and Linda looking to him for answers and him having none. Hurriedly he declared he would not interfere again and Georgie was free to do as she wished.

Grimly Georgie replied, tapping his chest with her finger as she did so, 'Thought that might remind you where your loyalties lie. Remember, he tripped and caught his head on a cupboard.' She saw the look of guilt in his eyes. 'You told Linda, didn't you? You did. I don't believe it. Blast it, I might as well have put an advert in the *Culworth Gazette*. That's it, then.' She threw her hands up in despair.

Alan cringed. Anything but that. 'I-I-I'm out, then?'

Georgie saw how cruelly she'd behaved towards someone who didn't deserve it. Poor inadequate Alan. It wasn't his fault. Only hers, for letting that thieving, conniving louse persuade her to . . . 'No, Alan, you're not out, but I warn you, one more piece of interference and you will be. Lock, stock and barrel. Understood?'

Alan nodded in gratitude. He'd have licked her shoes if she'd asked him to. He knew Linda would have told everyone she met, even though he'd said keep it to yourself. She was like that, was Linda. Well, he'd tell her at teatime just how close to losing their livelihood her chattering to customers had brought them and might still if she didn't watch her Ps and Qs. In future he wouldn't warn anyone about anything and then he couldn't be in trouble. Women! God save him from bossy women.

Chapter 7

Caroline and Harriet had a Christmas Bazaar to organise so they arranged to have their inaugural meeting at Harriet's. Coffee being the first item on the agenda, Harriet was pouring it out into some new mugs Jimbo had had designed for what he now called his tourist trade.

Caroline admired her mug. 'These are very attractive. I like the colour and the picture. He doesn't hang about when he has a new project in hand, does he?'

Harriet had to laugh. 'No, he does not. You know Jimbo, anything new and he moves heaven and earth to achieve it. That's what makes him so successful.'

'Which he definitely is. Let's hope Bryn's new project does as well. More business in the village can't be anything but a plus.'

As Harriet offered Caroline a biscuit she said, 'These are new. I'm thinking of selling biscuits mail order, I want to know what you think.'

The slightly misshapen biscuit, misshapen as in home-made, was a tempting golden mound of cinnamon and . . . and . . . syrup or was it honey? It smelled delicious and lived up to its promise when she bit into it. 'This is gorgeous! Absolutely gorgeous. How do you do it?'

Harriet showed her delight on her face. 'Trial and error.

It's an old recipe I found in a book of Mother's when I sorted through her belongings. It's purported to have been handed down from the seventeenth century, but I daren't put that on the packet as I'm not totally sure it is.'

'Well, it's lovely. A real treat.'

'Good. Wait till Bryn tries one. He's in and out of our door like a yo-yo at the moment, bursting with new ideas for his tourists. Let's hope it all comes off.'

'He's in Bath checking out hotels for his tours.'

'So he's well enough to travel, then?'

'I went to see him yesterday and he appears to have recovered. Still all black and blue but the swelling's gone down. It was an almighty bump he had.'

'Not surprising. I'd have an almighty bump if someone had swiped me with a cricket bat.'

Caroline, in the act of picking up her mug, paused, put it back down again and asked, 'Who hit him with a cricket bat?'

'Thought you'd have realised. It was Dicky.'

'*Dicky hit Bryn with a cricket bat?*'

'He did.'

'So . . .'

'Yes?'

'I thought he'd tripped and hit his head on the corner of the cupboard. I said so and no one denied it, but I knew there were undercurrents I couldn't pick up on. So that was it.'

'Also my dear mother-in-law saw Georgie coming out of Dicky's cottage the following morning.'

'No!'

'And she saw Georgie meet Peter going out for his run.'

'He's never told me.'

113

'And they've been away for a weekend together.'

'Bryn and Georgie . . .'

'No, of course not. Georgie and Dicky.'

'I see. So why did Dicky hit Bryn?'

'That's what no one knows.'

Caroline picked up her coffee and sipped it while she thought. 'Harriet! We really mustn't speculate, must we, that's how rumours start.'

'No, but isn't it fun?'

Caroline had to laugh. 'Yes. You know there's trouble about the dig, do you?'

'Can't work in a village store without hearing all the rumours.'

'Everywhere Peter goes he's being blamed for it when he couldn't stop it if he tried to. It's not on church land.'

'He shouldn't have offered to have a service and burial. That's what's got under everyone's skin. I wonder . . .'

'What?'

'I wonder, should I tell you that there's a protest meeting tonight.'

'Where?'

'At Willie Biggs's.'

'He hasn't told us.'

'Well, no, I don't expect he has.'

Caroline became indignant when it occurred to her that Sylvia had not said anything either. 'Sylvia hasn't said a word to *me*.'

'Apparently she's furious and is refusing to have anything to do with it.'

'Oh, dear. Are you going?'

Harriet shook her head. 'Of course not.'

'What time?'

114

'Er . . . well, *I* didn't tell you, right? Half past seven.'

'Right.'

Sylvia's opposition to Willie's determination to challenge the dig and the burial had boiled up inside her until she could no longer hold her peace, so two hours before the meeting was to begin she finally told him how she felt. 'You've known all along I agreed with the Rector, all along, and you've the gall to decide to hold the meeting here. Well, I'm sorry, Willie, but I'm leaving you to it.'

In a soft, wheedling tone Willie said, 'Sylvia! Now, this isn't like you.'

'Don't take that tone with me, because it won't get you your own way.'

'But I need help with the refreshments and things, and arranging the chairs and . . .'

'I'm quite sure you're perfectly capable of seeing to all that. You're not helpless. You managed for years on your own.'

'Sylvia, please!'

'You can wheedle all you like, I'm not staying for the meeting. Wild horses wouldn't make me.'

Willie watched her pick up her handbag and cardigan. When she went to the drawer where she kept her car keys, he knew she meant business. 'You don't mean you're really going out while the meeting's on.'

Those fine grey eyes of Sylvia's, which had attracted him to her from the first, looked at him with scorn. 'I have my principles. How can I be here? If I am, it means I'm in agreement with you, which I am not. And never will be. I honestly can't see why it's wrong to dig up the remains and give them a decent Christian burial. It's their right.'

'It's only because you work for the Rector, that's all. You're taking his side because of that, not because it's a principle.'

'Anyone would think I hadn't got a mind of my own. Well, I have. I won't oppose him on this.'

'But he won't be here; he doesn't know about it.'

Sylvia tapped the side of her nose. 'Don't you be too sure about that. He sees and knows more than we think.'

Willie cringed at the thought of a confrontation with Peter, for whom he'd always had the deepest respect. Goosepimples broke out all over him at the prospect.

'Sylvia! You haven't told him. Have you?'

'I may be against you, Willie, but I wouldn't do a trick like that. I need an apology from you for thinking such a thing.'

Willie realised how much he'd hurt her but he felt it counted for nothing in comparison with how he felt about her withdrawing her support from him. 'Sorry. But it's not like you, isn't this . . .'

'I'm sorry too, more sorry than you realise, but I will *not* stay for the meeting.'

Thoroughly cowed by her adamant refusal to give in to him, Willie asked sadly, 'Where will you be?'

'In Culworth at the pictures.'

Horrified, Willie stuttered, 'All by yourself?'

Sylvia nodded.

'Do I get a kiss before you go?'

Sylvia studied his woebegone face. 'Very well.' She gave him the merest peck, conceding in her own mind that she'd make it up to him when she got back.

At exactly eight o'clock Peter knocked at Willie's door

116

and walked in as he always did in village houses, calling out, 'It's Peter from the Rectory,' as he entered.

He was greeted by stunned silence. To a man the conspirators couldn't meet his eye, but he looked at each of them and said a cordial 'Good evening, everyone. Sorry I've arrived late.' Several of them blushed with embarrassment, others found their shoes more interesting than meeting Peter's eyes. They were occupying easy chairs, dining chairs and in some instances stools, which Willie had collected from various rooms in the cottage. The small living room meant they were shoulder to shoulder in as much of a circle as Willie could devise. No one moved a muscle.

Willie, from years of treating him with deference, leapt to his feet and offered him his stool.

'Thank you, Willie, but I'll perch on the end of the table if you don't mind.' Sitting there gave him an advantage, which crouching on a low stool wouldn't have done. 'Please continue. Just sorry I arrived late.'

Naturally Peter's arrival had taken the wind out of their sails and no one had the courage to continue. Finally Grandmama Charter-Plackett spoke. 'You know why we're here, Rector?' Peter nodded. 'We've all agreed we don't want the dig and we certainly don't think it quite right for you to be supporting it by offering burial. Already we've had a fire, which could have got out of control if it hadn't been for Willie's swift action, and we all dread what might happen next. I've been keeping an eye on it. They've only scratched the surface so far and found a few bones, but we want it closed up now and perhaps when they've done that you could say a few words appropriate for the circumstances and then we can forget about it.'

117

'You all know perfectly well that I have no jurisdiction over that land. It belongs to Mr Fitch. And then there's Gilbert.'

Jimmy spoke up. 'Look! Gilbert would dig anywhere whatever if he thought he could find something of value. Look at the trouble we had over the Roman ruins when we wanted to hold the Show. He didn't care a button that all our hard work would be in jeopardy. All he could think of was what he might find. He just gets carried away, he does. Also my Sykes knows a thing or two about that Dell. He won't go anywhere near it. Wild horses won't get him in there, not even if he thinks there's rabbits there. Animals is wiser than you think.'

There was a general nodding of heads at Jimmy's last statement.

Arthur Prior from Wallop Down Farm added his opinion. 'Two of my granddaughters have come down with violent attacks of chickenpox. They've blisters the size of a two-pence piece and they're very poorly. I just hope to God it is chickenpox and nothing more sinister. They've very high temperatures.'

Gasps of horror could be heard all round the room. A couple of the weekenders who'd been persuaded to stay on for the meeting voiced their protests too. 'There you go! You see, and this is only the start. Heaven alone knows what might happen next. Please, Rector, will you stop it?'

'I can't.'

Vince Jones had his say. 'You could, sir, please, have a word with Mr Fitch. We're all so afraid. They've got to stop.'

Arthur Prior got to his feet. 'I propose we make a deputation to Mr Fitch and go up to see him. The

Rector's quite right. He can't stop the dig but Mr Fitch could, and he's been much more amenable lately, so he might listen.' He sat down again, feeling that he'd exonerated Peter from any blame, but the others would have none of it.

Miss Senior's woolly hat bobbed again as she shuddered and, with a nigh hysterical tone in her voice, said, 'Think what might 'appen if they's buried in our own churchyard. I shan't fancy finding myself next to 'em when my time comes, believe me.'

A muttered 'hear! hear!' came from most of the people squeezed into Willie's tiny living room. A silence fell while they all looked to Peter for support.

'Those bones have been there for over six centuries already, and for most of that time they've been there unknown to anyone. Can any of you give me a sound reason for suspecting the bones are responsible for anything at all, either evil or good?'

'Don't think reason comes into it.' This from a weekender who guessed he was about to be persuaded by Peter that their protest was foolish.

Willie spoke up. 'Well, Rector, we know it doesn't make sense but it's how we all *feel*. It's not right and we want it stopped.'

'I'm afraid you haven't my support. I am still willing to see their remains decently buried in hallowed ground and so, too, should you be. They could be your ancestors, don't forget.'

Grandmama Charter-Plackett said firmly, 'You're a clergyman and I can see where you're coming from, but it won't wash with us. We want it stopped and I for one offer myself as a member of the delegation.'

119

'Hear! hear!'

'Who's willing to go with me?'

When it came to the point of standing up to Mr Fitch there was a marked reluctance on everyone's part to volunteer. In the end Arthur Prior said he would go with her and Peter realised he'd lost the debate. 'I'm certain in my own mind that Mr Fitch will say he wants the dig to go ahead, and quite rightly so. There's no harm in it, none at all, take my word for it.'

But they wouldn't be moved. They even begged Peter to head the deputation but he refused. 'I'm sorry I can't be at one with you about this, but there we are. I assure you, you are worrying unnecessarily about the situation and I have to say I'm disappointed in you. I thought you would have had more Christian understanding in you than to deny people a respectable burial. I'll leave you to it.'

Peter turned to leave but not before Miss Senior had said, 'And what about the chickenpox, a high temperature and sinister? What about that? I think it's very suspicious.'

There were grunts of agreement from almost everyone in the room.

'I'll say goodnight, then.' Peter left, feeling ashamed of them all and especially of Willie, of all people, spearheading it.

Despite high words between Mrs Charter-Plackett and Mr Fitch when he met with them in his office, he refused to withdraw his approval of the dig and both Arthur Prior and she were left in no doubt that their interference was nothing less than idiotic, and they weren't to come bothering him with prejudices and complaints more suited to peasants.

At this Grandmama Charter-Plackett drew herself up and gave him a piece of her mind, which left him in no doubt either that, although he might have money now, his origins were no better than theirs. 'Peasant? Huh! If we are, then so too are you. You can't pull the wool over our eyes, believe me. You're a self-made man, without that much good breeding in you.' She held up her thumb and forefinger scarcely half a centimetre apart. 'Good morning to you, Craddock. Let's hope nothing of a sinister nature happens to you in the next few weeks. If something does happen, such as you being run over by a bus, I for one will not be sending you a get well card. Come, Arthur, we're wasting our time here.' She sailed majestically out of Mr Fitch's study and stormed out on to the gravel drive. Looking up at the beautiful Tudor building which was Turnham House she said, 'This place deserves someone better than him. Had Sir Ralph still been in possession he would have treated us with dignity.' She remembered a word she'd heard one of Jimbo's boys use, which at the time she had thought distinctly common, but it fitted the occasion now. 'Mr Fitch is a scumbag, that's what he is. A scumbag.'

To emphasise his support of the dig Mr Fitch turned up at Deadman's Dell the same afternoon. He'd forgotten how distant and unmoved by money or titles Gilbert could be and he was received with no more ceremony than the local dustcart operator. This riled him and when he bent to pick up one of the bones with his bare hands intending to examine it, he received one of Gilbert's broadsides. 'Put that down immediately. Have you no sense, man? They've not to be touched.'

Mr Fitch straightened up and looked at Gilbert with a

nasty glint in his eye. 'I've a good mind to refuse you permission to carry on.'

'Have you? Too late. I've got your letter saying we can.'

'I can withdraw it.'

'You might be interested to know I've got the *Culworth Gazette* coming this afternoon. They should be here any minute.' Gilbert, head down, squatting in a shallow trench, smiled to himself.

Mr Fitch didn't answer. He watched the delicate process of removing earth from around a find, the gentle scraping away, the sensitive handling of the minutest scrap of material and became absorbed: the quiet throb of excitement was palpable. Just as he crouched down to get a closer look at something one of the students had found, the photographer and a reporter from the *Gazette* arrived. 'Excellent, Mr Fitch, stay right there and I'll take a picture.' The camera clicked and whirred, and Mr Fitch pointed and smiled until his knees gave out and he had to stand up.

'We understand you're funding this dig, Mr Fitch?' the reporter asked.

'Well, not exactly but . . . should the occasion arise I would be more than willing. Such happenings as this are very important to an ancient village like this one and if money can help in any way then I'm your man.'

'Excellent!' He scribbled on his notepad.

The reporter addressed Gilbert's back. 'Mr Johns, isn't it?'

Gilbert looked up and nodded. 'That's me.'

In all, Mr Fitch had an interesting and worthwhile interlude down at the dig, and felt justified in ignoring the stupid, childish pleas of Arthur and that old harridan Grandmama Charter-Plackett. Under a bus, indeed. Fat chance. He never went anywhere near a bus.

Bryn, when he came back from Bath, was horrified to discover how frightened the village was about the dig. There were now four of the Prior granddaughters suffering from severe chickenpox. The teachers at the school were finding their class numbers dwindling daily until, on the morning Bryn returned, only three-quarters of the school was present.

Beth and Alex were disappointed to discover they'd had chickenpox quite badly when they were very small, so their chances of being away from school for a couple of weeks were very slim.

Beth asked, 'Were we properly poorly, Mummy?'

'Very. Your spots were so close together I couldn't find a space to put my finger.'

'Really? Mum, did we have a temperature?' Alex remembered having a severe sore throat when he was eight and how funny his head had felt and how hot he'd been.

'You did. Daddy couldn't bath you, because he couldn't bear to see your spots.'

'You bathed us, though, didn't you, Mummy?'

Caroline nodded. 'I did indeed, Beth, just to help you stop itching. We used bottles and bottles of calamine to cool your spots down. You even had spots in your ears.'

Beth contemplated the thought and said sadly, 'So there's no chance of us getting it, then?'

'None, I would have thought.'

'Oh, well.' She'd quite fancied the drama of being really ill but apparently it was not to be. 'We'll be off, then, and see who's next to have got it. Come on, Alex, or we'll be late. They're all saying it's the dig that's made everyone ill, but it isn't, is it?'

'Of course not.'

Alex said, 'They're blaming Dad.'

'Are they?'

'Yes, they say he shouldn't have said what he did about a service.'

'Are they?'

'I nearly had a fight about Dad, Mum, in the playground yesterday.'

'I hope you didn't?'

'No, but I wanted to.'

'Well, don't. Please. It will all calm down in a day or two, you'll see.'

Quite out of context Beth remarked, 'Janine nearly got run over yesterday.'

Caroline broke off from clearing the table to say, 'Where?'

'Outside school, before school began. She wasn't being silly. There was a terrible screech of brakes.'

Alex said, 'There was, Mum, she isn't exaggerating. Poor Janine. They had to let her lie down for a while.'

'I'll leave this and go with you to school. It's getting beyond a joke, all those cars.'

Caroline had firmly believed that the crisis over Peter's decision to have a service would subside shortly but it didn't. Gilbert's two older toddlers caught chickenpox and so did Louise, who'd never had it as a child. Then Fran Charter-Plackett developed it and two days later Harriet went down with it. Even though there were columns in the papers about the epidemic of chickenpox in Culworth and the surrounding areas, none of the villagers believed anything other than that the dig was responsible for the Turnham Malpas chickenpox. Common sense quite simply did not prevail.

When Bryn next went into the Royal Oak, Georgie refused to serve him. 'I'm sorry, Bryn, but that is my decision. You are banned.' She stood, arms crossed, and waited for him to go.

But he didn't. He leaned on the bar counter and said confidentially, 'If Dicky hadn't come back the other night you know exactly where we would have been and don't try to tell me we wouldn't.'

'But he did and we didn't, and I don't want to, and you cause him too much upset and you're not welcome in this bar.'

Bryn tried putting on the charm. 'Come on, I'm not that bad. You were very close to me that night. Closer than we've been for years.' He leant over the bar and put a gentle hand on her arm. 'I rather thought you liked the new me.'

Georgie hesitated. He was right there, but . . . 'I don't, not at all, and buzz off or . . .'

'You wouldn't call the police, now would you?'

'Just go, before Dicky comes in.'

'Sir Galahad to the rescue, eh?'

'Do as I say.' At this point Alan came up from the cellar, saw Bryn, put down the crate of lagers, did a swift about turn and disappeared. He'd been told not to interfere so he wouldn't even give himself the chance.

'Just serve me a whisky and I'll be gone.'

'No. Alan, come please!'

'Please, just one and I'll be gone.'

'No. Alan!'

'Can I have a meal in the dining room?'

Georgie almost relented and opened her mouth to say it was all right but changed her mind. 'No. Now shift yourself or I really will call the police.'

'And there I thought you and I were business partners.'

'I promised Dicky . . .'

'Oh, well, if it was only that little squirt you promised that means nothing . . .'

'Right, that's it. Out!' Georgie started to walk round the end of the bar, calling 'Alan!' as she did so.

'OK! OK! I'll be off. How long am I banned for?'

She couldn't resist his chirpy smile nor the wink he gave her. She'd meant to ban him until his group came in August but she hadn't the heart. 'One week.'

'Right! Jug and Bottle here I come.'

Someone sitting at a table shouted, 'Watch out for that barmaid with the chestnut-coloured hair. She'll have anyone in trousers, she will.'

Bryn gave a thumbs up and went out with a final wink at Georgie, who was already regretting banning him. Alan appeared again as though by magic and she took her anger with herself out on him. 'Where the blazes have you been? I wanted you to help turn Bryn out and I called but you didn't come.'

'You told me I wasn't to interfere in your private life again, so I didn't.'

'Oh, I see. So that's how it is. I'll remember this.' She retired behind the bar again and continued serving as though nothing had happened but inside she wished Bryn were there. She enjoyed his flirting and the changes in him more than she liked to admit, and frankly couldn't understand how she could love Dicky and yet find the new Bryn so intriguing.

Dicky walked in to begin his evening stint behind the bar and immediately her heart burst with love. Of course this was him, the man of her heart. They didn't kiss in public but she wanted to so much. That divorce. She'd put things in motion immediately. First thing tomorrow. Dicky smiled at her with such love in his eyes and unknowingly his smile strengthened her resolve.

Unusually for them, Jimbo came in with his mother. Several people called out to him asking how Harriet and Fran were. 'Beginning to turn the corner, thanks. A slight improvement. We've just popped out to celebrate Mother's birthday. Can't stay long.'

The two of them chose a quiet table and Jimbo went to order their drinks. The flow of conversation went back and forth around the tables, people came and people went.

When Jimbo returned to their table with the drinks, Mrs Charter-Plackett said quietly, 'I see Bryn isn't in tonight.'

Jimbo raised his glass to her. 'Happy birthday, Mother, and many of them.'

'Thank you, you darling boy. I'm so proud of you, so proud.'

'And I of you. Still so full of spark and energy.'

'Less of the "still". I'm not that old!'

'Of course not. Of course not.'

'I can see you're worrying about Harriet and Fran. Well don't. Like you said, there's a slight improvement today.

127

Harriet was quite chirpy when I took her a cup of tea before we came out.'

'This business of the Dell. I see they were digging again today. Craddock Fitch was there too.'

'Blast that man. Thank heavens he didn't marry Harriet's mother. I couldn't be so vituperative about him if he had. He is so *rude*, in a way which leaves one with no alternative but to be very rude back. Which I was. I even said if he got run over by a bus I wouldn't send him a get well card.'

Jimbo laughed. 'It was a close-run thing, you know. She had more or less decided to say yes to his proposal.'

'I was sorry she died how she did, so suddenly. Terrible shock for Harriet and for all of us. Life is so short, one never knows, does one, when it will be one's own turn to be called.'

Seeing she was succumbing to what he called the birthday syndrome Jimbo said, 'You don't think like everyone else that the chickenpox is a result of the dig, do you?'

His mother snorted her contempt. 'Of course not! I'm not a fool, but then again . . .'

'I know just what you mean. Your head says it's ridiculous but the heart says something quite different. By the way, Mother, this business of Bryn and Georgie's divorce.'

'Yes?'

'I understand Bryn's trying to find out who is going to finance Dicky buying into the pub when Bryn and Georgie get their divorce. Thought I'd warn you, just in case he came fishing for answers from you.'

'He'll get no change out of me. In any case he'll be

more likely to think it will be you offering, not me. He's a scumbag. That's what he is.'

'Mother!'

'He's trying to get his feet under Georgie's table, the devious beggar. She's better off with Dicky. Lovely man, he is, makes two of Bryn.'

Amused by her close involvement in village matters Jimbo asked, 'Glad you came to live in the village?'

'Of course. I know I behaved badly when I first came but I have improved, haven't I?'

For fun Jimbo didn't answer immediately, then he said, 'Ye-e-e-s-s,' as though he had to weigh up the matter.

'You get more like your father every year. You bad boy.' Jimbo went to replenish their glasses and when he got back to the table his mother said, 'I'm not a superstitious person, but with all this going on about the ghastly effect the dig has had on everything, I must be off my head worrying about saying what I did about Craddock going under a bus. I should never have said it.'

'For heaven's sake, Mother, if something did happen to him how can it be your fault? You wouldn't be to blame at all.'

'No, but it does make you wonder sometimes just how much influence what you say has on people. I shall have to keep my tongue in check, I really will.'

'Well, that wouldn't be a bad idea.'

'I do hope so. I do hope so. I feel quite dreadful.'

'Are you ready? I've left Harriet for long enough.'

Fran was fast asleep but Harriet was awake when he got back. 'Hush, darling, don't wake her, I want her to sleep as long as possible. Oh, Jimbo, I can't remember feeling so

129

ill before. Can you get me a fresh drink? Did you have a nice time with your mother?'

'I did. She's getting quite mellow in her old age. 'Nother drink you said?'

Chapter 8

A feeling of impending doom permeated the village as the chickenpox epidemic continued to rage and the school numbers dwindled to a new low, trade at the Store dropped and attendance at church also suffered. It rained, too, day after day, with a relentlessness that seemed it would have no end. The pond on the green flooded and parts of the churchyard also went under water. Surrounding fields, good pasture and arable land alike, were flooded and the beck that ran through the spare land flowed wider, deeper and faster than had been known in living memory. Leaden skies became the order of the day and with them a depression descended everywhere. Somehow it made getting over the chickenpox harder than ever. Some sceptics said, 'Chickenpox! That's nothing, it can hardly be counted as a disease, that can't,' but this particular strain appeared tenacious in its infectiousness. Grown-ups and children alike fell victim to it.

In church on the Sunday morning Peter prayed for those who had been stricken so badly with chickenpox and that soon the village would be restored to its usual quiet everyday calm.

'Fat chance of that,' whispered Mrs Jones to a neighbour who nudged her and answered in a loud whisper,

'He doesn't know the half.'

A worshipper in the pew in front said, 'Sh.' While someone in the pew behind leaned forward and asked, 'What do you know that I don't know?'

The neighbour replied *sotto voce*, 'There's to be a demonstration at the dig.'

'No!'

'Really?' asked Mrs Jones.

'There is.'

'Sh!'

'When?'

The worshipper in the pew in front turned round angrily. 'Sh! Have some respect.'

Mrs Jones winked at her neighbour and said, 'Tell me later, Annie.'

After church she was told that the demonstration was to be the next morning and they'd be ready and waiting for the students when they arrived. 'I'm going to support the demonstration. It's downright disgusting what they're doing, disgusting. You'll be there, won't you? We need all the help we can get.'

'Come rain or shine, I'll be there all right.'

To Mrs Jones's embarrassment the neighbour insisted on making a 'Protest against the dig' placard for her.

Next morning it was raining harder than ever. Great fat raindrops fell incessantly, the dark-grey lowering clouds made it seem like an early January morning not a July one, so a lot of people who had promised to support the demonstration duffed when the time came to take their stand. Annie from church, Willie Biggs, Alan Crimble from the Royal Oak and Vince Jones were there, and the two Misses Senior but no one else.

Mrs Jones, Sylvia and Bryn arrived to represent the supporters of the dig. It all felt rather like a damp squib and the dejected representatives on each side of the debate huddled in two opposing groups.

Bryn yelled, 'It's pointless you standing there. The dig's going ahead come what may.'

'Not if we can help it,' Willie shouted in defiance. Sylvia blushed at his vehemence.

'You might as well go home right now.'

'We shan't till you've gone.'

'Look! They've almost finished, you know. They don't expect to find much more.'

'If that's right, why are you here?'

Mrs Jones piped up with, 'Because we got wind of what you were going to do, that's why we've come.'

Willie sniggered. 'I can see you've got lots of support.'

Sylvia felt ashamed of herself, but stuck to her guns. 'You're not much better.'

Willie, broken-hearted by their differences, didn't reply to her, but Vince did. 'We've got plenty of support as you well know. They're all frightened to death, what with this rain and the chickenpox and that.'

'Rubbish!' shouted Bryn. 'You're talking absolute rubbish. You all need a good shake-up. You've lived here too long. You're too set in your ways. Here am I, trying to bring business to the village and this dig will be a highlight and all you can think of is that it's evil.'

'It's not the dig,' declared one Miss Senior. 'It's the Rector threatening to bury the bones in the churchyard. We don't like it at all, do we?'

The second Miss Senior shook her head and muttered under her breath, 'I'm in agreement, fully in agreement. It's the work of the devil.'

Bryn roared with laughter. What fools they were. 'We've got to move with the times, you daft old biddies.'

Sylvia protested at his rudeness.

Mrs Jones said, 'Hey, hold on, there's no call for that.'

'Well, they are! We've got to move on, get modern. Onward and upward. So what if there's a few old bones in a coffin buried deep. What harm can they do, for heaven's sake?' Bryn laughed aloud at their dyed-in-the-wool attitudes.

'Doesn't look as if they're coming today,' Willie said. By now his faithful anorak, which he normally only wore in winter, was letting in the wet.

'They're usually here by now.' Vince adjusted the angle of his umbrella and it dripped down his neck. 'Blast!'

Alan Crimble spoke up for the first time. 'If you ask me . . .'

Bryn interrupted him. 'Nobody's asking you and what's more you should be on this side not that, you being an employee of my pub.'

'Your pub! That's rich.'

'Yes, my pub.' Bryn began to boil with temper. 'I gave you a home and a job when you'd nowhere to go, just you remember that. By rights, Alan Crimble, you should be standing shoulder to shoulder with me.'

'Well, I'm not, and I wouldn't be if it was the last job on earth.'

'You snivelling little . . . pipsqueak.' Bryn closed up his umbrella, laid it on the church wall and put up his fists.

'Oh, "pipsqueak", is it?' Alan shaped up to Bryn.

Willie said, 'Alan, stop it. We don't want a fight.'

Bryn shouted, 'I don't mind. Not at all. I'm a match for anyone.' Huge drops of rain fell from the branches above his head. He glanced up at the sky and wondered what the blazes he was doing here in weather like this, losing his temper with a fool like Alan Crimble. He lost all his fight at that moment and decided to leave. 'To be honest, there's not much point in us all standing here getting pneumonia. They're obviously not coming today. Let's agree to go home, shall we?'

There was a general nodding of heads from both sides and what had been intended as a fight to the death on the part of the objectors ended with them creeping home defeated and soaked to the skin.

Bryn rallied his troops. 'Round one to us, I think?'

'Definitely,' agreed Mrs Jones.

'But no more threatening to fight, Bryn, I don't want Willie hurt,' Sylvia begged, conscious that this was the first rift ever between her and Willie and not for the world did she want him injured.

'Pity there weren't more of us here, but it can't be helped. Thanks for turning out, you two.'

Bryn went home to change and decided there would be no more confrontations on his part. It was a complete waste of time. The dig would go on regardless of what they did and perhaps, once the bones were buried, life would get back to normal. Oh, God, now he was bestowing on the bones powers they most definitely had not got. Or had they? Nothing seemed to have gone right since the dig started. He'd better be careful or his wonderful plans would not materialise. If only the rain would stop. And if only the chickenpox epidemic would stop too.

Jimmy was one of the last to become infected and he lay for three days in his house, alone and ill, until it occurred to Grandmama Charter-Plackett that she hadn't seen him about and she went to investigate.

'Hello-o-o-o! Jimmy, are you there?'

She could hear Sykes scuffling behind the door. 'Hello! Jimmy?'

Sykes began to bark: his odd little noise which came between a yap and the bark of a much larger dog. Then he started to whine and scrabble at the edge of the door.

Mrs Charter-Plackett cautiously tried the doorknob and found to her surprise that the door wasn't locked. She spoke to Sykes so he could recognise who it was. 'It's me, Sykes. All right?' She pushed open the door and bent to pat him. There'd been no fresh air in the house for several days, she could tell that; the air was stale and smelt of dog. There was no water left in Sykes's bowl either, and not a sound from upstairs. She went to stand at the bottom of the stairs and called up, 'Jimmy? Are you there?' He must be, his car was parked at the end of his garden as usual.

Having reached the top of the stairs, she peeped into one of the bedrooms and found Jimmy fast asleep in a seriously tousled bed. The air offended her sensibilities so she crossed the room to open the window. It creaked and groaned and the noise woke Jimmy. She didn't think she'd seen anyone with as many spots as he had. Not even little Fran.

'Why, Jimmy! I didn't know you were ill. I hope you

don't mind, but I hadn't seen you about and thought I'd better investigate.'

Jimmy lifted his head from the pillow and groaned. 'It's Sykes. I haven't been able to feed him.'

'I'll see to that. It seems to me you need seeing to, too. First things first. I'll attend to Sykes and then you. A cup of tea. Eh?'

Her patient croaked a thank you and laid his head gratefully back on the pillow.

'You should have rung me, you silly man.'

Jimmy nodded a little impatiently. He was in no mood for Mrs Charter-Plackett's vigorous brand of jollying up.

By the time she'd fed and watered Sykes, and he'd rushed out of his cat flap into the garden and back in, and up to see Jimmy and generally decided life might have got back to something like normal, had the kettle boiling, had found a packet of porridge oats and made Jimmy a bowlful, Jimmy had been to the bathroom and flung some cold water on his face and dabbed it dry and run a comb very tenderly through his hair, desperate to avoid the spots on his scalp, and was back in bed.

'Why, that looks better. Now sit up and eat this. No argument. I like my porridge with golden syrup so I've put some on for you.'

She left him and went downstairs to do some bits of washing up he'd left. She wrinkled her nose at his carefree bachelor ways but manfully battled on with her tidying up.

A quarter of an hour later she was seated on his bedroom chair, watching him drinking the last of his tea. 'There, you must feel better. So you've got chickenpox.'

'I had every ailment under the sun when I was a boy but never chickenpox. Now it's finally got me. By Jove, but I've felt ill and not half. It could kill anybody, it could.'

'You realise why you've got the chickenpox, I suppose?'

'No.'

'Because you've opposed the dig. That's why, according to all the pundits who reckon they know it all.'

'It could be that. It could, yer know. There's stranger things 'ave 'appened, believe me.'

'You're soft in the head if you think that, Jimmy Glover.'

Jimmy smiled. 'You can scoff, but I bet they're right. Anyway, thanks for helping. I should be up and about tomorrow.'

'You haven't got rid of me yet. I shall cook a nice meal this evening and you shall partake of it. A nourishing chicken casserole, I think. On my way back from walking Sykes I'll call in at Jimbo's and see what he's got.' She stood up, brushed down her skirt, picked up his tray and noted with satisfaction that he'd eaten all his porridge. 'You look as if you need a sleep. Snuggle down. Sykes and I shan't be back till the casserole's ready, so you can relax. I won't lock the front door. Your cupboards look a bit bare of the essentials so I'll take the liberty of getting a few things for you. Jimbo will put it on the slate. Take care.' She didn't tell him he was as white as a sheet between his spots, nor that his long thin face was even thinner; he really was a sickly sight.

After she'd taken Sykes for his walk and become thoroughly wet, even though she'd worn her waterproofs, she tied him up outside the Store and went in.

Linda gave her an extra polite 'Good afternoon', having

in the past been at the receiving end of her sharp tongue and regretting it.

'Good afternoon, Linda. I can't be long, I've tied Sykes up outside and he's not best pleased.'

'Sykes?'

'Yes. Jimmy's ill with the chickenpox so I'm caring for him. Is Jimbo about?'

'He is, he's in his office, he said to call if it got busy.' She pressed her thumb on her emergency bell. One press for Jimbo's presence, two presses for a serious emergency. Jimbo came bustling through from the back immediately. 'Mother!' He kissed her on both cheeks as she preferred and said, 'Thank heavens we've got a customer; it's been so quiet this morning.'

'No wonder with this chickenpox. Jimmy's got it now and he's been very poorly. The silly man didn't ring anyone so I've only just found out. I can't be long, I'm soaking wet. I'm making a chicken casserole for Jimmy, so have you fresh chicken today?'

Just as she was about to pay for Jimmy's groceries Sylvia came shopping for the Rectory. She shook her umbrella vigorously and put it in the umbrella stand so kindly provided by Jimbo. 'Good afternoon, Mrs Charter-Plackett. The weather doesn't improve, does it. They've had to stop the dig, everything being so wet.'

'Oh, good! I'm glad.'

'You're one of the ones who doesn't approve, then?'

'I was at Willie's meeting.'

'Were you indeed?'

'Didn't you know?'

'No.' Sylvia intimated by the shrug of her shoulders that

she didn't want to know anything at all about 'that' meeting.

'So you agree with the Rector, then.'

'I suppose I have to say yes to that.'

'Of course, what else can you do when you work at the Rectory? You've got to be loyal.'

'I'm old enough to have my own opinions. I've never discussed the matter with him.'

Mrs Charter-Plackett looked askance at her.

'It's true. I never have, nor with Dr Harris. I just believe it's only fair to those poor unsettled remains for them to come home.'

'They should be left in peace.'

'Who says they're at peace where they are?'

'Well, they're certainly not at peace now they're being dug up. It's disgusting and it's irreverent.'

'You're not one of those idiots who thinks all our misfortunes are due to the dig. I would have thought you would have had more sense.'

'Well, really!'

'I mean it. More sense.' She looked up at Jimbo's clock above the door. 'Must fly. Shopping to do and the twins will be home soon.'

The discussion was abandoned by Sylvia just as Mrs Charter-Plackett was warming to her subject and she felt cheated. She exclaimed 'Well, really!' again and marched through to the back to find Jimbo. 'Some people are getting above their station.'

Jimbo looked up from his computer and said, 'I could hear you from here. I do wish you wouldn't be so antagonistic. "Above their station", honestly, Mother, it's no longer the rich man in his castle and the poor man at the gate, or hadn't you noticed?'

'Of course I have, but speaking to me like that, saying I should have more sense.'

'Well, perhaps you should have more sense. We both agreed the other night that our heads told us one thing and . . .'

'Our hearts another. So I'm listening to my heart.'

'Don't, it's causing too much trouble. Willie and Sylvia aren't speaking, you know, all because of this . . .'

'Still? I thought they'd patched it up.'

'Vince and Greta Jones aren't either. It's causing an awful lot of trouble and you're adding fuel to it. Please don't.'

'I will not have my son telling me what I can and cannot say. If I feel strongly about something then I shall speak my mind and I shan't ask your permission.'

'I was only appealing to your good sense, but obviously, as Sylvia found, you haven't any.' He turned back to his computer and, because of being thoroughly rattled by his mother's intransigence, deleted some figures by mistake and swore.

'Jimbo! That is disgusting! In front of your own mother. Really!'

'You are exasperating, Mother, and if you anger me much more I shall say even worse. Don't come to my Store if all you can do is upset the few customers I have left.'

'I won't, then. I shall condemn myself to travelling into Culworth for everything. I'm sure Jimmy will appreciate the business.'

'You've forgotten he has the chickenpox.'

Realising she had made a complete fool of herself, she drew her shoulders back, marched out of the office and stormed through the Store, remembering her shopping but completely forgetting poor Sykes who by now was soaked to the skin. Consequently, as soon as she got home she put down her shopping and began to take off her wet things, remembered Sykes and had to go all the way back again. The jerk he got on his lead as she set off home once more hurt Sykes's feelings, and he sulked and refused to walk properly so she carried him home, fuming at her strong-headedness and the mess she'd got herself into.

'Thank God he's not a bull mastiff,' she muttered as she put the key in her door, only to find she hadn't locked it in the first place. 'I really will have to pull myself together. Casserole first, cup of tea afterwards.' Then she saw Sykes's wet footprints on her beautifully polished floor and the marks on the wall from his wet coat as he tried to rub himself dry, and knew he had to be dealt with first. This was not a good day at all. Those bones had a lot to answer for. Bryn was delighted by the episode in Deadman's Dell only because it suited him for his groups, not for any other reason. Damn him. She'd have to sort him out because it was obvious no one else was going to.

Chapter 9

For the moment Bryn had more important matters needing his attention; primarily making sure that under no circumstances would Dicky get Georgie to the altar. He'd only another three weeks before he'd have to leave and go to London to meet his first American group flying into Gatwick. Therefore time was not on his side. His ban from going into the Royal Oak was up and he made free with his opportunities. Dicky didn't work every day, so he made a special point of being in there on his days off. But more significantly, he went in when Dicky *was* working, fixing him with a nasty glare, perfected in his bedroom mirror, at every possible chance he could. A threatening glare first, which he knew got Dicky's back up, then he'd set himself out to flirt with Georgie. The best of it was he sensed that Georgie enjoyed the flirting.

'Bryn! Behave yourself. You've seen me in this suit before. I've had it years.'

'But you've never filled it quite like you're doing tonight.'

'Bryn! That's cheek, that is. I don't weigh one ounce more than I did the day we married.'

'No! I hadn't realised. You were magnificent that day, Georgie. Truly beautiful.'

Dicky went to stand beside Georgie. 'She still is.'

'I didn't say she wasn't. I *meant* she still is. I remember it like it was only yesterday.'

'So do I.' Georgie went quite weepy at her memories.

Dicky sensed he was losing the game. 'Another whisky, Bryn?'

'Thanks, Dicky, I will.'

He tossed it back with a practised lift of the elbow. 'Tell you what, Georgie, my first group is up to twenty-five, a couple already booked are bringing two friends with them, I've had to close the list.'

This time Dicky took his glass from him without being asked and poured him another double. As he pushed it across the counter he gave Bryn a mean, challenging look. Man to man. Eyeball to eyeball. Bryn recognised the gauntlet Dicky was throwing down. 'And another.'

Dicky solemnly handed him his third and then his fourth. 'You're running up quite a bill. We don't have a slate here, you know. Remember, you wouldn't have one when your name was over the door.'

'That's right, I wouldn't. Here, barman.' Bryn laid a twenty-pound note on the bar counter, taken from a thick wad. 'Have one on me.'

'No, thanks, not when I'm working.'

By mistake Bryn said, 'The landlady won't mind.'

If there was one thing guaranteed to anger Georgie it was calling her the landlady.

'That's enough, the pair of you. I won't stand for it. Don't serve him any more tonight. He's had enough.'

'No, Georgie, I haven't had enough. 'Nother one, barman.' He sent his empty glass skittering across the counter and Dicky only just managed to stop it crashing to the floor. With a poker face he refilled the glass and handed it to Bryn. Seated now on a bar stool, Bryn accepted the glass and steadily downed the lot. The small area of his brain that from long practice could keep him in control no matter how much he drank swung into the arena. For that was what it had become: a gladiatorial confrontation, in public, for possession of the woman they both wanted. He downed his sixth and then his seventh glass, and Dicky, still poker-faced, poured him his eighth. The rest of the customers in the bar watched with breathless anticipation. Every eye was focused on Bryn and Dicky. The strange thing was that by the eighth glass neither of them was speaking. It had become a silent game of filling and emptying, filling and emptying. Georgie cringed with apprehension. He must have done some hard drinking in the past to withstand all this whisky. Someone's inane high-pitched laugh shattered the silence and should have broken the spell they were all under, but it didn't.

Suddenly Georgie banged her fist on the counter and said, 'Dicky! Don't serve him another glass. That's an order.'

The ninth and then the tenth glass, and still Bryn wanted more.

Bryn pushed his glass across the counter towards Dicky and signalled with a crooked finger that he wanted yet another double.

Georgie shouted, 'Don't you dare serve him. Do you hear me?'

But Dicky ignored her. Dicky who'd always been so . . . well . . . so *obedient* to her smallest wish. Bryn tossed back his eleventh double.

145

Dicky refilled Bryn's glass but instead of handing it to him he placed it well away from Bryn's side of the counter, making Bryn reach right across if he wanted it. Bryn crooked his finger again and beckoned for it to be given him. But Dicky, with a grin on his face which almost reached from ear to ear, didn't obey. Bryn overreached himself, almost caught hold of the glass but missed, overturned it and shot every drop of whisky down the front of Dicky's shirt, and he himself fell off the bar stool and on to the floor, unconscious. He lay flat on his back, his mouth wide open as though waiting for another whisky to be poured down his throat.

The entire bar erupted in hysterical laughter. They held their sides, wiped their tears, nudged each other, rolled about, pointed helplessly and roared with laughter all over again. As for Dicky, he simply spread his hands wide, shrugged his shoulders and looked as innocent as a newborn baby. The staff waiting on in the dining room came through to see what was the matter; some diners left their meals to see the fun.

Georgie stormed round the counter and knelt beside Bryn. 'Come on, Bryn, wake up. You've got to get home. Come on.' She shook him by the shoulders, slapped his face twice, to no avail. 'Dicky! Jug of water please.'

Without a word Dicky filled a large jug with water and handed it to her.

'You ought to have had more sense. I told you to stop serving him. What were you thinking of?' She threw the jug of water over his head and face, but to no effect.

Dicky said loudly, enjoying his audience, 'Round one to Dicky Tutt.' Everyone clapped their approval.

'Good on yer, Dicky!'

'Good for you!'

'Just what he deserved.'

Georgie snapped out, 'Get me a towel.'

Dicky found a not particularly savoury one from the bottom of the towel cupboard and handed it to her.

She vigorously rubbed his head and face dry. 'It's no good, he's completely out. He's not going to get home in this state.' She took hold of the front of his shirt and shook him briskly. 'Bryn, wake up! Come on!' But Bryn didn't.

Dicky laughed. 'Not much of a Romeo now, is he?' He got a round of applause for his remark.

'It's nothing to the credit of either of you. You call yourselves grown men. Huh! More like two little boys. I'm disgusted with the pair of you. It's all your fault, Dicky.'

Georgie's indignation soon turned to laughter and when Georgie and Dicky looked at one another they laughed louder still. So did the spectators – there hadn't been such an hilarious night in the Royal Oak for years.

'Them whiskies looked more like triples to me,' someone shouted.

Dicky gasped out, 'The last two were!' and everyone laughed louder than ever.

But they still had the problem of what to do with Bryn. 'We'll drag him into the back and he can sleep it off. I'll ring Neville and let him know.'

Bryn's planned night of romance had an ignominious ending. Dicky took one leg, Georgie the other, Alan caught hold of him under his armpits and between them they hauled him off stage into the back storeroom. Georgie found a blanket and covered him over. So Bryn spent the night squeezed between cartons of Tortilla crisps and toilet roll twelve packs from the cash and carry and not between the sheets with Georgie.

When he woke next morning Dicky was standing over him reliving his last night's triumph. 'So, you've woken up at last.'

'Oh! What are you doing here?' Bryn clutched his head with both hands and moaned.

'I work here, remember?'

Bryn opened his eyes and saw the word 'Tortilla' written only five inches from his eyes. His voice thick with sleep he asked, 'Where am I?'

'In the storeroom, sleeping it off.'

The events of the whole evening flooded back to him. 'You little sod. It was you.'

Dicky shook his head. 'No, it wasn't me. You did the drinking. Not me.'

Bryn tried to sit up. 'Ah! Get me a drink.'

'Hair of the dog?'

Though he was in agony, Bryn was sharp enough to see through Dicky's game plan. 'No. Black coffee. That's best.'

Georgie called out, 'Send him upstairs for a cold shower.'

Bryn shuddered. Cold shower. What did she think he was? He was far too frail for a cold shower.

'There's still some of your clothes in the wardrobe, Bryn. Put fresh on.'

Dicky didn't know this and he felt Georgie was disloyal to him, keeping Bryn's clothes as though she expected him back any minute. He half kicked Bryn's leg. 'Get up, then.'

'Steady on.' Bryn heaved himself up and, towering over Dicky, said, 'Don't for one minute think you've won. You haven't. Right?'

'Says you.' Dicky strutted out of the storeroom saying, 'Shall I show you where the bathroom is? Oh, of course, you know.' He grinned, considering he'd won another point. But at bottom he was bitterly angry. All he wanted was to get his and Georgie's and Bel's lives sorted out. They'd been in limbo far too long. He got through his routine with one ear cocked for Bryn. He heard him come down from the bathroom, caught a glimpse of him in an outfit he'd worn before he'd hopped it with Elektra, which did him no favours, listened for him talking to Georgie and then to his delight saw him cross the car park and go out into Church Lane. Good riddance to him. He'd thought she might give him breakfast but she hadn't. He just wished he'd died last night from all that drink. Obviously that wasn't the way to go.

He went to look for her. 'Georgie! There you are.' Dicky took her hand in his and said, 'There's something I need to know.'

'Fire away.'

'The divorce, is it going ahead?'

'Of course it is. I want rid of him as soon as possible after last night. I can't stand all this macho squaring up to each other. All this testosterone. Give me a kiss.' They kissed joyfully. 'Oh, Dicky, I do love you.'

'And I love you. Just let's get it all straightened out and then . . .'

'I can't wait. But listen to me, no more trying to finish him off with stupid tricks like last night. You mustn't, you know, it might backfire.'

149

'I know, I was daft, but the chance was too much to pass by. He knew exactly what I was doing and thought he'd win, but fortunately for me he didn't. It is stupid, the whole situation is stupid, and I want no more of it, believe me.'

'For the sake of the business I can't pass up those lunches on a Thursday, but from now on that's all it will be, him turning up from time to time with his punters. If he wants to put business our way then so what! All the better for us. That's all it will be and I mean it.'

'His clothes . . . get rid of them.'

Georgie had to laugh. 'OK. The new Bryn looked ridiculous in them, didn't he?'

Dicky hugged her tight. 'That's the problem, the *new* Bryn.'

'You've no need to be jealous, love. There's nothing there for him any more.' Georgie knew he needed reassuring about her love for him and she said what he needed to hear, but somewhere deep down came that hankering again, nudging at her, worrying at her. She sighed.

He sensed her hankering, felt she was wanting to be loyal to him but finding it difficult; just that little bit of conviction missing. But then again when he said he wanted no more of Bryn and his sparring he too didn't entirely mean it; well, almost but not quite. Just that little bit of conviction missing, the same as it was for Georgie. They'd been all right till Bryn turned up again, opening up old memories, looking more handsome then he'd ever done. Well, he for one wasn't giving Georgie up without a fight. Like he'd said once to the Rector, she was everything to him; on that matter he didn't lack conviction, not one jot.

'Coffee time?'

'Yes, please.'

Bryn kept a low profile the morning after his humiliation in the bar. He'd been an idiot, a complete idiot taking up Dicky's challenge. The only one to come smiling out of it had been Dicky himself. It simply wouldn't do. He had to have the upper hand not only in Georgie's eyes but in the eyes of the whole village. Damn and blast, he thought, as he showered yet again in the hope of restoring some semblance of equilibrium to his shattered body. He was getting too old for the kind of drinking he'd done last night. He carefully arranged the bath towel on the rail in Neville's guest bathroom and walked into the bedroom. He looked at the clothes he'd just removed and thought, where on earth was I coming from to be wearing a shirt and trousers like that? I even thought I looked good in them. Huh! No wonder Georgie had gone off him, no wonder at all. He must have been an idiot. Bryn bundled them up ready for the bin and selected a matching set of shirt and trousers from his extensive wardrobe. Then he settled himself in a chair by the window and looked out on to Neville's well-manicured garden, intending to take time reappraising his future.

He was right about doing this tourist business. Hour upon hour serving cruise guests on those damned liners had honed his skills to a fine point. He'd been out of his depth to begin with but by the end of the first year he'd found he could have them eating out of his hand. A combination of flattery and a good memory for faces and

151

what drinks the punters preferred had earned him more in tips than his wages and that was the way to go with his tourists. Barely three weeks and he'd be off to London to meet his first group. He rubbed his hands together in glee. From a file on the bedside table he took his list of Americans for the first group and sat lost in thought.

But somehow Georgie's face kept intruding, and instead of the words he saw an image of her laughing up at him on their wedding day, crying when she'd found she wasn't pregnant when she'd been confident she was. That had been a blow, that had; no children. But it had been a long time since he'd grieved about it. A long time. Down below him he spotted Guy and Hugh, Neville's boys, standing smoking by the summer house. Two huge great boys, well, men really, confident, well-educated, Oxford or somewhere similar now behind them, both heading out into the world. They'd only themselves to blame if they didn't succeed. Unbidden came the thought: if only he'd had their chances.

Somewhere below a door opened and he heard Neville calling for Liz. He wished he'd never thought to ask the slimy toad to help finance his scheme. In a rare moment of clarity he knew Neville would bleed him dry if he didn't watch it. That was what happened when you'd made your money, you could just sit back and do nothing and in the returns would roll. Well, damn moneybags Neville. He'd pay him his loan back as soon as he could, even if he had to go without to do it. He and Georgie together would conquer the world. He needed Georgie to enjoy the fruits of his plan, there'd be no point in being rich just for himself. Somehow he had to have her, come hell or high water. He'd never thought he could fall in love all over again but that was exactly what had happened to him. He only had to see Georgie and the blood was gushing through his veins, his heart making that leap it used to do whenever she walked into a room when they were young and starting out.

Bryn checked his watch. They'd be opening soon. He strolled downstairs, called out he wouldn't be needing lunch and left for the Royal Oak. He turned out of the gates to go down Church Lane and saw a surveyor standing on the pavement taking a bearing through a theodolite. He gave him a cheery 'Good morning' and a salute, and meandered past. Then Bryn stopped in his tracks. He turned back and went to pass the time of day with the chap. Friendly, kind of, the new Bryn. The new hail-fellow-well-met kind of Bryn.

'What are you up to this fine sunny morning, might I ask?'

His assistant some yards away glanced up. The surveyor answered, 'You can ask.'

Bryn thought aye, aye! Something's going on here he doesn't want us to find out about. 'Just wondered, you know, why you were here. Realigning the road or something?'

'No.'

'What then?'

The surveyor tapped the side of his nose with his forefinger.

Bryn began to smell a rat. 'I see. Mum's the word.'

He nodded.

'Surely we've a right to know; we are all ratepayers.'

'Look, I'm trying to do a job of work here. Would you mind moving on? Please.'

153

Bryn tried several diplomatic approaches but the chap remained annoyingly silent.

'There is such a thing as good manners when someone's speaking to you.'

'Look! I'm here to do a job. Just go away.'

Bryn was tempted to kick a leg of his theodolite, but decided against it. He wouldn't learn anything that way. He turned on his heel and went back to Glebe House.

'Neville!'

'Yes. I'm in the study,' came the reply in that reedy voice which could irritate so very quickly.

Bryn pushed open the door and there Neville sat in his gleaming study, at his obsessively tidy desk, fingers poised over his keyboard, peering at him over the top of his gold-rimmed half-glasses.

'In your position as councillor do you know anything at all about these chaps out here surveying the place?'

Neville paused only for a moment but Bryn picked up on it, then Neville said, 'Not a thing.'

Bryn thought, you liar. You absolute liar. You do. 'I'm surprised you don't, you being on the council.'

'I may be on the council but I don't know every jot and tittle of what's going on in other departments.'

'I thought you were in planning?'

'I am, but this isn't my kind of planning.'

'I see.' Bryn rubbed his chin while he considered. 'Do you know who might know? The chappie himself isn't forthcoming, which is suspicious in itself.'

Neville had returned to studying his computer and looked up impatiently. 'Sorry, Bryn, must press on. I'll ask around.'

I bet, thought Bryn.

Reluctantly he left Neville to his work and wandered off to the Royal Oak.

It was lunchtime and only Alan was about.

'Georgie not in?'

'Getting ready to go out. Her day off.'

'Ah! I'll have a whis— No, I'll have a tonic water. Choose something for yourself, anything you fancy.'

'No, thanks, too early for me.'

Bryn settled himself on a bar stool and quizzed Alan about where Georgie was going.

'I've been told not to interfere in her private life, so I've no idea.'

Bryn chuckled. 'Whoops!' He laughed some more and saw Alan beginning to go red in the face. 'How's the kid? Louis, or whatever his name is.'

'Lewis, actually. He's doing great.'

'Time you had another.'

'You can't rush these things.'

'Young virile chap like you.'

'These things take time and it costs money to bring up a kid. Two might just finish us off.'

'I bet. Tips you get in here. Cruise liners are even better for tips. I could earn more than my wages every week on the liners.'

Alan perked up at this, but then knew for sure that Linda would never tolerate his absences. 'Here's Georgie.'

She came through from the back, dressed for off, and what a picture she made, thought Bryn.

'My taxi'll be here in a minute. You can manage, can't you, Alan?'

'Of course.'

Georgie saw Bryn. 'You've turned up. Feeling OK?'

Bryn nodded. 'I'm just planning to go into Culworth. Can I give you a lift?'

He saw her hesitate, ponder and dismiss the idea. 'No, thanks.'

'Why not? I won't pester, I'll drop you off and we'll arrange a picking-up time.' He gave her a winning smile, saw her hesitate, than make up her mind.

'All right, then, but I'll have the taxi to pay.'

'Leave me to attend to that.' They heard the horn tooting outside. 'Won't be a tick.'

Bryn came back in and realised that Alan and she had had words; Georgie was flushed and Alan was sullen.

'I'll go and pick up my car. Won't be a minute.'

'I'll wait outside in the yard.'

'OK.'

After he'd settled her in her seat in the most gentle-manly way, Bryn roared off down the Culworth Road delighted to be able to show off his new car to her.

Georgie settled back on the luxurious leather seat and that nagging annoying feeling buried deep down struggled to the surface again. When she'd been so sickened by Bryn for so long, how could she possibly have any feelings left for him? But she had. They surged to the forefront of her consciousness and she revelled in them. He made her feel a million dollars. She glanced at him and he caught her eye.

'Watch the road, for heaven's sake!'

Bryn could only laugh, out loud, boisterously, joyfully. 'Let's lunch first, then we'll go our separate ways.'

'I don't know about lunch.'

Bryn nudged her. 'Go on.'

'Well . . . all right, then.'

'Good! The George for Georgie. Heh!'

'You've changed.'

'I needed to. Alan giving you grief?'

'Not really. Just thinks he's my guardian. Well, I've got news for him. He isn't.'

They drove in silence for a while, Bryn exulting in the chance to show Georgie what he was made of and Georgie enjoying the pleasure of escaping briefly from her workaday life. She looked at Bryn's profile and thought he wasn't the best-looking of men but there was something about him nowadays which had been lacking before. He'd become prepossessing, almost attractive. She said, 'It seems to me you're a hardened drinker. I didn't appreciate that performance last night.'

'Neither did I. It won't happen again. I'm not a hardened drinker, don't think that of me. It was Dicky's challenge that made me make a fool of myself.'

'Too right, you did make a fool of yourself. Why can't you just leave Dicky alone?'

'He annoys me, thinking he can whisk you off to the altar as soon as the divorce comes through. What's more, like I've said before, I shan't agree to it.'

'Hard luck, I'm going through with it.'

Bryn, having to pause at the traffic lights at the bottom of Deansgate, took his chance. He laid a gentle hand on Georgie's knee and said, 'That night . . .'

'Yes?'

'You and me in the lounge. You were very tempted. You and me making music together.' The lights changed and he drove on.

'I may have been tempted, but I'd never have forgiven myself. I'm marrying Dicky.'

Her throat seemed to fill up with emotion and tears

were very close. What was the matter with her? Blowing with the wind, she was. When she was with Dicky it was Dicky, with Bryn, out of the blue, she discovered emotions long since dead.

'You don't sound as convincing as you did.'

'Oh, but I am.' Liar, she thought, liar.

When they walked from the car park into the George she noticed one or two admiring glances directed at Bryn. His manners and bearing in a place like the George were exactly right, and she couldn't help thinking that Dicky would not have carried the whole situation off with quite the same style as Bryn was doing.

All through the meal Georgie endeavoured to keep the conversation as general as she could, avoiding all mention of Dicky or Bel or the pub, but after an hour of sustaining that Bryn inevitably turned the talk to Dicky.

'It's quite simple, Bryn, I love him and I don't love you.'

He looked keenly at her, noted the slight flush the wine had brought to her cheeks, the way her lovely blonde hair curled and swirled so naturally about her face, her mouth so sweet and yet showing strength, and he wished so very much that she were his. What an idiot he'd been.

'I sense doubt. I sense there's indecision.'

'Do you indeed.'

'I do.'

Georgie's eyes filled with tears. 'I do. I do. I do love him.'

'And me? What about me?'

A tear spilled over and ran down her cheek. Georgie found a tissue and wiped it away.

'Well, what about me?'

'Stop putting pressure on me. Stop behaving like a lunatic. I know what you're capable of. You make me afraid of myself.'

'What do you mean?'

'You make me not know my own mind. I want you out of my life. I want you to go. I don't want your lunch business and I don't want you in the bar. Right!' She stood up and marched from the restaurant blinded by tears.

He rushed after her, leaving two twenty-pound notes on the till as he went. Bryn caught her as she headed away from the hotel towards the station taxi rank. 'Look here, this is ridiculous. At least let me take you home.' With his arm round her shoulders he lead her towards his car and they sat there for a while until Georgie had command of herself.

'I was going to see my solicitor again with some papers he needs, to do with the business. You know, for the divorce. I'll tidy myself up and I'll go. I can't waste a day. I get few enough days off as it is.'

'Why bother, when you're not sure? I've found a whole new love for you, Georgie, a whole new love. I admit to being a fool in the past, but I've come to my senses now. I want you to leave things as they are. I'll do this tourist thing now I've got them planned and then after this summer I'll forget it and we can go back to being husband and wife running the pub, and we'll employ more staff so it's not so intense. You know, more time off. What do you say?'

Her answer was to stare out of the windscreen saying nothing. Bryn waited. And waited, until eventually he said, 'Well, all right then, you think about it.' He turned the ignition and started reversing out of the parking space.

'You're asking too much of me.'

Bryn stopped the car half in and half out. 'I'm only asking for the status quo.'

'Too much water under the bridge for that.'

'I don't see why.'

'How long till you become what you were before? How long till you kill what I have for you like before? How long till you forget the love bit and fancy the new barmaid? How long, I say, how long?'

Silenced by the obvious truth of what she said, Bryn drove her to the solicitor's office and remained outside like a condemned man awaiting his sentence. When Georgie came out and got back in, neither of them noticed the car which went past them in the busy street, nor did they see the wave the driver gave them.

Chapter 10

'Caroline! You'll never guess who I saw in Culworth today, outside a solicitor's office would you believe, you know, the one in the side street off Deansgate?'

'No?'

'Bryn and Georgie.'

Caroline turned from the cooker and looked at him. 'How odd, him driving her to the solicitor's to get a divorce from him.'

'It's curious, isn't it? It looked as though he'd sat outside and waited for her. She was getting into the car just as I passed.' Peter went to put his communion case in the study and came back into the kitchen closing the door behind him. 'Darling, we must come to some decision about . . . what to say to the children. We did say we would. Have you given it any more thought?'

'A little. I think I can face up to it better now than I imagined I would. But I still haven't thought out how to introduce it.'

'No, neither have I. What I don't want to do is give them the idea that their arrival was some dreadful murky underhand happening of which we are completely ashamed. I am ashamed of what I did, and rightly so, but I don't want them to feel that.'

'Even so, if it was rather less beautiful than we would have wished, neither of us has regretted it, have we?'

She turned round to look at him and he couldn't quite decipher what she was asking him, so he avoided a straightforward answer by saying, 'From the moment I first saw them I have loved them.'

'Me too.'

They were both silent for a while, then Peter said, 'It's amazing how one can help others with their problems and yet, with one's own . . .'

'Photographs. How about photographs?'

'Which?'

'In the parish albums. There must be some of her in there. Surely?'

'I don't know.'

Caroline answered quite clearly, 'You do, you know.'

Peter flushed. He poured himself a glass of water from the jug on the table and took a long drink before he said, 'I'll check that.'

'It will hurt me more than you to see them. Remember that. Tell the children, darling, they need to wash their hands.'

By the time the children had responded to this request the meal was on the table. 'Grace.' Peter waited for them to close their eyes and put their hands together, then said, 'By the grace of God we have food to eat, clean water to drink and a loving home. Praise God the Almighty. Amen.'

'I had hoped Bryn and Georgie might get together again. What about you?' Caroline asked him.

'I hoped so too, but considering the tales we've heard of the goings on I very much doubt it.'

'Oh, well! We'll have to leave it to them; there's nothing we can do about it. It's Dicky I feel sorry for.'

Beth enquired, 'Doesn't Mrs Fields want Mr Fields for a husband any more?'

Caroline answered her with, 'It's all very complicated, Beth, but I'm sure one day they'll get it all sorted.'

Alex said, 'I like Mrs Fields. She's nice, and I like Mr Tutt. I can't wait to get into Scouts proper, then we'll have him for our leader. He's always good fun.'

Beth emptied her mouth before asking, 'Where are Mr and Mrs Fields's children?'

'They haven't got any.'

Beth looked at Caroline as she said this and came out with, 'Perhaps she's like you, Mummy, and can't have children.'

'I expect that's so.'

'Will I be the same? Because you're my mummy?'

Caroline cupped Beth's lovely rounded cheek in her hand and skirted round the situation as usual by saying, 'Not necessarily. You'll probably have dozens of children.'

'Oh, I wouldn't want dozens, but four would be very nice, thank you. Think of all the washing. And the ironing.'

Alex said, 'I'm not having any at all, I'm going to explore the world in my plane, I shan't have time.'

For quite a while Beth ate her food without speaking. Caroline cast a few glances at her and, knowing her as she did, suddenly realised she was going to produce some devastating piece of information and felt sick to her stomach.

She did just that. 'But if you're not my mummy, and

my tummy-mummy could have Alex *and* me, then perhaps I *shall* be able to have babies.'

Peter answered on Caroline's behalf, 'Yes. It's very likely and I shall be proud to be their grandfather.'

Alex burst out laughing. 'Grandad! Grandad!'

Beth giggled. 'Granny! Granny!'

'Who is my granny?'

Peter looked at Alex and said, 'There's your Granny and Grandad Peterson who are Mummy's mother and father, but unfortunately my mother and father died a long while ago, so you've never known them.'

Beth declared, 'Those two sisters at school who dance, they don't know where their daddy is. They've only got a mummy. And there's Janine, she's only got her daddy and sometimes her mummy because she's usually in hospital. And there's Sean, he's got a dad at the weekends.'

Caroline asked Beth how she knew all this.

'Because I listen.'

Alex snorted his disbelief. 'Because you're a nosy parker. I've heard you asking.'

'I do not.'

'You do.'

'I don't.'

'You do, so there!'

Peter rapped on the table. 'Children, this won't do. Finish your dinner.'

Beth burst into tears. 'I don't want mine. He's horrid. I only wanted to know.'

Peter reached out to pat her arm. 'Of course you did. You needed to get it sorted out, didn't you. It's very sad that so many children haven't got both their mother and their father at home. Very sad indeed.'

Alex said in a belligerent tone, 'They look all right.'

Caroline murmured, 'But some of them must hurt inside.'

'Definitely. I'm sure they must. Now dry your tears, young lady, and count your blessings.'

This silenced Alex and Beth but it did nothing to quell the fear in Caroline's heart. Week in week out she felt as though she'd actually given birth to them both, she loved and adored them so dearly. So much so that for years she'd been able to dismiss from her mind the time when Alex and Beth would need an explanation of their origins, but as Peter had said only a few short weeks ago, the time had come. Whether it was harder for her than for him she wasn't quite sure. Whether or not they would fully understand the situation she didn't know. What she dreaded most of all was them wanting to know all about Suzy and their three half-sisters, Daisy, Pansy and Rosie. Their names were engraved on her heart. Even worse, though, would Alex and Beth still feel the same about her after they'd been told? She remembered the searing pain of the day when, thinking they were all away on holiday, Suzy had come back to the village. In her mind she could still see Alex running out into the road in his pyjamas and her snatching him up, and seeing Suzy standing by the lych-gate looking up the church path waving to Peter. It didn't bear thinking about.

Caroline looked at Peter and he saw how troubled she was. 'Children, if you give Mummy and me ten minutes I'll come and play a game with you. Your choice.'

'Lose Your Shirt,' shouted Alex.

Beth suggested Scrabble.

'Not Scrabble, I don't like Scrabble.'

'That's because you always lose.'

'I don't.'

'You do!'

'I don't!'

'Make up your minds. Ten minutes, then.'

He closed the kitchen door after them and began clearing the table.

Caroline asked, 'Just how far shall we go?'

'Play it by ear. They're both intelligent; they'll soon understand the whole picture. I've had a thought.'

Caroline said, 'Good. Because I haven't.'

'I think the photograph album is the best approach. We can casually find one of her and begin the explanation from there.'

'Oh, God!'

'You've nothing to fear.'

'Haven't I?'

'No, why should you? I bear the burden of guilt, don't I? They may never want to speak to me again, but that's for me to cope with.'

'Do they *have* to know everything?'

'As I said, I'll play it by ear. Go as far as they want to go. They know the mechanics. Believe me, Kate Pascoe has left no stone unturned in her sex education lessons. I know because she thrashed it all out with me before she started them.'

Bent over the dishwasher filling the racks, Caroline almost groaned aloud with anxiety at the prospect. She turned to face him. 'You must impress on them that they are adopted by you and me. That there's no going back. That Suzy wasn't able to keep them because she couldn't cope, with her husband dead and three children already.

Don't let them think she didn't want them, because she did. I think maybe I'm not ready for these revelations.'

'Is one ever completely ready? For something on this scale? But what I shall emphasise is that the two of them answered your prayers as well as mine. I don't want them to think Suzy and I foisted them on you. It was you who asked her for them, remember.'

The doorbell rang. It registered with neither of them so at the second ring it was Beth who opened the door and found Georgie Fields on the doorstep, looking distraught.

'Is the Rector in?'

'Yes, he is, Mrs Fields. Will you come into the study and I'll go and get him.'

Georgie crept in to the study, where Beth invited her to sit down and went to find Peter.

'That's our game cancelled.'

'Why?'

'That was Mrs Fields at the door. I've shown her into your study, Daddy.'

Peter put down the tablecloth he was folding and left the kitchen. He found Georgie sitting on the study sofa, weeping. Closing the door behind him, he seated himself at his desk and asked quietly, 'Now, Georgie, what can I do for you?'

Georgie couldn't answer. All she could think of was coming back from Culworth in silence because she was so confoundedly mixed up about everything and then finding herself alone in the lounge with Bryn . . . . she sobbed again at what she'd done.

'I'm sorry for interrupting when you're busy. I don't even know if I should have come. But I'm so mixed up. I can't ever, ever forgive myself for what I've done.'

167

Peter waited.

'I could kill him, I could.'

Peter waited.

'I've made such a mess of things.'

'There's an answer to be found to most problems.'

'Not to this.'

'Tell me.'

'I can't.'

'There's nothing I haven't heard about the frailty of human lives. The foolish, the downright evil, the absolute depths of depravity. I don't expect for one minute that your problem is any more dreadful.'

'It is to me.'

'Ah!'

Georgie dried her eyes. 'I should never have come here. I can't tell someone like *you*. Never. I'm an idiot, an incredible fool. I quite simply can't tell *you*. I'll go.' She stood up.

'That's all right by me, but sometimes it helps to speak to an outsider. Gives a new dimension to things, don't you know.'

'I . . .'

'Anything said in this room is entirely confidential; I don't even tell Caroline. You have my word about that.'

Peter waited.

'It's Bryn.' She sat down again. 'It's Bryn. Before he came back I was absolutely clear about Dicky. All I wanted was to get face to face with Bryn, sort out the business side of things, you know, the money side, get the divorce, marry Dicky and live happily ever after.'

'And . . . what's stopping you doing just that?'

'Me. I'm stopping me.'

'I see. How does Dicky feel?'

'Well, that's just it.' 'It' was Dicky finding out that they were in her bedroom with the door locked when he came to start his shift. He'd been looking for her and as he had free run of the upstairs rooms he thought nothing of going up there to find her. He'd tapped on her bedroom door as a last resort and found it locked, and had known instinctively what was afoot. She and Bryn were sleeping in each other's arms and they'd woken with such a jolt when Dicky had rattled the doorknob.

'He's . . . we've . . . Bryn and I have . . . slept together today and Dicky's found out.'

He'd stood hammering on the door, shouting and shouting. They'd both dressed and eventually Bryn had unlocked the door. Dicky must have heard the key turn because before Bryn could open the door he had pushed it open and was facing them, eye to eye, hands clenched by his sides. Georgie didn't think she had ever seen Dicky so wild with temper. She'd honestly thought murder would be done. He'd looked past them and seen the bed so obviously slept in, and he'd given Bryn a stare which had made her blood run cold. His face was contorted with such fearful anger, such terrifying despair, such horror. She shuddered at the thought.

Georgie heard Peter say something, but didn't know what it was. 'I'm sorry, I didn't hear.'

'I said I'm so sorry to hear that. So sorry.'

'So am I. I've run away to you because I'm so frightened. Just tell me what to do.' She remembered how Dicky had stormed off downstairs, leaving her and Bryn in shock. She'd hurried Bryn down the stairs and out through the back, and then she'd gone to the bathroom and showered and changed and redone her make-up and tried to pull herself together but she hadn't been able to face Dicky so, like a coward, she'd run to a safe haven hoping for some answers.

She mistook Peter's silence for an inability to give her an answer so she stood up again and made to leave. 'I'm sorry to have troubled you.'

'Wait, just a moment. I can't tell you what to do, that's for you to decide. There's nothing quite like removing oneself from a situation in order to get a perspective on it. Be honest, tell them or write them a note and tell them the *truth* of why you're going. When you're by yourself, think about what you want, not just for this year or next, but for *the rest of your life*. You won't have the answer the first day and maybe not even the second but eventually you will. When you've decided, come back and be absolutely up front about your decision.'

Georgie looked up at him. 'Do you know, I think you're right.'

'People might think it's running away from your problems, but it's not. What it is, is taking charge of your life again. Go today, tonight, straight away.'

'I will. Thank you. Yes, I will.'

'God bless you, Georgie, I shall remember you in my prayers.'

'Thank you for that.'

Peter opened the study door for her and saw her out. He watched her walk away towards the Royal Oak and thought, what a mess human beings make of their lives. Then he thought about his own problem of the twins' birth and knew he was no different from the rest of humankind.

Dicky had walked down the stairs knowing he was capable of murder. He imagined the feel of his hands round Bryn's neck, sensed his own inhuman strength, slowly, slowly strangling him, almost felt Bryn's body suddenly lack resistance as he collapsed at his feet. A grim smile crossed his face and a tear trickled down his cheek. He stood at the foot of the stairs gripping the newel post, trying to come to terms with what he'd found out. His mouth felt like a piece of arid desert, his teeth so dry they stuck to the insides of his cheeks. He could hear Trish and Alan talking, the sound of laughter from the bar, the clatter of cutlery and china in the dining room; none of it made any sense. Dicky felt black inside, emptied, voidlike. From upstairs came sounds of life, voices and movement. He couldn't bear to be standing there so numb when they came downstairs, so he hurried to the storeroom and, leaving the door ajar, sat down on a case of something or other to brood and listen.

But he heard nothing except scurrying feet and haste, the bolt shot back, the door open, shut and the bolt refastened, and Georgie's feet climbing the stairs again. He remembered how he'd loved to massage those same feet for her when they ached after a day behind the bar. But there was one thing for certain: he, Richard Tutt, wouldn't be massaging her feet ever again. When he could hear the water running in the bathroom, moving like an automaton he went to where he had hung his jacket, took it down from the peg, laid it over his arm, took hold of the knob of the door bolt and thought he could feel the warmth of her hand still there, so he caressed it for a moment, a lump rising into his throat as he did so, then he

171

opened the door and left the Royal Oak, vowing it was for the last time.

He flung himself down on the sofa in his tiny cottage living room, lying there for what felt like hours, filled with black despair. His mind racing and racing through what had happened, trying to find reasons, while all the time his imagination shied away from thinking of them in that bed, together, touching, thrilling . . . everything which had belonged to *him* now besmirched by Bryn. Such an agonising betrayal, he couldn't believe Georgie was capable of it. But she was. He groaned out loud and wept.

He woke when he heard Bel's voice saying, 'I've got away for half an hour, Dicky, love.'

He didn't answer her. There wasn't anything to say.

'She's gone. There was this letter on the mat. It's from her, I recognise the writing. I'll put the kettle on.'

It seemed only one tick of the clock when Bel came back in with the tray. She poured out his tea and pushed it close to him.

Dicky picked up the cup of scalding tea and burned his lips trying to drink it.

'Silly boy, it's straight from the pot. Put it down. Have you read the letter? No, I can see you haven't. You'd better read it. I can't, it's got your name on it. I'd like to know what's happened.'

'You don't know?'

'No. I might be your sister but I'm not a mind reader. All I know is she's packed her bags and gone. For a few days, I understand. I've been too busy in the dining room to get away any sooner. I do know she's been to see the Rector and then come back and said she was taking a few

172

days off. She didn't tell me, it's only what I've learned from Trish and Alan.'

'She and Bryn have . . . slept together today.' He spoke as though he was having to prise the words out of his mouth.

Bel gasped with shock. 'Oh, Dicky, love, I'm so sorry.'

'As far as I'm concerned that's it. I'm finished with her. The love of my life. Over. Done. Finished.'

'Oh, Dicky!' She kicked off her shoes and lay back in the easy chair, lost for words. All she longed for was his happiness. His total happiness. And here he was, broken to pieces. Gently she prompted him into action. 'See what she says in her letter.'

Dicky handed it to her. 'You read it.'

'I can't, Dicky, I can't. I mustn't.'

'Read it!'

'I . . .'

'Do as I say.'

Bel opened the letter and swiftly read it through.

'Out loud!'

'Out loud? But it's private.'

'See if I care. Read it, please.'

Bel cleared her throat and in a shaky voice read out:

Dearest Dicky,

Can you forgive me for one moment of wrongdoing? It didn't mean a thing to me, you're all I care about. I'm so muddled. Peter said go away and think, and I am. But it's you all the time.

All my love,
    your Georgie

Dicky snatched the letter from Bel and read it through for

himself. 'Hah! "*I'm so muddled.*" She's not the only one. Muddled? I should say. So am I. I can't understand the signals I'm getting. Does she or doesn't she love me?' Dicky's voice broke as he asked that last question.

'Oh, Dicky, I don't know the answer to that one and neither does she apparently. Like she says, give her time.' She went to get some biscuits from the kitchen, desperate for something to do to cover her distress. How could Georgie do this to him? Her loving, kindly Dicky didn't deserve this. So patiently waiting for a divorce which never materialised and this was his reward. But sleeping with that creep, Bryn. God! How could she? How could she? Bel peeped round the kitchen door and saw that Dicky was still clutching the letter, lost in thought. He needed something to do. 'They'll be glad for you to get back to work; they were busy when I left. We'll walk back together, eh? What do you think?'

Dicky refused a biscuit, looked up at her and said, as though making a public announcement, 'I, Dicky Tutt, am not setting foot in that pub again.'

'Dicky! Don't be ridiculous. You must.'

'There's no must about it. I'm not.' He swung himself round on the sofa and laid his head on one arm, his feet not quite touching the other. 'See yer.' He put his arms across his chest with the letter still in his hand. Briefly she thought he looked as though he'd been laid out.

Out of fright she said, 'Dicky, don't do this to yourself. The only one to lose out will be you. You've got to hang on to something. You can't go back to that dreary, boring job you had, you hated it. In any case you've been too long away, it won't be waiting for you, not now.'

Dicky ignored her.

'Do you hear me?'

Dicky still ignored her.

'Right, well, I've got to go. I'll sleep here tonight, I'm not leaving you on your own. So if you want to go to bed before I get back, make up the sofa bed. Right?'

Dicky nodded. Bel threw up her hands in despair and set off back to the Royal Oak with a heavy heart.

At Glebe House Bryn had just been handed Georgie's letter. Guy gave it to him with an amused smile on his face. Bryn didn't give him the satisfaction of opening it in front of him.

'A billet-doux from the wife, no doubt.'

'Probably.' He tossed it on the table without so much as a glance, but he knew whom it was from and longed to open it. He'd no idea what the situation back at the Royal Oak was, because Georgie had whisked him out in a trice after Dicky had seen them both. Bryn had a prickly feeling down his spine still, after that glare Dicky had given him when he'd twigged what they'd been up to, the two of them. My God, there was still the old magic there. He couldn't help a satisfied smile, forgetting that Guy was still watching him from the door.

'Looks to me as though the cat has been at the cream. Good luck to you, man.'

Bryn waited for the door to close behind Guy and aimed a rude gesture at it. That Guy got more like his father every day. He opened the letter from Georgie and read:

Bryn,

I'm going away for a few days. When I come back I shall

have made up my mind what I want to do. The situation is tearing me apart.

Georgie

In Bryn's mind there was no quandary for Georgie: he, Bryn Fields, was the obvious and only choice. Women! Ah, well, nothing but good would come out of her being away.

He turned his mind from Georgie and thought about the men he'd seen in the village street earlier that day. A visit to the pub might prove valuable. He was skilled at turning a conversation in the direction he wanted it to go and he remembered that when he'd lived in the village, before Elektra, there'd been someone down Shepherds Hill who had a son in the council offices. What was his name? He dredged his memory and came up with Kevin. That was it, his mother called him 'our Kev'. If Dicky was there, well, so what, he presented no serious threat with the pub full of customers, not likely.

He heard Liz calling everyone for dinner. He sprang to his feet shouting 'I'm coming' and went downstairs to yet another of Liz's beautifully prepared meals. He really couldn't take advantage of their hospitality much longer. Maybe when Georgie came back she'd be ready for him to return to live above the pub.

When he got to the bar he found his luck was in. There, to his total delight, was Kevin's mother ensconced on the settle, everyone's favourite seat because it gave such a good view of the bar. He stood in front of her and said, 'Can I buy you a drink for old times' sake? What will it be?'

'Why, it's you. Throwing your money about, aren't you?'

Bryn shrugged his shoulders. 'So long as you're on the receiving end I shouldn't worry too much. Well, can I?'

Kev's mother nodded. 'A double vodka, please.'

'Orange with it?'

'No, ta. I like it neat.' Her small, brown, closely set eyes watched him march across to the bar counter. She knew only too well she wasn't getting the drink for the good of her health; there'd be a catch somewhere. But what? she asked herself.

She toasted him and downed half the glass in one gulp. 'Excellent.' Bryn could see he was in for an expensive night if he didn't watch his step.

'They seem short-staffed tonight. They say Georgie's gone off for a couple of days. And Dicky! Well, he's nowhere to be seen, let's put it like that. So I expect he's gone with her. I don't suppose you know anything about it, do you?'

'Nothing.'

'Have they gone together?'

'Shouldn't think so. How's your . . . what was his name? . . . the one who works at the council offices. I know . . . your Kevin.'

So that was it. He was after some information from their Kev. Well, he'd have to pay for it.

'He's doing fine. Been promoted. He's in media and communications now.'

'He'll need to know everything about everything then, won't he. A good chap to know.' Quite by chance his fingers strayed to his wallet, which now lay on the table beside his glass. He fingered it delicately and looked at our Kev's mother with a single raised eyebrow.

'He's well informed, oh, yes.' She emptied her glass and put it down in the middle of the table.

'Fancy another one?'

'That's very kind of you, Bryn, very kind. I don't mind if I do.'

At the bar he asked Trish where everyone was tonight. 'Dicky's not turned in and Georgie's gone to the coast, last-minute thing.'

It hit him like a massive clout on the side of his head. Dicky missing! They hadn't gone together, had they? Surely not! He'd ignored what Kev's mother had said about Dicky, but she might be right after all. Perhaps they had gone together. But not after he and she had . . . he'd left his wallet on the table alongside Kevin's mother. In his confusion he grabbed the wallet, tried to take a note from it and fumbled it so out spilled the whole wad of fifty-pound notes and twenties. Kevin's mother eyed it with relish.

Bryn paid for the drinks, took them to the table and said, 'Shan't be a minute.'

He fled to the dining room and found Bel clearing a table. He caught hold of her elbow and spun her round. 'Your Dicky, where is he?'

Bel looked at him, hating every bone in his body, and said, 'Are you worried about him, then?'

'No . . . well, yes, well, no, not really, just tell me where he is.'

'That's his business. After what you've done to him I wish I could crush the life out of you with the heel of my shoe. You're scum.' She picked up the loaded tray and stalked straight past him.

'Don't walk away when I'm speaking to you.'

Over her shoulder she said, 'Well, I'm not speaking to you' and pushed open the door into the kitchen.

Bryn ground his teeth with annoyance, remembered Kevin's mother and hastened back to sit with her. 'Sorry about that. Where were we? Oh, yes. Your Kevin's promotion. I'm wanting to know why those council chaps were round the village this morning.' Was it only this morning? 'A chap with a theodolite and an assistant taking measurements. Surly, he was, and wouldn't answer my questions.'

Kev's mother eyed his wallet, still prominently displayed on the table. 'I could ask him, of course, but I can't guarantee he knows the answer.'

'You bring me the answer and then . . .' His own eyes deliberately wandered to his wallet. He picked it up. 'I'll make it worth his while to find out,' he told her.

The small brown eyes sparked with an avaricious glint. 'I see. He's no fool, our Kev. Hope you're not thinking small.'

Greedy woman. 'Of course not. I just need to know. After all, in the interests of the village we don't want changes, damn signs and things. No, definitely not, so we've to be prepared, haven't we?'

'D'yer think that might be it, then? By Jove the toffee-nosed around here won't want that, will they? Spoiling their precious village. Eh?' She grinned.

'No. That was what I was thinking. Sir Ralph and the like won't take kindly to it at all. We, you and I, we'd be doing them a good turn.'

Kev's mother stood up. 'Don't make it sound as though you have the interests of the village at heart, the only thing in your heart is worrying that double yellow lines and road signs will spoil the village for your tourist scam. You can't kid me. I'll ring soon as I get home. I might be in here tomorrow night if I've got anything for you.' She squeezed out from the settle, went to speak to a neighbour and left.

Bryn finished his drink while he applied his mind to finding out if Dicky had gone away with Georgie. His stomach churned with the thought that they might have gone together. But she had said she needed time to think away from them both, so she wouldn't have written that if she didn't mean it, though she might have if she didn't want him to know Dicky had gone with her. Red-hot pokers seemed to burn their way into his guts at the thought of them together.

He leapt to his feet, called out 'Goodnight' to Alan and Trish, and left. As he approached Glebe Cottages he looked to see if there were any signs of life in there. He couldn't tell. So he began cautiously creeping up Dicky's path. He looked towards the front window and could see nothing. He crept closer, slowly, carefully, until his nose was inches from the window. Was that a figure lying on the sofa? He shaded his eyes and peered in with his nose now almost touching the glass. It was. It was Dicky! Staring into space, totally helpless and so, well, so lifeless. Relief flooded through his body. Thank God. They hadn't gone together then. But there was something terribly defeated-looking in Dicky's posture. He looked like a whipped dog, thrashed almost to death. Completely crushed.

Bryn slipped softly back down the path and went into the garden at Glebe House. He sat for a while on the seat in front of the summer house and lit a cigarette. It wasn't often that he smoked but tonight he needed one. Bryn dragged on it, drawing the smoke into his lungs with relish. He rejoiced in his knowledge that Dicky wasn't with Georgie, but underneath that came a sense of sorrow, a deep regret for Dicky's plight. The poor chap was ... was ... destroyed, and it was all down to him, Bryn Fields, for wanting to satisfy his own selfish pleasure with Georgie. A small voice inside him argued and why not; after all, she was his wife. Then his conscience kicked in and he knew he'd no rights where Georgie was concerned; it was he who'd gladly exchanged her for that dreadful Elektra. He must have been mad, completely mad to have fancied that tart.

Someone called out from the open French windows, 'Drink, Bryn?' It was Neville. 'Whisky?'

'Thanks.' Bryn stubbed out his cigarette, picked it up and took it to the outside bin, remembering even in his distress about Dicky, not to litter Neville's immaculate garden.

'Coming.' Bryn realised that losing Georgie wouldn't affect him nearly so badly as it had Dicky. He, Bryn, would bounce back far quicker, being a different kind of person from Dicky. The poor chap was in pieces. With a heavy heart he joined the family for a nightcap and hoped he'd be able to sleep tonight, but he was aware it wasn't a certainty.

Chapter 11

He went to bed to think. He'd some e-mails to send off tomorrow, courtesy of Neville, to his lunch and coffee stops on the tour confirming numbers, and reconfirming the hotels en route. Check with Jimbo about the souvenirs. Check with Willie about the tour of the church. See Jimmy about the geese and rehearse what he had to say. Stroll round to Deadman's Dell to see what progress was being made – if no one was there he'd ring the county offices and speak to Gilbert himself. See Bel about the dining room and the meal. Ring the coach company confirming times and dates et cetera; probably send them an e-mail to make sure they had no excuses for being late at the airport. Decide what to do about Georgie.

He turned over and thought about her in bed that afternoon in the bedroom which had always been theirs. She'd responded to his need for her so willingly, so wholeheartedly, he'd been overwhelmed. Much of the cherished feelings of their earlier years had returned to them both and he came close to worshipping her. Him, Bryn! Feeling like that about a woman. Surely not. It wasn't part of his psyche to come even close to worshipping a woman. But he had. He shouldn't have, though;

seeing Dicky so destroyed had cut right to his heart and taken most of the joy out of his encounter with Georgie.

If he took Dicky out of the equation then how did he feel? Pleased, elated, thrilled, triumphant even. But taking that peep at Dicky had affected him more deeply than Bryn cared to admit. That secret view of him lying on the sofa had made him realise he couldn't play with other people's feelings, couldn't carelessly meddle in their lives without a qualm.

With Dicky in the equation he felt selfish, inconsiderate, thoughtless. If he truly loved Georgie he should want her happiness, so if that meant her marrying Dicky, so be it. He wouldn't stand in their way. When she came back he'd tell her that. It would mean selling his share of the pub to Dicky. It would mean he had no permanent home. It would mean depending on his tours for income and that seemed exceedingly shaky. No, he'd have to get another pub. Settle for second best with someone else, a hard worker, and the two of them would make a success of it. He finally closed his mind to a reunion with Georgie. It would be so much easier to have that reunion with her, though: a ready-made business, settling back into the old routine, familiar faces. Just before he fell asleep he'd reverted to the idea of making a new start, for Dicky's sake. Dicky obviously loved her and desperately needed her ... for once in his life he'd do the right thing, no matter how hard it would be.

Kev's mother was, as she had promised, seated on the settle with an orange juice in front of her when Bryn entered the bar. He waved to her, mouthed 'vodka' and she gave him the thumbs up.

'Thanks for this.' Again Kev's mother tossed back half her vodka in one gulp.

'Have you any news for me from your Kevin?'

'Ah, well. It's not definite. What was the word he used? Yes, exploratory it was. There's been complaints, yer see, about all the traffic round the school gate mornings and when they finish. Such a jumble, which it is, cars parked all over the place, on the green, in the road. So-o-o they're thinking of double yellow lines and one-way traffic, street lighting and a zebra crossing across the top of Shepherds Hill.'

Bryn almost choked at the prospect. 'Street lighting! Zebra crossing! My God, have they gone mad?'

'It's true, though, they need something at school time, or there'll be an accident before long. They can't help coming in cars from Little Derehams and Penny Fawcett, can they, since the education cancelled the school minibuses. Scandalous, that was. It's too far for children their age to walk and there's no footpaths neither, so they'd be walking in the road round all them blind bends. Dangerous. Spoil the village, though.'

Bryn sipped his whisky.

'It's Miss Pascoe what's asked for the one way.'

Bryn took another sip of his whisky while he had a good think.

'Loads o' signs they'll put up. Them postcards showing ye olde Englishe village won't be no more. There'll be bloody great one-way arrers all over the place.'

'Not if I can help it. No, siree. They're not riding roughshod all over Turnham Malpas. We've got some big guns, you know, to fight this. Mr Fitch for a start.'

Kev's mother added the name of another big gun: 'His nibs, Sir Ralph.'

'Exactly. They neither of them will want the village spoiling. If the council want a fight, a fight they are going to get.'

'Miss Pascoe at the school 'ull have a lot to say about that.'

'Who else besides her will want it, then? I can't think of a living soul.'

Kev's mother sniffed derisively. 'Nor me. Damned waste of time, the council. Don't know why we bother to vote 'em in. Street lights might be a good idea, though, you know. Help people to get home safe who've had too much to drink.' She said this with a sly smile on her face, which let Bryn know they were all talking behind his back about his night with Dicky and the double whiskies. He wished he hadn't been reminded of Dicky, it only recalled his pledge to give Georgie back to him. Make amends to the poor chap.

Kev's mother said, 'Well?'

'Well?' Bryn saw her rubbing her thumb and forefinger together. 'Oh! What I promised.' He dug in his back pocket for his wallet, and slipped her a fifty-pound note. 'Say thanks to Kevin for me. Much appreciated.'

'That all?'

Bryn raised his eyebrows.

'I went to a lot of trouble for you and I didn't need to.'

Bryn thought about the cost of her vodkas and her delight at the news she had to impart, and weighed it against the cost of the local phone call she'd made and thought, stuff you. But his newly awakened conscience pricked and he took out a ten-pound note, folded it and put it into her hand as he patted it. 'Pay for the phone call. Thanks for all you've done. Would you be on side if we started a campaign?'

'Might, but then again . . .' Kev's mother picked up the ten-pound note and pushed it into her pocket. 'Thanks, anyway. If I've any further news I'll let you know.'

'Good. I'll be glad to hear. There's more where that came from if it's useful news.'

Kev's mother tapped the side of her nose, slid out from the settle and went to join a neighbour over the other side of the bar.

Bryn looked at his watch. Still quite early. He eyed his empty glass, almost went to get another and thought this new Bryn with his spanking-new conscience is having only one tonight. Purposefully he marched to the bar with his glass, paused as though debating something in his mind, decided to leave and, calling a loud 'Goodnight!' to everyone, left and headed for Glebe House. As he approached the cottages he slowed his steps. There were no lights on at Dicky's, though it was still only twilight, so maybe . . . Bryn went up the path, as he had the previous night but instead of peering in the window he tried the door handle. It wasn't locked. He put a foot on the doormat and called softly, 'Dicky! Dicky!'

He walked into the living room and saw Dicky lying on the sofa, just as he had been when he'd last seen him. 'Dicky?'

Getting no response, Bryn went to sit in an easy chair, facing Dicky. There was such a terrible stillness about the chap he could almost have been dead. He hadn't shaved, that was obvious, he hadn't combed his hair and by the grey, drawn look on his face he hadn't washed either. In front of him was the coffee table with sandwiches, a mug and a flask on it, which, as far as Bryn could see, were untouched. Presumably Bel knew, then, that at least he was alive.

I owe him a lot, he thought. I nearly murdered the fellow; would have done, too, for murder was in my heart at the time. The least I can do is put his life back together again, if he'll let me. Bryn must have sat an hour while the twilight deepened into real darkness. With no street lights to illuminate the room it had become pitch-black and he could no longer see Dicky. He heard a stirring sound of cloth against cloth, a slight creak of bones, a small cough.

'Don't be alarmed, Dicky, it's Bryn. I'll put a light on.'

He drew the curtains and fumbled his way to the light switch. The bright light showed to what depths Dicky had sunk. It emphasised the shadows on his cheeks, the world-weary look of his eyes and the appalling fragility of the man. It had only taken him twenty-four hours to shrink to a shadow, his bustling energy completely gone.

'I've been waiting for you to wake, Dicky. I've something to tell you. Will you listen?'

Dicky simply stared.

'I want you to know that Georgie is for you. I've always known, but I wouldn't acknowledge it. But I do now. She belongs to you. She hasn't belonged to me for a long time.'

Dicky slowly raised a hand and gestured his acknowledgement of what Bryn had said.

'When she comes back in a day or two I shall tell her I want a divorce.'

It was hard work telling someone life-changing things

and getting no reaction. Bryn tried again. 'Have you heard me? Do you understand what I mean?'

But Dicky didn't respond.

'Look here. Let me pour you a drink. What is it? Coffee? Get this down you.'

Bryn opened up the thermos and poured some coffee into the mug. He put it within reach and waited. Dicky half rolled on to his side and looked at the steam coming off the top of the coffee.

'Sit up. You'll manage better.'

So Dicky did and drank from the mug. Slowly at first and then in great gulps. But he still wasn't for speaking.

'You see, Dicky, I'm a greedy beggar, always wanting more of whatever it is I can't have. Well, I've been doing a lot of thinking and I'm going to change. I have changed I should say. If marrying you makes Georgie happy then . . . so be it.'

'I *can't*. Marry her.'

Bryn cast him a startled look. 'Why ever not? What do you mean?'

'Not after what she's done. She's yours. She betrayed me.'

'Damn it, man, it was me betrayed you. I persuaded her. I made it so she couldn't say no.'

'I wanted everything between us to be honourable, without stain. Perfect. Beautiful. After what you did, all that's been destroyed. There's nothing left between her and me.'

'Without stain? Honourable? Destroyed. What are you talking about, man? She's sure to come back and beg forgiveness and go ahead with the divorce, and then you and she can settle down at the pub to married life and a business partnership. I understand you can find the money to buy a half-share.'

Dicky shook his head.

'Go for it, Dicky, please. Make her happy.'

'No. It's all too late now.'

Bryn saw him look with interest at the generously filled sandwiches, so he leant forward, took the cling film off them and handed him the plate. 'Go on. You'll feel better. You've nothing more to fear from me. I've treated you rotten and it's all stopped. I've called you names that I shouldn't have and I'm ashamed.'

'Squirt. Dwarf. Tiddler. Stunted little specimen.' Dicky stirred uncomfortably against the cushions as if saying the words brought back all his pain. 'Well, I'm not setting foot ever again in that pub. Not for anything.'

There was such finality in his voice that Bryn was forced to believe he meant it.

'I walked out after I'd opened the bedroom door and seen what I saw, and I said to myself, "I'm leaving the Royal Oak for the last time." I've spent the happiest time of my life in there these last four years, but they've come to an end. I know now you can't expect lifelong happiness.'

'But they need you. You and your jokes. You're good on the stand-up comic bit, much better than I ever let on to you. It was jealousy made me object to you doing a turn, sheer jealousy. They need you still. Georgie needs you.'

'No. Not any more.' The last of the sandwiches consumed, Dicky lay down again. He closed his eyes and ignored Bryn. Bryn stood up and looked at Dicky thinking, he might say that now but wait till Georgie comes home. He'll change his mind. At least Dicky looked less of a dead man than when he'd come in. 'I'll go, then, I'll leave Georgie to persuade you. I can't do any more than say what I've said.'

Bryn closed the front door behind him thinking, he'll come round to my way of seeing it, he can't do any other. By tomorrow, that's right, by tomorrow he'll be feeling better when it's sunk in that I mean what I say. He didn't know how wrong he was.

Georgie came home at lunchtime two days later, her first priority being to speak to Dicky as soon as time would allow. But of course he wasn't working. 'Trish, where's Dicky?'

'Well, he hasn't been to work since the day you left. Bel says he won't come.'

'Won't he, indeed? I'll soon sort him out with what I've got to tell him. Soon as this rush slows and you've had your lunch, I'll buzz round there to see him.'

'Don't tell Bel. She'll likely bite your head off.'

'Ah, I see. Right. Mum's the word.'

So Georgie slipped out quietly by the back door at about half past two and sped down Church Lane to Glebe Cottages. There was no need to use her key, the door was unlocked. The living-room curtains were drawn and when she peered through the gloom she saw Dicky lying on the sofa in his dressing gown. 'Dicky, what's this? Still not dressed. Are you ill?'

There was no reply. Dicky could have been waiting for the undertaker he was so still; not even by so much as a flutter of his eyelids did he show recognition of her presence.

'Dicky, love.' Georgie bent over him to kiss his cheek. Which she did, but it was like kissing a marble statue.

190

'Dicky! I've come to tell you that I'm still divorcing Bryn and marrying you like we've wanted all this time. Come on, love. Stir yourself.' She stroked his hair in the way she'd always loved to do; his thick, springy hair, so extravagant on a man of his size. 'Come on, love, speak to me, your Georgie. They're all wondering where you are. Bel says you won't go to work. Now that's not right, is it? You know how we depend on you.'

Dicky heard but chose not to reply.

'I've done my thinking, love, and of course I know and you know that we were made for each other. You and me. Together. Married. A good business. Equal partners. Like we said. Perfect. Just beautiful.'

At the words 'perfect' and 'beautiful' Dicky gave a choking kind of groan so full of anguish that Georgie's eyes brimmed with tears.

'Oh, Dicky! I know what wrong I've done you, a terrible wrong, worse than I would ever have thought possible of myself, a moment of madness I hope you can forgive me for. Please, Dicky, please forgive me.'

'I can't.'

'You must. You must. Please.' Georgie knelt beside the sofa resting her forearms on the cushions alongside Dicky. 'Please, love.'

'Just go away. You betrayed me. The thought of you with *him* . . .' He groaned again. 'I can't bear it. Go away. Back to Bryn.' His right arm flicked sharply at her arms where they rested on the cushion beside him and the glancing blow made her take her arms away from his side.

'Dicky!'

'I loved you more than I've ever loved anyone in all my life. Like first love. The love of a much younger man, really. Such passion I had for you, you were the light of my life, the beat of my heart. You knew that and still you did what you did. You dirtied our love for each other with that man. It's finished.'

'Finished? What do you mean? Finished! You can't mean that.'

'I do.'

'This is ridiculous.'

Dicky sat up. 'Don't lay the blame on me by belittling how I feel. It is not ridiculous, it's the truth, Georgie, the absolute truth. I told Bryn and I'm telling you, I am not going back into the Royal Oak ever again.' He lay down and closed his eyes once more.

'You've seen Bryn? What for, for heaven's sake?'

'Ask him.'

'I'll talk to Bel first, right now. She'll talk you round if anyone can.' Georgie got up and left the house.

On the sofa where he'd lain since that first terrible day, Dicky wept.

Georgie set off for the Royal Oak, then spun on her heel and returned past Glebe Cottages to Glebe House and rang the doorbell for the first time ever.

Liz came to the door. 'Oh, hello, Georgie. What a lovely surprise. I've just put the kettle on, do come in.'

'Hello, Liz. It's Bryn. Is he in?'

'Yes, he is. He's in the garden enjoying the sun, smoking.'

'Can I go straight to see him? I'll go through the side gate if you don't mind. It's personal.'

'Right. OK, then. It isn't locked.'

Georgie opened the gate as quietly as she could, wanting a glimpse of Bryn before he saw her. There he was, as Liz had said, seated in front of the summer house, smoking. Not so tanned as he had been at first, though still much more prepossessing than when he'd gone away. She carefully latched the gate and went towards him. He heard her footsteps crunching the gravel and looked up. His face broke into a restrained smile and he moved up to make room for her on the seat.

'You're back, Georgie.' He patted the seat beside him, inviting her to sit with him.

'Yes.' She sat down, leaving a space between them.

'You've decided.' He stubbed out his cigarette in the flower pot beside the seat, and as he flicked soil from his fingers, he asked somewhat cautiously, Georgie thought, 'Which one of us is it to be?'

Georgie nodded. 'I've decided. Yes.' She took a deep breath. 'It did me good getting away. It was Peter's idea and he was right. Away from the pressures, you learn what really counts. He said, "Think about what you want not just for this year or next, but for the rest of your life" and, of course, I've chosen . . . Dicky.' Georgie expected a huge explosion of temper from Bryn but he sat quite still and there was nothing but silence. 'Bryn?'

'Have you told Dicky?'

'I have, but . . .'

'He isn't interested.'

'You knew.'

'I've been to see him. That's what he told me.' Bryn explained about his visit.

Georgie was appalled. 'You mean you don't want me?'

'To be honest, I do in a way, but not like I did. When I saw what I'd done to him I knew I couldn't take you from him.'

'I see.'

'He's being so stubborn, so damned stubborn. He can have all he wants on a plate, and he won't take it because of some stupid idea about perfection and beauty in your relationship. He's a romantic.'

For a moment Georgie didn't reply. She appeared to be admiring a rambler rose ablaze with blossom, but in her heart she was loving Dicky for being a romantic and hating Bryn for being so scathing about Dicky's ideals. 'But then, of course, you wouldn't know anything about his kind of loving. He's all heart and you've none.'

'I'm changing all that. I've found my heart while you've been away. Or maybe it's my conscience I've found. I do know you belong to each other and I've no rights whatsoever. Elektra saw to that.'

'Hm, I see. Well, I don't know what we're going to do to bring him round. He's desperately hurt. We were terribly wrong.' Georgie stood up and bent to kiss Bryn. 'Thanks for finding your conscience.'

'It's Dicky you should thank; he found it for me.'

She walked away from him, paused by the rambler in full bloom and turned to wave goodbye. A frightening lump came into his throat at the sight of her looking so lovely against the flowers but he managed to smile and wave in return. God! Was he turning into a romantic too? Heaven forbid. He'd the tour to lead. Money to make. Things to do. Things to do. Mr Fitch to get on side when he returned from the Far East. Sir Ralph to persuade. A campaign to organise. A whole new career to tend. But as he listened to Georgie crossing the gravel drive the other side of the gate he pondered the might-have-been, which had now become the never-will-be.

Chapter 12

Bryn went to London to collect his group of tourists and left the situation about Dicky still in limbo. The sole good news was that he was eating again, just small meals under persuasion from Bel but it was a matter for hope. He kept the bolts on the doors so Georgie couldn't get in and watched television for most of the day, only getting up to open the door when Bel peered in at the window.

They were eating their evening meal and Bel couldn't hold back any longer; she had decided to speak her mind. 'You can't go on for ever like this, Dicky. You can't expect Georgie to keep paying you to work when all you're doing is lying flat on your back ignoring everyone and everything. Bryn's gone now, so you can come out from under and show your face.'

Dicky carried on eating. He still hadn't shaved but he was looking better and was showering and dressing each day, but he refused to go out.

'When the money runs out, how are we going to pay the mortgage on this place? You know we need both our wages to keep going.' Then she played her trump card and wondered why she'd never thought to mention it before: 'There's no Scouts next week.'

Dicky hadn't been listening properly but suddenly it registered. 'No Scouts?'

'No, Gary told you he'd be in hospital having his foot done and you said you'd be there, no need to worry.'

'We can't have no Scouts.'

'Well, apparently you can, because there isn't.'

Dicky sat silently shaking his head and repeated abruptly, 'We can't have no Scouts.'

'No, we can't, but we have.' Bel quietly went on eating her dinner. Balancing it on her knee wasn't very easy, but to encourage Dicky to eat she'd taken to having her meal in front of the television too.

Dicky cleared his plate, laid his knife and fork side by side, took a drink from his glass of water and said, 'It's Scout night tonight, isn't it, Bel?'

A wicked kind of grin crossed her face. 'Yes. But you're far too ill to go. Puff of wind would blow you over. It's quite chilly out. Before I go back to the dining room I'll get a blanket for your legs. Don't want you to catch a cold.'

'Anybody would think I was in my dotage.'

'They'd be right, wouldn't they.'

'I'd have to shave.'

Bel put her empty plate with Dicky's and handed him his dish of stewed plums and custard. Silently she ate hers, leaving him to come to his own conclusions.

'Tea or coffee?'

'Have I time?'

'Just about.'

Dicky thought for another moment. 'Neither, thanks.' He hauled himself off the sofa and went gingerly upstairs. She heard the bathroom taps running and rejoiced.

He came back down after twenty minutes, dressed in his uniform, scraped as clean as a new carrot from head to foot, his clothes immaculate, his face solemn.

He explained himself: 'Well, you know, I can't just turn up next week and not know what's going on, can I?'

'No, no. Don't forget your key. I might be late tonight.' Bel watched him pick up his Scout file and head for the door. 'Your key! See you.'

Dicky hesitated. 'Should I go, Bel?'

'You might as well, you'll feel an idiot sitting watching television all night dressed like that.'

'I can't let them down, can I?'

'Not you.'

'Not when it's all I've got left.'

As he closed the door behind him Bel clenched her fists and shook them at the ceiling in triumph.

Dicky, by exerting enormous self-control over his feelings, endured the whole evening with, outwardly at least, his usual style; a healthy mixture of authority, laughter and camaraderie.

They were putting all the equipment away in the Scout cupboards and preparing to leave when Peter came in. 'Good evening, boys, Gary. You look to have had a good evening.'

Gary answered, 'We have, sir, very good indeed. We won the canoeing at the weekend, by the way. Did anyone tell you?'

'No. I'd no idea. Well done. Second year running. Full marks.'

'County championships next month.'

'Excellent. Good luck. Let me have the date and I'll try

to get there. All the best for your op next week, Gary. Is Dicky here?'

'Locking up at the back. Goodnight.'

'Thanks. Goodnight.' Peter found Dicky bolting the back door.

'Hello, Dicky. Time for a word?'

Dicky had realised Peter had come in and hadn't known what to say to him, so he'd dallied by the back door. He still didn't know. 'Yes.'

'Let's sit on the bench out here. Everyone's gone.'

There was no gainsaying Peter. He opened the inner door and held it open for him. Dicky was tired. Keeping control of his feelings and on top of that this being his first night out of the house for over a week had taken a lot out of him.

'Here, sit down. You look exhausted. It won't take long.'

Dicky collapsed rather than sat beside Peter. He rested his elbows on his thighs and, clasping his hands together, stared at the floor.

Peter went straight to the nub of the matter. 'Church hall, funny place for a heart to heart, but you're not out and about and I've tried your door a few times and it was locked. I've seen Bel. Well, rather she came to see me. You've got her very worried.'

Dicky stared at the floor.

'And me. I'm worried.'

Dicky shifted his weight a little but didn't answer.

'I'm glad to see you out, though. That's a start, isn't it.'

Dicky clasped his hands a little tighter to stop them shaking.

'You see, love is the strangest thing, Dicky. It takes us

by surprise and then when we've got it, sometimes we don't know what to do with it. It should make us strong, happy, loving, forgiving. It should make life a joy, it should be a pulsing, throbbing thing which colours every hour of our day. Then something cuts right across that and love makes us unhappy, bad-tempered, jealous, envious, revengeful, murderous, to name but a few. Sometimes we have love offered to us and for whatever reason we reject it, and then we reach the deepest of depths and feel the worst it's possible to feel, but pride or resentment or distrust makes us stubborn and we suffer.'

Dicky straightened up. 'I can't bear it. You know they . . . one afternoon . . . well, they got it together?'

Peter nodded.

'It's broken my heart.'

For a while the two of them stayed silent, then Peter said, 'Some time ago I had my heart broken too. But I realised that I had to learn to forgive, generously, if I was ever to regain what I had almost thrown away. Georgie's offered you a lifetime of loving. Don't you throw it away.'

'He says he's the one to blame. He persuaded her to. No one seems to remember that he nearly murdered me and yet she could let him persuade her to . . .' Dicky surreptitiously rubbed his eyes.

'They haven't forgotten, not really. I certainly haven't. But that has nothing to do with Georgie loving you, has it? It's not Bryn, it's Georgie who wants to marry you and heal the wounds.'

Dicky nodded and almost smiled at the memory of her.

'I remember meeting you in the Store at the start of it all and you saying, "She's the cream in my coffee, the fizz in my drinks, the sherry in my trifle, the icing on my cake." I've never forgotten those words. So simple, but so meaningful. Think about what life without her will be like if you don't forgive her and wipe the slate clean.'

'Terrible.'

'Only good can come from a love as great as yours, Dicky. So let it. Love given freely, despite everything that happens between you, is a wonderful, worthwhile thing.'

Together they got up and walked towards the main entrance. Peter waited while Dicky turned off the lights. They stood there for a moment in the darkness. 'Do you know, Peter, I've had some of the most rewarding times of my life in here at Scout meetings.'

'Good. That's excellent. It's what makes for quality of life, isn't it? Just think how many lives you have influenced for the better.'

'I hope so.'

As Dicky locked the outer door Peter said, 'Glad to see you picking up the threads again, Dicky. If you need to talk confidentially, you know where I am. The Rectory door's always open to you. Any time. Goodnight. God bless you, Dicky.'

Dicky watched his tall figure striding away down the path and remembered how Peter had almost lost his marriage over that actor fellow and Caroline fancying each other, and yet now they were as one again as though it had never happened. Maybe they were more emphatically one person than before; as Peter had said, forgiving had made their love stronger than ever. Georgie! Georgie! His hand reached out to touch her and for a moment he thought he could feel her hand in his. How he loved her. But he couldn't quite, not quite . . . bring himself to . . . perhaps in time.

Dicky went home to find Bel already making herself a bedtime drink. 'How's things, Dicky? Go all right?'

Dicky tossed down his file and keys on the sofa with a gesture more like his old self and said, 'Fine. Absolutely fine. I'll have hot chocolate, Bel, please.'

'Great.' She came into the living room, planted down his drink on the table and flopped into her favourite chair, cradling her mug in her hands.

Without looking at her Dicky said casually, 'I think it's time you went back to keeping Georgie company at the pub at night.'

'You do?'

Dicky nodded. 'I do. I've talked to Peter tonight and I'm feeling better. In fact I might . . . just . . .'

'What?'

'I might, just might, start work at the pub on Monday.'

'Sooner than that. She's thinking of finding someone else.'

'See how I feel tomorrow, then. I can't go back to my old job, couldn't face all that boredom. In any case the money's not as good.'

Bel sipped her hot chocolate for a while, then said tentatively, 'I wonder if Mrs Charter-Plackett is still of the same mind.'

'I didn't say I was going to buy that half-share. That's a whole different ball game.'

'Oh!'

'Don't push me, Bel, I'm not ready for it.'

'Never mind, then. Sorry. I'll move my things back to the pub tomorrow if that's all right.'

He nodded firmly. 'It is. Got to pull myself together.'

'Can I ask?'

Dicky looked hard at her.

'Can I ask if going back means anything? You know, should we draw some conclusions from it?'

Wide-eyed with innocence Dicky said, 'None.' But in his heart he knew differently. As Peter had said, you can't carelessly throw away the offer of a lifetime of love. Maybe, just maybe, he'd been too hasty.

It was Alan's late-turn shift and Georgie was wondering how on earth she and Trish would manage without some muscle on the premises to heave the bottled drinks in and bring supplies up from the cellar.

'Don't worry, Georgie. You and me, we can manage. We don't need men, they're just handy from time to time.'

'Are they, indeed? Well, we'll have to, we've no choice. I just hope we can cope tomorrow with Bryn's group coming. Twenty-five all at once. I'm starting to get nervous about it. I wish, in the circumstances, I'd never agreed to it, but I did and we need the trade. Bel says the kitchen is all organised so all we've got to do is keep the drinks coming. Anyway, I'll make a list of what we want for today.' She found a crumpled piece of paper right at the back of a drawer, smoothed it out and laid it on the bar counter. 'Right. Mixers. Yes.' As she wrote 'mixers' at the top of the paper the back door shut with a tremendous bang. If she hadn't known it couldn't be, she would have thought that was Dicky. He always managed to let the heavy back door get caught by the wind. She wrote down 'sparkling water' and glanced around to see which other shelves needed filling up. She smelt his aftershave first of all; that fresh lime and tea tree she'd given him on his birthday. Her heart gave a lurch and began to beat erratically. Slowly she turned round and found she was right. It *was* Dicky. Thinner, leaner, more grave, but Dicky. 'Hello, love.' His eyes didn't light up when she spoke, but there was something there, a kind of strength, she thought, which she hadn't noticed before.

'Realised it was Alan's morning off. Thought I'd better give a hand.'

If that was how he wanted it, unemotional, casual, then so be it. 'Thanks. We were just debating who'd be getting the beer up from the cellar.'

'Right. Done the list?'

'Almost.'

'I'll wait, then.'

Trish decided to pretend it was no surprise to see Dicky there. It was easier than having to find something embarrassing to say. 'Morning, Dicky. Put Coke on that list, Georgie, there's hardly any on the shelf.'

'OK.'

'It's the hot weather.'

'Not before time. We deserve it hot.' Georgie looked at Dicky from under her eyelashes and found he was covertly weighing her up. She gave him a cautious smile, but he didn't respond. No wonder, Georgie thought, no wonder, after what I've done to him. 'There's the list, I don't think I've forgotten anything. Thanks.'

They worked all day like this, saying the minimum, pressing on, till Georgie thought she might burst with frustration. She was relieved when he went home for his meal at five, but he came back to work an evening shift, which he wasn't scheduled to do.

By closing time Georgie couldn't take it any longer,

making up her mind that enough was enough and she was having it out with him. As she opened the safe to put in the cloth bag she used for storing the takings overnight she said, 'Dicky Tutt! I want a word.'

Alan said a hasty 'Goodnight!' and disappeared.

Dicky stood silently, waiting while she locked it.

'There was no need to come back tonight; you weren't due on.'

'I know, but I've got to make up for my absence somehow.'

'No need.'

'I feel there is. If you pay me a wage, then I've to work for it. It's only right.'

'We can't avoid what's happened between us. We can't ignore it, disregard it. Someone has to say something.'

'No, they don't.'

'Yes, they do.'

'I'm off. See you lunchtime tomorrow.'

Georgie daren't say she didn't want him to come tomorrow because of Bryn, but she had to say something to stop him coming in. 'Dicky!'

Before she could come up with a credible excuse he'd said 'Goodnight', turned on his heel and closed the door sharply behind him.

At eleven thirty precisely the following day, right on schedule, the tour coach pulled into the village to disgorge its load. It had begun as one of those eternal village mornings blessed by peace and serenity as it had been for more than a thousand years, the only sounds those of the geese on the green honking at a feral cat, the delightful singing of the children in the school floating out through the open windows and the spasmodic chatter of the people in the queue outside the Store waiting for the lunchtime bus into Culworth. But the quiet was to be blown apart by the thrum-thrum of the coach engine and the noisy, excited babble of its occupants.

They disembarked from the coach with an eagerness amazing to behold. They scattered hither and thither like a host of vividly feathered parrots just released from captivity, exclaiming at the green, the houses, the pub, the geese. Best of all for the queue at the bus stop was the sight of Bryn marshalling his flock. Over white trousers and shirt he wore a navy blazer. They could just see a badge of some sort on the pocket and the regimental tie which completed his outfit. The white moccasins on his feet induced a burst of giggled comments from the queue. 'What does he think he is?' 'Looks the part, though, don't he?'

Then they spotted Jimmy emerging from his garden on to the green. He was carrying a basket they were sure they'd last seen displayed in Jimbo's window full of Easter eggs, but what he wore was the most amusing of all. It was a very old Victorian farmer's smock, a work of art to the eye of a collector but to the people in the bus queue he made a highly rib-tickling picture. On his feet he wore a pair of old boots from his poaching days and to top it off a soft black felt hat with a wide wavy brim.

They watched Jimmy walk steadily towards the seat beside the pond, observed him touch the brim of his hat and call out a greeting to the tourists. 'Good morning to ye all. You be welcome to feed my geese, you be.'

All twenty-five of the tourists leapt at the opportunity, cameras flashing: 'Hold the bread. Merle, turn this way.'

'Hi, sir. Can I photograph you for my album?'

'Sue-Ellen, smile!'

'What a souvenir! So genuine!'

Jimmy turned this way and that, obliging the Americans. The geese took exception and began to hassle one of the men by noisily pecking at his trouser seat as he crouched to take a picture.

'Hey, Marlon, watch out!'

Before Jimmy could distract his geese with another chunk of bread, Marlon was racing across the green with two of the geese in full pursuit, the man's huge stomach shaking and shuddering like a firm jelly as he ran. By this time the queue was having hysterics, but the twenty-five Americans were wielding their camcorders and their digital cameras as fast as they could, loving every moment of the chase.

Bryn was boiling with temper. Between clenched teeth he bent over Jimmy's shoulder and muttered, 'Stop those damn birds, or else.' Jimmy leapt up and, putting his fingers to his lips, he emitted a piercing whistle. To his surprise it worked, the two geese put on their brakes and came racing back half flying, half running, leaving Marlon to stagger back as best he could.

Finally Bryn got his tourists assembled and suggested they might like to hear from Jimmy, whose ancestors had lived in the village for something like six hundred years.

'Gee! No!'

'Can that be true?'

'Really.'

'Amazing.'

Unfortunately the queue couldn't quite hear what he was saying and only occasionally a snatch of his well-practised discourse drifted across the green: 'My family name's on the memorial plaque in the church . . . given their lives for old England . . . so we been 'ere my ancestors all them years, poachers mostly. I've poached these wood man and boy . . . this 'ere is my dog Sykes . . . my family's bred Jack Russells for generations.'

'The liar! His dog's a stray!' muttered someone in the queue. 'What a load of rubbish.'

'See that old oak tree yonder . . . a hundred years ago . . . terrible storm . . . it lost a third of its branches . . . but it survived . . . once the old oak dies so will the village.' He used such sepulchral, doom-laden tones that the tourists were reduced almost to tears. Some took notes, others filmed Jimmy sitting lost in gloom.

Unfortunately the lunchtime bus rumbled into the village at that moment and the queue had no alternative but to climb aboard and miss the fun.

Bryn decided Jimmy would soon be over-egging the pudding if he didn't move everyone on pronto, so he assembled his charges and suggested they wander across to the church, where they would be treated to a talk on its history, a history going back over a thousand years.

'You mean that very church?'

'There's been a church on that site for well over a thousand years. The present church has parts going back to the eleventh century, the rest is fourteenth century. But let's go and hear all about it. You can find Jimmy's ancestors' names if you like.'

Jimmy called out as they left, 'Don't forget to visit the plague pit,' his voice once more laden with doom. Once they all had their sights set on the church, Jimmy threw all the leftover bread in the pond and went as fast as he could to the pub for a restorative drink.

Georgie had to congratulate him on his costume. 'You look so authentic, Jimmy. Absolutely right for the part.'

'Thanks. Like the smock? Genuine, you know. Harriet's lent me it, and the basket.'

'Did it go well?'

'They were delighted. Nice folk. Very nice. I shall be on all their pictures.'

'Talk go well?'

'Oh, yes. Very well. They've gone across to the church now, so half an hour and they'll be ready to eat.' Jimmy took his real ale over to the settle and Sykes crept under it as he had always done, ever since he'd adopted Jimmy.

He was still sitting there when the Americans came in for their lunch. Three of them offered to buy Jimmy another drink, two of them sat on the settle with him for photos and they enticed Sykes out for his share of glory. Another asked if he knew where they could get a smock like his. 'How long has it been in the family?' The moment had come when he either lied or told the truth and spoiled the fantasy. It was a question he hadn't quite prepared himself for. 'Being poachers, we didn't own things like this to pass down the generations, but this belongs to someone in the village who comes from farming stock.' Half-lie, half-truth and he got away with it.

Bryn took them through to the dining room, got them settled and came back into the bar for a word with Georgie. 'Going like a dream. Like a dream. They're paying for their own drinks, you know, apart from the half-bottle included with their lunch. Pour me a whisky quick, I need it.'

He tossed back the whisky, slapped down the glass on the bar, then spotted Dicky talking to a customer at one of the tables. Bryn glanced at Georgie and raised an eyebrow. In reply she very slightly shook her head.

Bryn watched Dicky for a moment and went across to speak to him. There didn't seem to be quite so much naked hate in Dicky's eyes as there had been and Bryn took hope from that. 'OK, Dicky? Glad to see you picking up the threads. One step at a time, eh?'

Dicky looked at him but didn't respond to his question.

Bryn put out a hand and patted his arm, but Dicky dusted off his sleeve where Bryn had touched it. 'Too soon yet for the friendly gesture. Just keep out of my way.'

Bryn stood back. Palms exposed and held up in reconciliation he said, 'Fine. Fine.'

'Bryn! Hi, baby!' One of the American tourists approached them.

'Hi, Lalla! How can I help?'

'Marlon's wanting souvenirs. Where do we go?'

'The Village Store. We'll all go across there in a moment.'

'Right! I'll be powdering my nose. Don't go without me.' Lalla pattered off, twinkling her fingers at him as she went.

They were all charmed by the Store and most especially by Jimbo. A real English gentleman, they declared, and were exceedingly impressed when Bryn let out that Jimbo had been to Cambridge. He did a roaring trade with his souvenirs and items of food they bought to keep them sustained while on the coach.

'It must be wonderful living here.'

'You've made us all so welcome, fancy living here all the time. Great!'

'Everyone's been so kind. Just another picture! That's it!'

'I don't want to leave.'

'I guess it's like going back in time.'

'Nothing's changed, ever.'

'Not a road sign in sight. Wonderful!'

'And the church ... well ... I can't wait to get back home and tell them all about it. So old. And the tombs! And the ghost! They'll be so envious.'

'That lovely man who guided us round. Such a wonderful tale to tell.'

'You won't let them change it, will you? Keep it as it is.'

Bryn wholeheartedly agreed with these sentiments and, catching Jimbo's eye, said, 'We'll keep it like this, won't we, Jimbo?'

'Of course.'

'Not even an advertisement of any kind. Marvellous.'

'We'll be telling our friends. They'll all be coming.'

'Come along, Bryn, baby.' Lalla, clutching her two Turnham Malpas Store carrier bags to her chest, hooked her free arm through Bryn's and led him out of the Store, the others following reluctantly.

Georgie had decided to wave them off and took Trish and some of the customers out with her into the car park.

''Bye! 'Bye-bye!'

She came in for some serious embracing before they all left, and compliments about the food and the ambience of the Royal Oak flowed back and forth.

Lalla squeezed Dicky's arm and said, 'That joke! You

naughty boy. I could come back just to hear some more. Only wish I could squeeze you into my case. Be seeing you!' She climbed up the coach steps and turned to wave for the last time. "Bye, everyone. You lucky people!'

Before he climbed into the coach Bryn put his hand on Georgie's shoulder and whispered, 'Brilliant! Absolutely brilliant. Food wonderful, they're all so impressed. It's the start of something big for you and me, I'm sure.' Georgie smiled up at him, pleased by his success as well as her own.

Dicky's hand closed in a vicelike grip on Bryn's elbow. 'Unless you're wanting to do the rest of the tour with a black eye, let her go and get on your way.'

Bryn prised Dicky's fingers from his elbow and said quietly, 'When I get back, you and me's going to have a talk. Man to man. Clear the air. Right?'

Dicky shrugged his shoulders.

'See you both. Thanks for everything you've done. We've made a great start.'

As the coach backed up and swung round to leave the car park Georgie waved brightly to them all. The Americans responded enthusiastically and Georgie had the feeling that some of them at least would be back. The moment they were out of sight she turned on Dicky. 'Dicky Tutt, grow up! He's trying to made amends. He wants the divorce and he's going to get it. Whether or not you want to marry me afterwards is up to you, but I want to marry you, remember.'

211

Chapter 13

'Caroline, I'm home! Just got some things to put in my study and I'll be with you. Good day, darling?'

Caroline felt that lift to her heart which only Peter's presence could bring about. 'Fine, thanks, and you?'

'All right. Tell you later.'

Caroline brought the Bolognese part of their evening meal out of the oven and called the children to wash their hands. 'It's ready, don't delay.'

Peter, Alex and Beth all arrived at the table at the same moment.

Beth said loudly, 'You haven't washed your hands, Alex.'

'I have.'

'He hasn't, Mummy.'

'Only Alex knows if he has or not, so if he hasn't, he can wash them at the sink.'

As she drained the spaghetti Alex came to turn on the taps and run his hands underneath.

Triumphant Beth exclaimed, 'You see, I knew he hadn't. You've started telling fibs, Alex.'

'That will do, Beth. Alex's conscience is his own responsibility.'

Caroline served the spaghetti Bolognese and after Peter had said grace she asked him if he'd seen the Americans.

'No. I didn't leave Little Derehams until well after lunch, but Willie told me almost every word of what he'd said on his guided tour. They were deeply impressed by the war memorial plaques and all the names on there, and seeing Willie's uncles and grandfather and Jimmy's four uncles, and our wonderful banners and the architecture and how old the church was. He seemed to have thoroughly enjoyed himself, to say nothing of the tips he got. He told them everything, even to the ghost he vows is there by the tomb.'

Beth shuddered. 'I've never seen a ghost in there.'

'Neither have I, but I'd like to.' Alex made ghost noises and waved his arms at Beth, who hit him hard on his leg. 'That hurt!'

'Good, you know I don't like scary things.'

'Stop it the two of you! I want my meal in peace.' Caroline soothed Alex's leg with her hand and mouthed a kiss to him.

Peter said, 'After we've eaten I'm going to catch up on the parish photo album. I'd be glad of some help.'

Both Alex and Beth volunteered.

With his mouth full of food Alex muttered, 'It's ages since we did it, Dad. Mr Prior came the other day with a load. He likes being our photographer. He said he'd been taking parish photos since he was twelve. That's positively historical.'

Peter laughed. 'Well, that means he's been doing it for about sixty years.'

'Sixty years! He's seventy-two, then. That's old.'

'We did have a lady called Mrs Gotobed and she lived

213

to one hundred. She died about a year after you were born. Now that really is old.'

Peter noticed, but the children didn't, that Caroline had gone quiet. Without her the three of them chattered on about age, and grandparents and what changes Mrs Gotobed had seen in her lifetime. Without speaking Caroline served the cheesecake Sylvia had made for them before she left that afternoon. When the time came to clear up she said, 'We'll clear the table and then you can start on the albums in here. I've some letters to write. I'll leave you to it.'

Quite deliberately and with every intention of getting his own way Peter said, 'I think it would be nice if you helped us, darling. The children and I haven't seen you all day. How about it?'

'I'd rather get the letters written.'

'I know you would, but they can be done any time.'

'No, really, I must get them written.' Caroline folded the tablecloth and went to switch on the dishwasher. 'You always do it, the three of you.'

'Get the albums out, children, and find Mr Prior's envelope. They're on their special shelf in the study.'

As the children darted off on their errand Peter went behind Caroline to put his arms round her. He nuzzled her hair and held her close. 'It's got to be the two of us. It mustn't look like something you can't talk about. It needs to be in the open between us all.'

'You've sprung it on me; it's not fair.'

'I just feel the moment is ripe.' Peter turned her round to face him. 'It has to be faced.'

Alex came back in, staggering under the weight of the

albums, with Beth coming up behind carrying Mr Prior's envelope.

Peter released Caroline and went to pull out a chair for her. 'Here you are, darling, you sit here.'

She couldn't refuse, it would be too obvious. But when you've kept a secret for more than ten years . . . 'OK, then.'

'Is there a photo of old Mrs Gotobed, Daddy? Which one will it be in? This newest one?'

'No, the last full one.' He stood up and heaved the one he wanted out from the bottom. 'Here we are. This one.' Eventually he found Mrs Gotobed in a Harvest Festival photograph taken, he guessed, about two years before she died. 'There she is with her daughters, Lavender and Primrose. Both very dear ladies.'

Alex burst out laughing. 'Lavender and Primrose. Help!'

Beth peered at the photograph through Peter's magnifying glass. 'I think they're very pretty names. Look how old she is. Just look. All wrinkly and thin. She looks like a little bird. Like a wren.'

They played a game of guessing who all the other people were in the photo and then Peter let them ramble along through the pages till they came to the page he wanted them to look at.

'These are of the village show. Nineteen ninety-one, I think. Yes. Can't quite read it.' The two of them identified several people, including Lady Bissett wearing an astonishing hat, and Venetia from the Big House when she was going through her Quaker dress period. Then Peter said casually, 'There's someone there who belongs to you.'

'Belongs to us?'

'Yes.'

'Just us?'

'Yes. You and Alex.'

Alex looked hard at the picture. 'Is it Grandma and Grandad? I can't see them.'

'No. It's this lady here.' He pointed to someone with long fair hair, wearing a smart red-and-white dress and obviously serving behind a stall.

Beth protested she didn't know her. 'Do I know those three girls sitting on the grass in front? They don't go to school.'

'That's their mother standing behind the stall. They'd be too old now for your school, wouldn't they, Caroline?'

Alex asked, 'Who are they? What are they called?'

Caroline answered his question. 'Daisy, Pansy and Rosie. That's Daisy, that's Pansy, I think, and the little one kneeling up is Rosie. They'll be something like eighteen, sixteen and fourteen now.'

Beth found the tone of her mother's voice oddly unlike her normal one, but still she had to ask, 'But they don't live here. I've never seen them, so how can they belong to us.'

Peter took the plunge. 'They were three lovely girls, so sweet and pretty and shy. I expect they still are. They are actually related to you, they're your half-sisters.'

'Really? Honestly?' Beth was intrigued.

Alex was more cautious. 'What does that mean?'

Caroline was sitting with her hands resting on the table, gripped tightly together, her head down. Suffering. 'They have the same mummy as you.' Alex hid his shock while he worked out whether it meant what he thought it did.

Beth thought this over for a moment, took the

216

magnifying glass and carefully inspected the girls and the lady standing behind the stall. 'So where's their daddy? Is he here somewhere?'

'He didn't used to join in things. He was a scientist and always preoccupied.'

'So there's not just Alex and me. There's Daisy, Pansy and Rosie. That's five of us.'

'I expect you could say that.' Peter added, 'They left the village, though.'

'Where have they gone?' It was Beth doing all the asking; Alex had withdrawn from the conversation.

Caroline, in fear she might ask to go to see them, said, 'A long way away.'

Still peering through the magnifying glass Beth said, 'The mummy looks pretty. I like her hair. It's the same colour as mine and her cheeks are round like mine. Oh! Just like mine!' She glanced at Caroline as though assessing whether or not there was anything of Caroline in her own face.

Alex, by now, was standing beside Caroline, his face inscrutable.

Peter said, 'Yes.'

Then Beth asked the question Caroline had been dreading. 'Daddy, could we see them some time?'

'Perhaps when you're eighteen.'

'You always say that. You said the same when I wanted my ears pierced and when I wanted to wear make-up. Well, I shall wear it before I'm eighteen, Daddy. I'm sorry but I shall.' Still scrutinising the photograph, Beth came to a splendid conclusion. 'I wish we could see a photo of those flower girls' daddy, then Alex could see if he's like him.'

217

'He wouldn't be like him, though, would he?'

Beth stared hard at him. 'Why?'

'Because I'm your daddy.'

'Oh, of course you are. I'm getting awfully muddled.'

Peter was trying to lead them to their own understanding of the situation but felt he was floundering. He turned to Alex and said, 'You're very quiet, young man.'

'Just thinking.'

'I see. Come and have a look at the flower girls. Come on.'

Alex shook his head and pointed to Beth. 'No, thanks. They're not really my sisters. She's my sister.'

Beth, still greatly intrigued by her discoveries, ignored him and asked, 'So what's her name?'

'Whose?'

'The flower girls' mummy.'

'Suzy Meadows.' There, it was out, thought Caroline. She'd said the name she'd dreaded to hear on the children's lips.

'Suzy. Suzy. Suzy Meadows.' Beth repeated it time and time again until Caroline's head swirled with it and she blurted out, 'She was a lovely, kind, generous person.'

'You knew her, Mummy?'

'Of course. I asked her if I could have you both. She knew there was no way she could feed and clothe three children and look after two new babies and earn money for them all.'

Beth, who'd been kneeling on her chair to get a better view, shuffled down on to her bottom and looked set for hearing a story. 'Go on, then.'

'Well, I knew she was expecting twins and I knew her

husband had died and she already had three girls to bring up, so I asked her if she could possibly let us have you.'

Alex, ever sensitive to his mother's mood, put a hand on her shoulder to comfort her and leant his weight against her.

'She said that was what she had planned and she wanted us to take you.'

'So she gave us to you.' Beth's eyes grew wider. 'Did she love us?'

'I know she did.' Caroline put an arm round Alex's waist and hugged him, as much for his comfort as for her own. 'You were born first, darling.'

'Then me?'

'Alex was screaming his head off, really screaming.'

'Did I?'

'No, you were all quiet and composed, and you were sucking your thumb even then.'

Rather smugly Beth reminded her she'd stopped now.

'I know, but you were then. You were small and neat and beautiful.'

'What about me?'

'Alex, I remember thinking what big feet you had and that you were long and gangling. I thought to myself, he's definitely Peter's boy and he's going to be just as big.'

Alex posed as he'd seen strong men pose and Beth laughed. 'I was beautiful! You weren't.'

'He was, just as beautiful. You were both beautiful.'

'Did the Suzy person think we were beautiful?'

Caroline was instantly back in that delivery room witnessing Suzy's bravery. Felt again her own extreme joy mixed with the terrible fear that Suzy wouldn't be able to part with them. How had Suzy lived through it? Should she tell them Suzy couldn't bear to look at them, fearful that she wouldn't be able to give them up if she did? Caroline hesitated while she weighed up the merits of telling or not. 'She was so full of pain at giving you up to your daddy. So full of pain.' Without warning Caroline was crying. Unspoken and unrecognised anxieties tore to the surface and ten years of persuading herself that now she had the children it didn't matter about not being able to bear children of her own, that it didn't matter about Peter's unfaithfulness, all came pouring into the open along with her tears. She was inconsolable. Her heart-rending, gut-wrenching sobs shocked them all.

'My darling girl! Hush! Hush!' Even Peter's arms round her gripping her firmly didn't assuage her distress.

The children clung to her and Beth wept. 'I'm sorry, Mummy, I didn't mean . . . '

'Come on, Mum. Don't cry. Don't cry.'

But she did cry. She'd been too brave all along. In her gratitude for the chance to take the children for herself she'd been too accepting of what had happened. She should have raged and stormed, and made Peter's life hell. She'd no idea that all of it, the whole terrible mess, had been secretly boiling and bubbling in her and the tears pouring down her cheeks, for herself and for Suzy and for the children, wouldn't stop coming.

'Darling, you're frightening the children. Please. Please.'

Alex couldn't bear to hear her anguished weeping. He closed up the flower girl photo album with a bang and carried all the albums back to the study. But instead of putting them neatly on the shelf where they always sat he flung them to the floor and kicked them across the carpet. Then he went back into the kitchen and picked up the envelope with Mr Prior's latest contributions, took it into the study, shook the pictures out all over the floor and stamped on them in a wild frenzy. If Beth didn't understand what had happened he did. Stamp. Stamp. Dad had done with Suzy what you did to get children, like Miss Pascoe had explained, like Dad had explained, too, very simply, years ago. Stamp. Stamp. Stamp. Which Beth seemed to have forgotten all about. Stamp. Stamp. Who cares about half-sisters and all that rubbish, they were old anyway. Stamp. Sta— He stuck his fingers in his ears so he couldn't hear his mother's sobbing. She loved him tons more than someone who could give him away. His heart felt as though it had broken into a thousand pieces. Slowly his own tears surfaced and ran down his cheeks, and he locked the study door so no one could discover him crying. Alex felt so alone; more deeply distressed and perplexed than he had ever been in all his life.

Peter, later that evening, went to his study and found the albums and the photographs lying where Alex had left them. He realised then, as he had suspected, that this was Alex's reaction to understanding fully the implications of what he'd learned, whereas Beth had only accepted without appreciating what was behind it all. Caroline was in bed, exhausted, and at last he'd got the children to bed too, though whether they would sleep . . . The trauma, brought about by the disastrous revelations, was mind-numbing.

He knelt down and began to pick up the pictures, straightening out the more crumpled ones and wondering what on earth he could say to Arthur Prior about them. Small matter, compared with what he had to face now. A son who probably loathed him and a daughter more confused than she deserved. And a wife . . . it didn't bear thinking about how she felt. Peter paused for a moment and felt again the pain of Alex not being able to look him in the eye.

There was the sound of someone on the stairs. At the moment he didn't think he could cope with anyone, but they were coming down whatever he thought. Standing in his navy-and-white pyjamas in the study doorway was Alex. 'I can't sleep, Dad.'

'Come and sit on the sofa. I won't be a moment doing this.'

'Sorry I made that mess. Beth's asleep in your bed and Mum's asleep too.'

'That's good. They'll feel better in the morning.'

'Dad . . . '

Peter reached across to put Arthur's envelope on the shelf and then stood up. 'Yes.'

A frightened face looked up at him. 'Did you do it on purpose? To get a baby for Mum?'

'That's how it turned out.'

Alex didn't allow his eyes to look at his father. 'So it wasn't on purpose for a baby for Mum?'

'No.'

Vehemently Alex declared, 'I don't want to see them, those girls, nor that Suzy person, even if Beth does. You won't make me, will you?'

'Of course not. Only if you wish. For Mum's sake . . . I'm glad you don't.'

'Dad . . . does everyone in the village know? About us.'

'At the time they didn't, then they did, but they never say a word and for that I have always been very thankful.'

222

He sat down on the chair at his desk. 'You couldn't be loved more by your mum and me, you know that, don't you? You're properly adopted, no one can take you from us, you are ours for ever and a day. Praise be to God for that.'

'I . . . you don't love this Suzy person, do you, instead of Mum?'

Peter shook his head. 'I loved her only for the moment. Mum is the one I truly love and always will, no matter what.' He went over to sit beside Alex on the sofa. 'Do you want to know anything else? I'd rather you asked now than kept worrying.'

'Not right now.'

'If Beth wants to talk to you about it all, be careful what you say. I'm certain she hasn't realised as you have.'

'I'll have to be truthful to her?'

'Of course. How about hot chocolate, you and me, mm?'

'Will Mum be all right? I've never seen her so upset.'

'It will take a while, I'm afraid.' He got up and asked again about hot chocolate.

'Yes, please. Mum's great. I never think she isn't mine . . . you know . . . it's like for real.'

'What you have learned about tonight is not for discussion outside this house. It is an entirely private matter which Mum and I *never* talk about to anyone, for your sakes as much as our own. We can talk about it between ourselves, of course, if we wish, so you and Beth are absolutely free to discuss it with either Mum or me or each other. And your grandma and grandad know about it too, so you can talk to them absolutely freely if you wish. You understand?' Alex nodded. Peter bent over, looking

223

as if he were intending to kiss him but Alex dodged away so he couldn't.

Peter left Alex to drink his hot chocolate in bed and turn out his own light. He went into their bedroom and found, as Alex had said, that Beth had gone to sleep with her mother's arms round her. He stood, looking at them both. As he watched, Beth sat up and said 'Toilet'. She climbed out of bed, disappeared to the bathroom and didn't come back. He found her fast asleep in her own bed.

So he was left with Caroline. He drew the duvet up around her bare shoulders and lay on his side looking at her. Her eyelids were still red from weeping and they appeared swollen, too, and there were shadows where there hadn't been shadows before. She stirred in her sleep as though searching for Beth. 'She's gone back to bed, darling.'

Caroline stretched, clutched her head and muttered, 'Aw! I feel terrible.'

'I'm so sorry. Can I get you anything?'

She shook her head. 'Alex, is he all right about it?'

'So-so. His problem is he has understood, which Beth hasn't. She's just intrigued.'

'She's not a fool. She will in a day or two.'

'It didn't go quite as I intended.'

Caroline turned away from him saying, 'I'd no idea I would react like that. I've always thought I had it under control. Accepted it, you know.'

Peter pulled the duvet around her shoulders again. 'I didn't want them to think their conception had been something . . .'

More sharply than he had ever known, Caroline

snapped out, 'You can't find the word, can you? You honestly can't find it. Well, I'll find it for you, shall I? Sordid? Would that fit the bill? Or how about shoddy, or shameful? No, I think sordid was the word you were looking for.'

'Caroline!'

'Caroline nothing! Whatever brought it about?' Her question was met with stunned silence. 'Well? Lost for words? It's time we talked about it. I was so thrilled at the idea of at last having babies and ridiculously pleased that they were yours and not a stranger's that I never bothered to enquire or even think how it had come about. I simply closed my mind to stop myself getting hurt any more than I was.'

'My God.'

'Well? I'm waiting.'

So quietly his voice was almost inaudible Peter said, 'I . . . do you really want to know?'

'I wouldn't have asked if I hadn't.' Caroline turned back to face him. 'Well?'

Peter rolled over on to his back and stared at the ceiling. 'I noticed her at my first service here. Then I saw her passing the study window and couldn't believe how devastatingly attractive I found her. I took you out to lunch to make myself stop thinking about her; to help me cling to sanity. Her face seemed to be everywhere I looked: on the page, in the mirror, on the computer screen. I went to sleep with her face inside my head. She would not go away. Then the police arrived to tell her Patrick had committed suicide. Her parents arranged to take the children out and I was to pop round to discuss the cremation and such with her because she didn't want the children to overhear. So I did.'

'And . . .?'

Ever so quietly he murmured, 'It was lust, Caroline. Sheer lust.' He saw Suzy's beautiful sad face and felt the touch of her hand on his arm as she begged him to comfort her, her intention absolutely plain. Remembered his own overpowering surge of sexual appetite. 'Alex asked me tonight if I loved her still. I never loved her, only craved her.' He recalled the sweet, scented smell of the palm of her hand as he'd kissed it. 'Craved her.'

'That was a sin.'

'Yes. Over, literally, in minutes, because our need for each other was so powerfully urgent. But a sin nevertheless, which I shall take to the grave.'

Caroline absorbed what he said, then replied, 'So that night when she rang very late for your help and you wanted me to go too . . .'

'Because I couldn't risk being in the house with her alone.'

'I must have been completely naïve not to have sensed that in the air. Talk about rose-coloured spectacles.'

'Saying how sorry I am is totally inadequate. But I don't know how else to apologise.'

In a dangerously strained voice Caroline answered, 'It makes me sick to my stomach to hear all this. If she hadn't conceived then, you wouldn't have told me about it, would you?'

'No, I don't think I would. But it would have been to save you the pain.'

'And that's he who values truth so highly. Well, I've nothing to confess about Hugo. We never made love. I wanted to, but didn't, for your sake. There was always that something indefinable which held me back.'

'I'm eternally grateful for that. I sensed you hadn't made love, but it's wonderful to have it said. You must be a vastly better human being than I.'

'Mm. It's half past one and I've surgery tomorrow – no, this morning. Goodnight.'

'God bless. Thank you for your love and for your loyalty. I certainly don't deserve you.' Peter switched off his light.

'No, you don't. Strange thing is I still adore you. How does that come about?'

'Don't know, but I am deeply grateful. Goodnight, my darling girl.'

Minutes later he said, 'I adore you. Utterly. Can you ever forgive me?'

It must have been a whole minute before she replied, 'As I said at the time, I forgave you soon after I learned you were their father. I had no option, because I wanted them so much and I couldn't allow myself to be in a position of you being grateful to me on a daily basis. But tonight I ask myself what you would have done if I had *not* asked Suzy to give them both to us. If I'd said definitely *no* to that and you'd had to watch her leave with your children. Would you have gone with her?'

Peter gave her her answer immediately. 'No. She said herself that you were the one for me, that you were my soulmate. I can say with my hand on my heart that, without any hesitation, I know I would have had to let them go.'

'You would never have asked me to be a mother to your children either?'

'Never. I love you too much to ask that of you.'

'Thank you for that. I love you too, so very much. No matter what.' She saluted his love with a gentle kiss on his forehead.

Next morning when the twins came down for breakfast it appeared as though last night had never happened. They entered the kitchen to find everything as normal: the kettle singing on the hob, the table laid, their mother pouring milk into the huge jug they used at breakfast time, the one patterned all over with spring flowers, their chucky-egg egg cups with their very own chucky-egg spoons, the special cereal bowls they'd bought when they were holidaying in Portugal. They could hear Dad above their heads singing in the shower. Their mother appeared to be as she had always been until last night, happy and cheerful.

Before they knew it Dad was sitting down to eat his breakfast, and they heard Sylvia's key in the front door and her calling out as she always did, 'It's only me.' To Beth, last night had become a strange dream to be thought about another day. As for Alex, he was glad to find things appeared to be back to normal, when he'd thought nothing would ever be the same again.

Chapter 14

The day Bryn came back to Turnham Malpas after seeing off his American group at Gatwick happened to be the day that, unknown to him, Mr Fitch returned from the Far East. Bryn had a hurried lunch in Liz and Neville's kitchen, and went off to the Big House, not knowing, but hoping against hope, that Mr Fitch might be back.

Bryn pulled up with a screech of brakes, sending the gravel flying. Just as he leapt from his sports car, full of his success and desperate to find an influential ally to stop any possibility of the council deciding to modernise Turnham Malpas, Mr Fitch came out of the front door. 'Good afternoon, Mr Fitch. Very, very glad to see you home safe and sound.' Bryn shook hands vigorously. 'I must say you're looking in excellent health for a chap who's just put in hours of flying time.'

'Thank you, Fields. I must say I'm very glad to be back. If you've come to talk to me let's walk about the garden for a while. After all those hours in that damn plane I'm longing to see some countryside, my countryside. You know ... come through into the rose garden, it's my favourite place. When I first came to live here, had the flat made and got the staff training school organised, it was simply a place to live. Now, well, I love it. I've had a lot to learn, a lot, but I think I finally know how privileged I am to live in such a place as this.'

'It's certainly a lovely estate now.'

Mr Fitch's icy blue eyes became angry. 'I don't just mean the estate, I mean the whole place. I just wish I owned every house in the village and then . . .' Mr Fitch's thin, severe face and those ice-cold eyes of his warmed for a moment. He touched a glowing rose in full bloom and savoured its splendid scent. He looked at Bryn with such joy in his eyes that Bryn became embarrassed as though he'd been privy to some tremendous secret to which he had no right at all. 'You see, it isn't just money. It's knowing that one is only a trustee of land like this and it, the land, is far more important than anything else. I hold it all very close to my heart.' He picked up a handful of rich, crumbly soil and let it trickle very slowly through his fingers.

Besides being unaware that Mr Fitch had a heart, Bryn had never seen him in such a mood and was at a loss to know what to say. Finally he answered, 'I suppose after being abroad so much you're more than glad to be home.'

'I am, I am, but I wasn't meaning that. I was meaning that the land itself affects you after a while. I learned about how to care from Ralph, you know. Great chap. His heart belongs to the land. Oh, yes. A man of powerfully sympathetic understanding where the land is concerned. I admire him.'

Mr Fitch looked almost mistily into the distance and Bryn, considerably surprised, blurted out, 'I thought you two were sworn enemies.'

'Certainly not, Fields. What gave you that idea? We're

the best of friends, he and I. Let's have a look in the glass houses. Follow me.'

Mr Fitch chattered on with such enthusiasm that Bryn became almost enamoured of the vines and the peaches and the . . . 'You see, it's the seasons, coming one after the other never mindful of man, just doing their own thing. There's such a reliability about the seasons, don't you think? Such an assurance.'

'Oh, yes. There is.'

'Century after century, always the same and it doesn't matter what man does or doesn't do; it happens. One's part of history, you know. Had you ever thought about it like that?'

Suddenly Bryn realised that with Mr Fitch in this mood it wasn't going to be difficult to persuade him to become a powerful ally. As they turned to leave the glass house Bryn said, 'Talking of history and centuries and such, I have a mole in the council offices and he informs me that the council are doing exploratory investigations into modernising the village.'

If he'd drawn a gun on Mr Fitch he couldn't have looked more horrified. 'Modernise the village? My God! What do you mean?'

This was more the Mr Fitch he knew and Bryn took a step back. 'One-way signposts, street lighting, numbering the houses, yellow lines . . .'

'Yellow lines! Lighting! Never! I won't allow it.' Mr Fitch began to boil. His snow-white hair almost sparked with indignation and horror. 'One-way signs! What are they thinking of? They'll be putting up advertising hoardings next. Traffic lights! What brought this about?'

'Miss Pascoe at the school saying how worried she was

about all the cars pulling up to drop the children off in the mornings. She's been on about it for months. Mayhem, she claims. Parking on the green and such.'

'I'll give her mayhem, the bloody woman. This is what comes of giving women positions of authority. Wait till I see her! I'll give her mayhem.'

'If I might suggest, I wouldn't use that argument.'

'What argument?'

'The one about women in positions of authority. It doesn't go down well in the present climate.'

'Well, you may be right. Diplomacy, eh?'

'Exactly. In any case it's the council we need to get at, not Miss Pascoe. I wondered if you had any influence?'

'The last time I tried my kind of influence, Sir Ralph shamed the officials into changing their minds with no one ever taking up battle stations. Have you tried him?'

'They're in Singapore and then they're going on to Japan. The whole job could be done and dusted before he gets back.'

'Pity. These people with their inherited titles seem to get their own way in the countryside in the most gentlemanly fashion. Scarcely a word in anger and Bob's your uncle, the whole matter is cleared up apparently to everyone's satisfaction, and both sides believe it's they who have brought it about. I admire that.' He stood, hands in pockets, gazing across the lawns towards Sykes Wood. 'This mole. It wouldn't be our Kevin, would it?'

Bryn had to smile. 'Yes. Our Kev.'

'I classify him as a rat rather than a mole. However, needs must . . .' Mr Fitch turned on his heel and began to walk towards the house. 'Surprised to find you of all people interested in preserving the village. It couldn't be a vested interest because of your tourists, could it?' He looked up at Bryn with an amused grin on his face.

This old codger saw more than was good for him, he'd have to admit it. 'That's right. Just got back from a very successful trip with my first group of tourists. They loved it. Second group next month. I'm really on to something big.'

'Back with Georgie, then?'

'No. I've given up all rights there. That damned Elektra . . . burned my boats, you know.'

'Women can be the very devil. Leave it with me. Need some sleep to bring me round. Jet lag, you know. Don't bother me again with this, Fields. I'll ring you.' Mr Fitch abruptly dismissed him with an impatient flick of his hand and disappeared into the house.

Bryn became distinctly disgruntled when he thought about that final piece of arrogance. And there was he, thinking for a while that he and Mr Fitch were associating on level terms. Bryn felt he'd been dismissed with less grace than Mr Fitch would have spoken to a dog of his. 'Fields' indeed. Did he need Mr Fitch's help with the entire village just waiting to shoulder arms to prevent their enemy from modernising their precious village? Well, better two strings to one's bow, so he'd stir up the villagers and see what happened.

He tried the Village Store first, running into Mrs Jones who was picking up a jar of 'Harriet's Country Cousins' Lemon Cheese' made with real lemons and fresh barnyard eggs, from the preserves shelf. 'How would you feel about it? Could I count on your support?'

'To be frank, in letters of one syllable, no.'

'No?'

'That's what I said. It's nothing short of criminal the chaos on Sunday mornings at morning service and during the week at the start of school. There's cars all over the place. Do we have to wait for someone to get run over before something's done?'

'But do you want yellow lines and road signs all over the place?'

'If it saves lives, yes I do.'

'But there has never been an accident nor anything anywhere near it since the year dot.'

'What about Flick Charter-Plackett and that little Janine outside the school the other day?'

'As you well know that wasn't because of chaotic traffic, but little girls running out into the road without looking.'

Mrs Jones came down from her high horse. 'Well, maybe you're right about that, but the fact remains it all needs organising.'

'So I can't count on you?'

She shook the jar of lemon cheese in his face. 'I've something better to do than stand here arguing.' She marched off to attack her parcel tape with renewed vigour.

Next he tried Sylvia who was shopping for the Rectory. 'What do you think about this business of yellow lines and one-way traffic?'

'To be honest I shudder to think about there being accidents outside the school. I hardly dare let the twins go on their own, just in case. So one-way traffic and some yellow lines would go down well in my book.'

'And in mine.' This was Jimbo joining the discussion. 'We always take Fran to school and put her right inside the gate. There's so many cars coming from all directions.'

It wasn't until Bryn spoke to Jimmy that he found an

ally. 'I'm on your side, definitely.' He nudged Bryn and gave him a conspiratorial wink. 'Can't have our little scam spoiled can we?'

'So how much did you get in tips?'

'That'd be telling. But quite satisfactory, thank you.'

'So if we hold a protest outside the council offices you'd be with me?'

'Count me in.'

'They all thought you were great. If your tips don't come up to scratch one time don't come looking to me for recompense.'

'OK. OK. I enjoyed it. Easy as pie it was. Nice people, too.'

'Only don't go on about the plague pit quite so long, just enough to whet their appetites.'

'Right. Did they go to see it?'

Bryn nodded. 'I spun a bit of a tale there, actually. When is the burial taking place? We need a headstone up.'

'Ask the Rector. He'll know better than me.' Jimmy whistled up Sykes and left Bryn standing alone in the middle of the road.

Suddenly Grandmama Charter-Plackett's cottage door snapped open and there she was, beckoning him in. 'Time for coffee?'

Now she really was a formidable old bat and he needed her on board. 'Good morning! I have indeed. Just what the doctor ordered.'

'I've got the kettle on.'

Her kitchen was at the back of the house overlooking her charming garden. While she busied herself with the cafetière he stood at the back door admiring the view. 'By the looks of this you're a gardener, not just someone who gardens.'

'What a delightful compliment. I consider myself just that, a real gardener. It's so rewarding.'

Bryn took in the whole of her view, noticing she could see the old oak tree as well as the stocks if she stood on tiptoe, and the whole lovely vista of some of the best houses in the village as well as the Village Store. 'You've a lovely view of the green.'

'Exactly. I keep intending to *buy* a house when one comes vacant, but then I'd lose this view. I don't think there's a single house with a better view. Some are as good but definitely not better. Come and sit down.'

She went out through the back door to her small group of table and four chairs on her little terrace. 'Some people call this my patio, but that's so common. It's a terrace.' She put down the tray on the snow-white wrought-iron table and sat down.

'You wanted to see me?' Bryn asked.

'Yes. About Dicky.'

'Ah!'

'Is he marrying Georgie?'

Bryn shrugged his shoulders. 'Who knows? Dicky certainly doesn't.'

'I hear it's all your fault.'

'Dicky thinks it is.'

'I'm very fond of Dicky. Lovely little chap. He and Georgie are well suited.'

'If he does marry Georgie I understand there's someone in the village willing to help him buy my share of the pub.'

Mrs Charter-Plackett organised her cafetière and carefully filled his cup. 'There we are, cream and sugar? I would have thought that the money you took from your joint account when you skipped with that hussy would have been enough for you. You left Georgie in a mess.'

Bryn was surprised she knew as much as she did, but he didn't miss the fact that she hadn't taken up his remark about someone lending Dicky the money. Could it be her?

'I've felt sorry about that. You could be right. But the stubborn fella won't have anything to do with her. He's gone back to work because he needs the money, but he reckons that Georgie and I . . . well . . . I have besmirched their love.'

'Hm. I heard about that. You were an idiot.'

'Maybe. While I'm here, I'd like to ask if you approve of this business of the yellow lines, and street lighting et cetera.'

'No, I do not, and if you're starting up some opposition then count me in, as they say. It would ruin everything. Imagine! Huh!' She shuddered.

'You're the first one I've spoken to, apart from Mr Fitch and Jimmy, who's against it.'

'Oh! He's back? I'll do some campaigning for you. That Kev everyone talks about . . .'

Bryn tapped his jacket pocket. 'I've got him right there.'

'Good. Good.'

They drifted on to talk about all manner of things and Bryn found her an entertaining woman. Eventually she signalled that he should be moving off so he stood up and carried the tray inside for her, but before he left she said, 'I'll have a word with Dicky. See what I can do.'

'Thanks.'

'You're not interested in staying married, then?'

'No. Divorce is going through.'

'Good man. I've enjoyed your company.'

'And I yours.'

Bryn's luck was in that day for he found Peter at home. He was sitting in his study reading a prodigious tome the size of which quite intimidated Bryn. 'Sorry if I've interrupted . . .'

'Quite glad of an excuse, actually. Sit down. What can I do for you? I hear your tour went well.'

'It did. Yes, it did.' Bryn sat on the sofa wishing Peter were wearing mufti. This clerical collar bit and the cassock felt like a barrier to normal conversation. He'd be confessing his sins if he didn't watch it. 'It's like this. You know the plague pit; well, are we any nearer to having a service and a burial? If so, will there be a headstone saying who − or is it what? − is buried there?'

'Two weeks today. I'm paying for the stone, I feel so strongly about it.'

'That's more than kind, that is, more than kind. I just wondered because those Americans of mine were fascinated by the pit and the idea of a burial. Yes, indeed they were. Does everyone know?'

'It will be in the weekly newsletter on Sunday.'

'Right. I see.'

'How's Dicky?'

'Working. He said he'd never set foot in the Royal Oak again, but he has, so maybe there's hope for him and Georgie.'

'I sincerely hope so. They need each other. I'm just so sorry it all went wrong.'

Here we go, thought Bryn, confession time again. 'He's being stubborn.'

'With good cause, I think. But I have talked to him and tried to get him to see reason.'

'Well, old Grandmama Charter-Plackett is on the case so watch out. With her . . .' They both laughed. 'The other thing is did you know that the council are thinking of modernising the village? Zebra crossings by the school, lighting et cetera?'

'I had heard rumblings.'

'How would you feel about that? For or against?'

'Half and half, actually. Lighting. Zebra crossings, possibly even one-way traffic . . .'

'But not the whole hog surely? Think of the signposts. And whatever kind of lighting standards would they put up? Ruin the . . .'

The telephone rang and Peter lifted the receiver. 'Turnham Malpas Rectory, Peter Harris speaking.'

Bryn watched his face change to complete puzzlement, then concern. 'No, no, you're all quite busy enough. I'll come. Tell her I'm coming right away.'

Bryn stood up. 'I'll go. I can record you as half and half, can I?'

Peter didn't appear to know what he was talking about. 'Got to go. Sorry. Do you mind?'

'Not at all.' The two of them left together and Bryn stood in Church Lane to watch where Peter went. Mm, he thought, I wonder what's happened?

Then he had a stroke of luck: one of the weekenders staying over for the week was setting off for a walk. He called a cheery 'Good morning to you!' as he passed.

'Good morning! You won't know me . . .'

'I do. Bryn, isn't it, used to be landlord at the pub. How's things?'

'Fine, fine.'

'Coming back to take over again, are you, though that Dicky's doing a great job.'

'No, just back for a few days. I wondered . . .' Bryn explained his mission and the weekender nodded his head in agreement. 'Oh, I wholeheartedly agree with the protest. Disgraceful. We're sick to death of government interference, sick to death. It's diabolical what they think they can do with the country nowadays. Your life isn't your own. We haven't bought this cottage to find ourselves in a wilderness of signposts and traffic lights. Certainly not. You've got my support, definitely.' The weekender strode away in his imitation Barbour jacket and walking boots towards Sykes Wood with a cheery wave and a thumbs up shouting, 'Leaflets, leaflets, that's what you need. And a big protest meeting to discuss strategy.'

Bryn rubbed his hands with glee. He appeared to be having a more profitable morning than he had first thought. Leaflets, though. He went back to Glebe House to rough one out. Perhaps even posters for windows.

Peter could hear Beth screaming as he crossed the school playground. He lengthened his stride and arrived full pelt in the hall, where he found her having the most terrible tantrum he'd ever seen her have. Miss Pascoe was struggling to calm her down but to no avail. The classroom doors were open and children were spilling out to witness this phenomenon.

Peter scooped her up and carried his grunting, snarling daughter into Miss Pascoe's office. He closed the door behind him with his foot, sat in the chair and hugged her hard. 'Hush! Hush, my darling child, calm down. Hush! Hush!' He tried to rock her but she was fighting him like a hell-cat. She beat her fists on his chest, grabbed his hair to pull it, pushed at his chest with her fists to be released but none of her strategies worked because he held her so firmly. Finally her strength ran out and she burst into tears, flushed and exhausted by her outburst.

Peter stroked her hair and gently rocked her, allowing the tears to flow. Slowly the crying lessened and he was able to get a tissue from Miss Pascoe's box on the desk to wipe her eyes. 'There we are. There we are.' The two of them sat quietly hugging each other until Beth relaxed against him, shielding her face with the tissue. She'd laid it fully open so that it completely covered her face. He could feel her shuddering as she strove for control. 'There we are. That's better. How about going home for the rest of the day, eh?'

He thought he detected a nod.

'What do you think, eh?'

He got a positive nod this time.

'They're all out playing, your class. Shall we wait till they come back in?'

Beth nodded again from under the tissue. She laid her head on his chest and enjoyed the security of his arms round her helping to make everything right. Gradually the love he felt for her reached her innermost turbulent being and she began to relax. 'Daddy?'

'Yes, my darling.'

'Sorry.'

'You must have had good reason.'

Beth nodded.

'Are you able to tell me?'

'No.'

'I see. Does Miss Pascoe know why?'

'No.'

'Is it something you've done and shouldn't have?'

His answer was a shake of Beth's head.

'Well, then. I think she'll be needing her room. Let me dry your eyes again and we'll leave. Blow everyone out playing. Head up and we'll march home. How about it?'

'They'll all see me.'

'Of course they will, but who cares? You and I, we're tough.'

Beth took the tissue from her face and he could have wept at the sight of her distress. Her sweet rounded cheeks were streaked with dusty tears, her eyelids swollen, her lashes still dripped a tear. Carefully he reached out and wet a fresh tissue under the washbasin tap and cleaned her face. 'There, that's better. Let me straighten your hair. Now you look like new. I think we'll say sorry to Miss Pascoe tomorrow, shall we?'

Beth nodded. She got off his knee, and prepared to show herself to all and sundry.

Peter opened the office door and found Miss Pascoe in the book corner picking up the books Beth had apparently flung about.

'There you are! Going home? What a good idea. We'll talk about it another day, shall we, Beth?'

Peter answered for her. 'Thank you. I'm so sorry.'

'Don't worry, Rector. We've seen worse, believe me.' She patted Beth's cheek. 'See you tomorrow, Beth, bright and shining new.'

Beth refused to look at her because she was so

embarrassed. How could she explain to Miss Pascoe that she'd realised that very morning what it was her daddy had been trying to tell her on the evening with the parish photo albums? Tell her that she'd seen a photo of her real mother but at the time hadn't understood what it meant, but now she did? That they had the same colour hair and the same rounded cheeks. Tell her how she'd made her mummy cry like she'd never cried before, tell her she, Beth Harris, wasn't what she thought she was and that she'd three sisters she hadn't known about. That when she looked in the mirror she didn't know who she was. Was she Elizabeth Caroline Harris any more? Now she *knew* she wasn't normal would they let her sit the exam for Lady Wortley's after Christmas? Maybe they wouldn't want her, not when they knew she didn't belong. If she'd got it right her daddy must have done what you did to get babies . . . So was she Beth Meadows, really, and one of those flower girls? But she couldn't be because Elizabeth wasn't a flower name. So she didn't even belong to them either. Her daddy slotted his key into the Rectory door and together, hand in hand, they went in.

'Would you like a nice cold drink, darling? You must be thirsty.'

'Yes, please.' Daddy went into the kitchen, poured two glasses of that fizzy real lemonade they both liked, and together they went into the sitting room to sit on the sofa and drink it. Daddy pulled the coffee table closer so she could put her glass on it when she'd finished. She'd better say it. Might he be cross? She glanced at him and saw he wasn't cross, only hurting. 'Sorry, Daddy, for screaming.'

'That's all right. I feel like screaming sometimes when

things get too much. The thing is to get out in the open *why* you screamed.'

Daddy was so gentle when things were upset He always understood. She couldn't bear making Mummy cry again as she had that night; she had to sort it out with him, not her. Very softly she told him why she'd screamed and cried and thrown the books about. It had boiled up inside her into a huge balloon and it burst at school. 'I was crying because all of a sudden I understood what you meant.'

'I thought perhaps it might be so.' Daddy was being so careful not to hurt. But he had hurt her that night, though she hadn't realised at the time. She needed to get Daddy to sort it out. He'd always said they could ask anything they wanted and he'd try to answer truthfully.

'Daddy, you're my real tummy-daddy, aren't you?'

'Yes.'

'But Mummy isn't my tummy-mummy?'

'No, because Mummy's place for growing babies till they're ready to be born isn't there, so she can't. It's like I said when you were very small.'

'So instead, this Suzy person had us.'

'Yes.'

'I see. So was my mummy pleased when she knew?'

'She wanted you both so very much.'

'So am I a Harris or a flower girl?'

'You're a Harris because Mummy and I adopted you, for ever and ever and ever. You are ours by law. It's all written down.'

'I'm glad about that. I'm glad I'm a Harris.' She felt a sharp pain of fear in her heart. 'That Suzy person can't come and get me, then?'

'No, she can't.'

'I don't think I'll bother to see the flower girls and the Suzy person. I won't have to, will I?'

'Definitely not.'

She'd asked as much as she could. She couldn't be bothered to try to understand any more of it at all. She was worn to a shred with the whole thing. 'I'll watch TV now.'

Beth switched it on quickly to put him off explaining any further. Oh, good, that was the phone ringing again. As her daddy went to answer it she lay back against the cushions and prepared to forget the whole thing. But couldn't, at least not quite. This *Teletubbies* was ridiculous. There was nothing on. Maybe she'd go back to school after lunch. But what would they all think? They'd tease her. No, she'd go back tomorrow when she felt better. Mummy would be home before long. Mummy. Mummy. Mummy. Mummy. The word ran like a well-beloved tune through her head.

Having run off far more copies of his leaflet than he'd any right to do on someone else's computer, Bryn set off to push them through every village door. He was surprised at how vicious some people's letter boxes were; his knuckles became quite tender. At some doors a dog snatched it straight out of his hand, which served to remind him not to let his fingers linger the other side of the letter boxes for too long. It was quite soothing wandering along in the sun stuffing the leaflets in every door. The blasted council mustn't succeed or it would ruin everything he'd planned. Bryn decided to give our Kev a call, ask him about further developments. Now the council had changed their routines and become less keen on allowing the general public to attend their meetings it was becoming increasingly difficult to learn about future plans, so our Kev had to be kept sweet. As he reached the bottom of Shepherds Hill and was crossing over to do the other side and so back to the village he thought about inviting our Kev out to a meal. But he felt that was going too far. No, he'd simply hand over more dosh, that was the best way. Money spoke to rats.

He met quite a group of mothers coming home with their children from the school. 'Good afternoon, ladies, would you be so kind as to take time to read one of my leaflets. You may live outside the boundary of Turnham Malpas but it will, I'm sure, be of interest to you, with your kiddies attending the school.' He smiled sweetly at the children; he even chucked one little boy under the chin as he'd seen politicians do and began handing out leaflets, but he hadn't bargained for their vigorous reaction. 'We want some traffic control, it's our kids' lives that are at risk.' He thought this particular mother was about to strike him.

'Is that what it's about?' another asked.

'Thank you, but no.' The third mother stuffed his leaflet down his shirt neck.

Bryn protested. 'I say, I say. Please.'

'We'll stuff them all down your neck if you want.'

Bryn backed off. 'Sorry, ladies, but it's a free country . . .'

'Not so's I've noticed. Buzz off.'

Disconcerted by their opposition, Bryn finished putting leaflets in letter boxes when he arrived at the last of the new cottages in Hipkin Gardens. He was hot and sticky and thirsty. He'd done every house including those down

Royal Oak Road and Church Lane and the Culworth Road. Was it worth it? Honestly, was it worth it? Then he thought about the delight his group of Americans had expressed about the village and decided, yes, it was. So he popped into the Royal Oak for some much needed refreshment and while he was there distributed the last of his leaflets to what turned out to be several very enthusiastic supporters of his protest, and felt tremendously heartened.

Chapter 15

It had been mentioned twice in the weekly church newsletter that the funeral service for the bones was being held on Tuesday morning at ten o'clock and that afterwards there would be coffee served in the village hall. Peter rather suspected that he would be the only person present apart from Mrs Peel at the organ and Caroline. He'd written a special funeral service as there were large parts of the normal one which would be inappropriate, and he'd laboured long and hard to get the wording exactly right.

'Caroline! I've finished it. Would you read it through before I print it out?' Getting no reply he went in search of her. He found her in the attic looking through small baby clothes belonging to the twins.

'Do you remember when we bought these? No, of course you won't, but I do. I was so excited. The twins were coming home from hospital and I was hurrying to get things ready.' She held up two very small premature baby sleep suits, each with a tiny rabbit embroidered on the front. 'I loved these. Still do. They are lovely, don't you think?'

Peter took hold of them and held them up to the light. 'Indeed they are. Beautiful. Weren't we excited?'

'Oh, we were. And these! Remember these?' She was holding up a pair of bootees she'd made for Beth because her feet were always cold. 'I loved every stitch of these, every single stitch.' She kissed both bootees before she replaced them in the box along with the other early baby clothes and put on the lid. 'I'm sorry for all those tears that night. It spoiled the telling, didn't it?'

Peter had to smile. 'A little, but it was understandable. They were horrendous times.'

'They were, but at the same time so joyous. I wouldn't have had it any other way, though. After all, I've got the babies I wanted and you've got children of your very own.'

'I have. Thanks be to God.'

'Exactly. Poor Suzy. I wonder if she ever thinks of them and what they're doing. It hurts me still thinking about how brave she was, but they are turning out to be terrific people, aren't they?'

Peter kissed the top of her head. 'They are.'

'What did you want me for?'

'To read the funeral service I've written for the remains.'

'Ah, right. I doubt there'll be anyone there but thee, me and Mrs P.'

'I know, but we've got to do it right whatever.'

'Of course. I'll be down when I've tidied up. Really all these things should go to someone in need.'

'Keep them a while longer.'

'I think I will.'

'Why not bring the children up here and let them see?

Make them feel as though they belong . . . or something, I'm not quite sure.'

'That's an idea. By the way, this afternoon we're going boating on Culworth Lake. Might as well take advantage of the good weather while we can. Are you able to come with us?'

'Sorry, urgent sick visiting.'

'OK, then. I'll be down in a moment.'

Peter went down the narrow attic stairs and on to his study, and left Caroline to her memories.

The sun was even hotter that afternoon. Caroline packed plenty of drinks and sunhats, which the two of them hated but being so fair she had to insist upon, and with the sunroof open to its fullest extent they set off for the lake. It was on the Turnham Malpas side of Culworth so the journey there was not lengthy. In no time at all they were parked beside the lake and getting their hats and drinks out of the boot.

Alex had a favourite boat, and he ran down the slipway to search for her and found her tied up as he had hoped. She was called the *Mary Rose* and shone with layers of marine lacquer, over a lovely golden-brown stain. On her side the words *Mary Rose* were painted in bright royal blue with a Union Jack sticky transfer alongside her name. The brass oar locks seemed to shine more intensely than the other boats' and, well, he just plain loved her.

Beth arrived beside him. 'I want to go in that other one called *Elizabeth*.'

'We're not. It's this one and no other.'

'You always get your own way.'

'It's our boat is this. Ours. See.'

'Mummy! Alex wants to go in the usual one.'

'We will today and next time we'll go in the *Elizabeth*.'

Seeing Beth beginning to work herself up into a rage, which had become more frequent since the night of the photo albums, Caroline hastily gave her the money and sent her off to the boat office to pay.

The boatman came down to see them safely aboard and to shove them off. 'Nice day for it, Dr Harris.'

'It certainly is, Tony. Looks busy.'

'Yes, thank goodness. It's a short season.'

He shoved off the *Mary Rose* with his bare foot and they splooshed out on to the lake. Caroline had become very proficient at rowing and they were soon speeding down the centre of the lake heading for the long arm off to the right where the trees bent down to the water and where the children loved to tie up under a particular willow which dipped the ends of its twigs into the water to form a delightful secret hideaway.

They sat there under its cool canopy sipping their drinks and talking about school starting soon, and it being their last year at the village school, about beginning at their new schools and about uniform and new friends and a myriad other things of interest. After a little while Caroline decided to untie the boat and row back into the main part of the lake.

They were smoothly making progress round the big open area at the far end where the water was deep and where sometimes the two of them spotted fish in the dark depths when a crowd of youths in a bigger boat than theirs came racing down the lake yelling 'In . . . Out . . . In . . . Out . . .' at the tops of their voices. Caroline, trying to keep to the rules of the water and pass on the right, became worried that they were taking no notice of where they were going. She shouted to them and so did Alex but they couldn't hear. She swiftly directed the boat to pass them on the left, then saw another boat approaching her and before she knew it she was trapped between two boats both heading straight for her, one from the front and another from the rear. The second boat took evasive action and pulled away but the boat with the youths in it kept going and Caroline couldn't row strongly enough to get out of their way. They hit her full on with their surging bows and rocked the *Mary Rose* so that Beth, who'd been covering her eyes with her hands from fear of what might be going to happen, suddenly tipped out of the boat, hitting her head on the edge before she disappeared from sight.

An oar slipped from Caroline's grip.

Alex stood up.

'Sit down. Sit down.'

He did.

Caroline looked into the depths of the water.

No Beth.

Terrified, she could hear Alex bellow, 'Beth, Beth.'

Caroline saw Beth's fair hair rise to the surface.

Too far to reach.

'Stay in the boat.' Caroline carefully lowered herself over the side into the water.

Alex by now was screeching, 'Help! Help!'

Caroline swam to where she'd seen Beth's head come to the surface and dived.

One of the youths jumped into the water and swam to help.

Can't find Beth. Too dark.

Have to go up for air.

Go down again.

Too dark.

Go up for air, there's Beth going down yet again, further away.

Swim towards her.

The dark waters closed over her again.

Find her. Find her. Find her. There!

Grasp her.

Hoist her to the top.

Hold her head out of the water. Lungs bursting.

One of the youths swam towards her, took hold of Beth, swam with her to the boat and heaved her in.

Beth lay in the bottom, frightened and exhausted, choking and spluttering.

Desperately Alex held out the oar for his mother to grasp.

But the youth came up behind her and gave her the most tremendous push up so that she was half in and half out of the boat. Caroline pulled herself up but was too paralysed with fear and too heavy with water to manage the last push up into the boat. 'Oh, God! Oh, God!'

The youth came behind her and manhandled her into it, grabbing her body anywhere at all to achieve his objective. She collapsed in the bottom of the boat alongside Beth. By now they were floating well away from the lost oar and all she could think about was how to get back to the shore with only one oar. 'Beth! Beth?'

As they tried to get themselves seated without upsetting the boat, Caroline heard the phut phut of a motor boat engine. Thank heavens! It was Tony coming.

He circled round, rescued the oar and came alongside.

'Dr Harris! Young lady! OK? I'll tow you back. Hold tight. Sit up. That's it. On the seat. I've got you, don't worry.'

Caroline began to shake, not so much with the chill of the water on her skin but the full horror of what might have happened. Beth was unable to speak. Alex was deathly white from shock.

Tony switched off his motor boat engine, tied up and then tied up the *Mary Rose*. 'Come on, now. I'll switch the fire on in the boat office. Warm you up. Just wait till I get hold of those bu— beg your pardon, Dr Harris.' He hustled them into the boat office and turned on the fire. Out of a cupboard he brought towels somewhat the worse for wear and a collection of dry clothes kept for the purpose. Tony went out, shutting the door behind him, and they could hear him ranting and raving at the top of his voice and using fearful bad language at the youths. They heard their boat bump into the side and Tony still raving at them.

Caroline stripped Beth of her clothes and rubbed her hard with Tony's rough towel. She still hadn't spoken. Alex was channelling his fear into looking for something suitable for Beth to wear. 'Here we are, look, shorts and a shirt with dolphins on it. You'll look all right in these, Beth. Bit big but . . .'

Caroline was quickly becoming chilled right through to the bone. She left Beth to dress herself and began stripping off her wet clothes. 'Look for something for me, Alex, please.'

'There's not much, just this funny dress or a pair of man's shorts and a football shirt.'

'They'll do.'

They were much too big but she wasn't going to let that bother her.

'Look! I've lost a sandal. My best sandals!' Beth began to wail. 'My best sandals!'

Caroline put on the shorts and football shirt saying, 'Never mind about your sandal. We can always buy another pair, but we can't buy another Beth.'

Beth took hold of her hand.

Alex grasped the other. 'Let's go home,' he said.

'That's the best place. I'll get my bag and we'll go straight home. But we'll thank Tony first.'

Tony knocked at the boat office door and shouted, 'The wife's made a cup of tea for you. Sit on this seat out here in the sun. She'll be out in a minute.'

Beth wanted home more than anything. 'I want to go home.'

'Hush, darling, we will when we've had a nice cup of hot tea.' They emerged into the sun, thankful they were all alive. 'Thank you, Tony, that will be lovely. I found a plastic carrier bag in the office and I've borrowed it to put our wet things in. Where's the young man who jumped in the water to help us? I'd have liked to thank him.'

'They've all gone. I gave them a telling off and no mistake. They won't be back here for a bit. Idiots. I'd no idea they had drink in the boat. It's forbidden, really, but the moment your back's turned . . . Ah, here's your tea.'

The tea was welcome, it was sugared but it didn't matter, because it tasted like nectar.

'Ring Dad, tell him.'

'He's sick visiting, darling.'

'Please ring Dad, he'll want to know.'

'I don't want to worry him, it'll keep till we get home.'

Caroline put an arm round Alex and hugged Beth with her free arm. 'Feeling better?'

Beth held up her feet. 'One sandal's no good.'

'Never mind, you can wear your flip-flops for a day or two. We can't go into Culworth to buy new sandals looking like this, can we?'

Alex looked at the two of them and burst out laughing. It was infectious. Both Caroline and Beth joined in and laughed till their sides ached, but it was such a relief. Laughing took some of the fear away.

They drove home singing silly songs from when they were small. Caroline put the car in the garage at the end of Pipe and Nook Lane and they went into the Rectory by the back door so no one would see them looking like freaks.

Peter was back and the children ran into the study to tell him their adventure.

His first words were, 'Whatever are you wearing, Beth?'

She explained, with Alex putting in his pennyworth where she hadn't explained clearly. 'And when I was under the water I could see fishes and nasty bits and the water tasted dreadful!'

'Beth! My darling! Where's Mummy, is she all right?'

'She's putting the kettle on. The water was so cold and dark, Daddy. I've never thought about water being dark before.'

'Did you try to swim?'

She shook her head.

'Why not? It's because of accidents like this that we taught you to swim.'

'I tried but I was so frightened. I kept going up but then

I went back down again. I felt so heavy. I couldn't stay up and I couldn't see Mummy anywhere. It was so cold.' She shuddered at the memory. 'Worse than the swimming pool. I've got a huge, huge bump on my head, Daddy, look.' Beth pushed her hair away from her face to show him a black-and-blue patch close to her temple. 'I bumped it on the edge of the boat when I went in. It really makes you so you can't think.'

'Thanks be to God, you're safe and sound.' Peter hugged her.

Alex declared he'd tried to help. 'Mum wouldn't let me dive to find Beth. She told me to stay in the boat.'

'Very wise, else she'd have had two of you to rescue, wouldn't she.'

'*I* could have swum back to the boat and climbed back in, Dad.'

'I expect you could, but it's as Beth says: it's very different from the swimming pool.'

Caroline came in still dressed in her borrowed clothes. 'Peter! Am I glad to see you.'

Peter stood up and put his arms round her. 'And I'm glad to see you too. There I was, visiting my housebound sick, totally unaware of the danger my entire family were in. Darling! I'm so sorry I couldn't come with you. Are you sure you're feeling OK? It must have been a terrible shock. You were so brave.'

'I jumped in without thinking. She kept coming up and going down again. I was scared to death. I don't call that being brave.'

'Well, I think you were brave anyway.'

Beth said, 'She was. She dived dozens of times to get me, didn't she, Alex? Dozens. She was brave. I'll need new sandals. I've left one of my best ones in the lake.' She held up her bare foot to show him.

'I'm hungry. Is it nearly time to eat? It must be.' Alex wandered off into the kitchen.

Peter volunteered to start the meal while Caroline changed, so she and Beth went upstairs to find fresh clothes. They sat on Beth's bed, had a long cuddle to comfort themselves and giggled at their outfits. 'Mummy, I was so scared. I thought I was going to die.'

'Don't, darling, don't even think about it.'

'But I did.' She curled her arm more tightly round Caroline's neck. 'It's terrible down there. I go under the water in the swimming pool with my eyes wide open but under there, under that lake ... there's swimmy things and black bits, and it's so dark you can't see, and even when I went down I didn't touch the bottom. I couldn't even *see* the bottom.'

'I know, darling, it's very deep at that end of the lake.'

'Have you ever drowned?'

'Not even nearly.'

'Has Daddy?'

'Not that I know of.'

Beth kissed her cheek very hard, again and again. 'I love you, Mummy. I truly do.'

'And I love you.' Caroline wound her arms round Beth and hugged her more tightly. 'I love you so very much.'

'And me you. And I love Daddy. Do you love Daddy?'

'Of course I do. You know that.'

Beth sat up and loosened her hold on Caroline. 'I love you like you really were my mummy. Which you're not, but you are and I want you to be for ever. Daddy says no

258

one can take me from you. They can't, can they, if it's written on paper?'

'No. Never ever. Was that what the screams were all about at school the other day?'

Beth nodded. 'Yes. All of a sudden I understood. But I want to live with you all the time. Mr Glover said he wished you were his mother too, because you're so lovely. Well, that's how I want it to be. I'm going to be yours for ever. I'm not going to bother about those girls with the flower names, not for now anyway.'

'Thank you, darling, I like the sound of that very much. But you can when you wish, you know, when you're older.'

Beth shrugged her shoulders. 'Perhaps.' She stood up. 'I think I'll put on my blue shorts and that white top.'

'Fine. I'd better get changed myself.'

'I've got things sorted out now.'

'Good, I'm glad.'

'I'm your girl because I must be because you said you jumped in the water without giving it a thought, so you must love me the very bestest. Mustn't you?'

Caroline smiled at her. 'I expect I must.'

'Well, I *know* you do.'

Beth disappeared into the depths of her wardrobe searching for her favourite blue shorts and said no more, so Caroline crossed the landing to her own bedroom, overwhelmed with joy.

There'd been rain over the weekend, for which every gardener in the neighbourhood was very grateful, but on the morning of the bones service – for that was what everyone called it whenever it got a mention – a weak sun appeared and bathed the village in a kind of mystical hazy light from first thing.

Peter was approaching the service with trepidation. Not because he wasn't well prepared for it, but because it had occurred to him that he could very easily have been conducting a funeral service for his own daughter. As he tucked his cross into his leather belt and made the chain comfortable round his neck he looked at his reflection in the bedroom mirror. Behind him he could see Caroline standing by the dressing table putting on a necklace.

'Caroline, come here, darling.' Through the mirror he watched her come to stand beside him. They looked gravely at each other in the glass and Peter said, 'Thank you for being utterly wonderful and for loving me.'

'Thank you for loving me. Because I do love you. This funeral is getting to you, isn't it?'

Peter nodded. 'The thought occurred to me that but for you I might have been conducting Beth's . . .' He felt as well as saw her shock.

'Oh, my God! Don't even think it. And don't let her hear you say that. She really thought she was going to die.'

'I'm sorry. Sometimes, though, it is salutary to remind ourselves to be grateful for His mercy.' He found her hand, grasped it and took it to his lips to kiss. 'Thank you for coming with me this morning. Is my congregation ready?'

She smiled back at him, checked her appearance and said, 'It is.'

They got downstairs to find both Beth and Alex ready and waiting. 'We're going to be late.'

Caroline asked, 'Why, where are you going?'

'To the bones service, Mum.'

Peter protested, 'I'd arranged for you to stay with Willie while . . .'

'We're going. We want to.'

Peter saw that determined look in Alex's eye which experience had taught him meant he, Alex, was set on having his own way and that nothing, but nothing, would change his mind.

'We're both going, aren't we, Beth?'

'Oh, yes.'

Peter couldn't face the ensuing battle if he refused to allow them to be there; he was in no mood for an uproar. 'Very well. Pop next door and tell Willie. I've got to go. We'll see you in church.'

Alex knocked at Willie's and Sylvia's door, pushed it open and put his head round it, just as he'd seen his father do, saying, 'It's Alex from the Rectory.'

Sylvia was standing with her handbag on her arm, obviously about to leave for the service. Willie was ensconced in his chair by the fireside trying to read the paper.

'Willie! We're going to the service. Dad says we can, so we shan't need to stay with you. Thank you all the same.'

Willie nodded his agreement without looking at the pair of them.

'Are you coming with us, Sylvia?'

'You go on. I'll follow in a moment. I need a word with Willie.'

Alex left without closing the door. Sylvia pushed it shut and went back to stand in front of Willie. 'This has gone on far too long. Get up and come with me.'

'I shan't.'

'You will.'

'I won't.'

'After all you've said in the past about how Peter is so close to God he knows the rightness of things without even having to debate about it, and you're *still* flying in the face of his decisions. How can you? How can you?'

'Because I can.'

'Willie Biggs, you've been fooling me all these nine years we've been married. I thought you were a good, upstanding man, a man young in mind and body with modern ideas. I can see how wrong I've been.'

'Just a minute!'

'You're a silly, stubborn old man, that's what. I'm disgusted with you. What Peter will think I can't imagine.' Sylvia marched towards the cottage door with tears brimming in her eyes.

'Hold on a minute, then, and I'll come.'

She had her hand on the catch and didn't look back to see if he followed because she knew he would; he was as tired as she was of their conflict. Arm in arm they hastened up the path into the church and arrived just as Peter announced the first hymn.

Peter's beautifully chosen words, the tremendous feeling he imparted with every sentence he spoke, lifted the heart. 'God of peace and compassion, make bright with Your presence the path of those who have walked in the valley of shadows.' Mrs Peel played 'Abide with me', with such soulful passion no one could fail to be moved. Peter's closing words brought tears to their eyes, so powerful and heartfelt had been the service. 'Father God, they have journeyed beyond our sight many years ago, but we, Your children of today, entrust them to Your keeping, with complete and utter faith that in Your infinite mercy, You will transform the fearful terror of their deaths into a bright new healing dawn in Your everlasting Kingdom. Amen.'

The service had been difficult enough, but the sight of the coffins being lowered into the grave was almost his undoing. He said the final blessing with tremendous relief and was able at last to see who besides his own family had come, for he'd been aware the moment he'd walked into the church that there were far more people present than he had ever hoped for. He realised as he blessed them that there was a representative from almost every family in the village and felt a huge sense of triumph. So, despite half the village setting themselves against him so vehemently, they'd finally come round to his way of thinking. He smiled at them all and they all smiled back.

Duty done they went from the churchyard into the church hall for their coffee. Mrs Jones laid a firm hand on his arm. 'One thing's for certain, Rector, they'll be resting in peace now. We shall have no more troubles, not after that beautiful service. How you think up all those lovely words I shall never know. Like poetry it is, sheer poetry. Gets you right there.' She thumped her chest as she spoke. 'As I say, we can look forward to peace now. Ever since Gilbert dug up them bones there's been nothing but trouble but I can feel right here' – she thumped her chest again – 'that things are going to be right now.'

'Thank you, Mrs Jones. Thank you. I'm glad you approve.'

'Of course I do. It could well have been Flatman bones you've just laid to rest. You know, my family go back a very long way.' Her large brown eyes scanned the crowd. 'I notice even Willie turned up and he was dead against it.

Mind you, I understand Sylvia's had a lot to say about his attitude. She must have won!'

'I was a bit surprised, I must say. Here's a coffee for you . . . Greta.'

It was the first time he'd called her Greta and whereas at one time she would have been indignant at his familiarity, today it seemed a lovely friendly gesture, a kind of acceptance that she belonged to the inner fold. 'Thank you . . . Peter. No sugar. I'm quite sweet enough! About the council and the road safety, how do you stand on that?'

'I certainly don't think things should stay as they are. We need something, unobtrusive certainly, but something, because one day there's bound to be an accident; it's unavoidable.'

Smugly Mrs Jones declared, 'Then we're on the same side, Peter.'

'Good. I'm glad.'

Bryn came to talk to him, so Mrs Jones moved away. 'Thank you, Rector, for the service. Excellent. Lovely hymns, too. I'd like to go halves with the headstone if you'd agree.'

Gravely Peter studied Bryn's face and pondered his motives. 'Why?'

'Why? . . . because, well, because I feel I should.'

'Why should you?'

'Because I think everyone in the village should donate money to it. It belongs to all of us. You can see that, all those people turning out for it.'

'I have to confess to being surprised at how many attended the service. I just wish I could believe your motives, Bryn.'

'I know it looks as if I've only come because my tourists love the idea of it, and that it enhances their tour, but I really want at least to give some money towards the headstone.'

'Greta Jones, for instance, Greta Flatman that was. Descendant of an old village family, it could be one of her ancestors we've buried today. She has genuine reasons for being interested. But you . . . ?'

Bryn didn't like the sceptical expression on Peter's face. He'd as much right to be here as anyone else. 'I'm still very fond of the village. I've lived here – what? – ten years.'

Peter sighed. 'Oh, Bryn!'

'Will you let me go halves? Please.'

'Very well, then. I've ordered it. I'll let you have the bill, then you can do as you wish. Who am I to deny you your heart's desire? Talking of heart's desire, have you done anything about your divorce?'

'It's going through; takes time.'

'Good chap.'

'Though there's not much point in it. Dicky won't even talk about marrying her. So it might be that Georgie finishes up with neither of us. And a lonely life that will be.'

'He'll come round, given time. I've read your leaflet. I'll be at the meeting, not on your side, though.'

'We need open debate. I'll be glad for you to put your side.'

'Good, because I shall.'

Chapter 16

On the day of the meeting Mr Fitch went to school. He was there by eight forty-five. Propped against the school wall, he watched the children arriving. He saw the chaos of drivers trying to pull up to let the children out, the haphazard parking, the difficulty of pulling away without bumping into another vehicle and the risk the children ran if their parents couldn't find space close to the entrance. He was given the occasional 'Good morning' by parents taking their children on foot through the school gate and certainly got some odd looks when all he did was acknowledge their greeting with the briefest of nods. All in all, though, there was no hurried screech of brakes or even the slightest chance of one of the children being mown down.

He stood there, still propped against the school wall looking at the village, listening to the joyous sound of the children's hymn singing coming through the open windows. Back to school. Those were the days, he thought, those were the days. He thought about his own two boys and realised he'd been so remote from them that he'd never even once taken them to school or gone to a school occasion to support them. Sad, that. He'd been a fool. Too busy concentrating on his career. He'd missed out there.

Missed out on everything of any real value. Precious lives passing by him till they'd gone for ever. The singing stopped and he could hear the tramp of feet, the closing of classroom doors, the rustle of paper, the squeak of chalk. Those were the days.

No good facing her until break. Or was it still called playtime? Such a happy word, 'playtime'. Tag, and chain tig, and hopscotch. Marbles! Remember marbles? Then on dry days in the summer the headmaster teaching cricket. He must be turning in his grave now at the thought of rigged cricket matches. Pity that. Pity. We had such fun. He fancied coffee so he went into the Store to see if they'd got their coffee pot on the go. Couldn't remember the last time he'd been in there, either. As he opened the door Jimbo's bell dinged a cheerful ping and the aroma of baking assailed his nostrils. Jimbo must have studied psychology: he'd created such an ambience it became compulsive to shop, one must, one couldn't help it, one needed to have a share of . . . what? Happiness? Comfort? A slice of childhood?

Mr Fitch felt out of place. He was at least twenty-five, maybe thirty, years older than the other customers. Well, he needn't let that worry him, he still had a contribution to make. He still made things tick, if not tock!

'Coffee, Jimbo!'

Heads turned. Turned back when they saw who it was. What the hell did he want?

'Good morning.' Jimbo raised his boater. 'Coffee in the jug freshly made. Help yourself!'

So he did. Added half a teaspoonful of multicoloured coffee sugar – such a nice touch, he thought – and seated

267

himself on the chair by the side window to watch the world go by.

The rush subsided and Jimbo took a moment to speak to him. 'Are you needing a word?'

'Not really. You've a little gold mine here, Jimbo. Such style.'

Jimbo raised his boater for a second time. 'We have.'

'Ambience, that's what you've created. I do believe your customers feel better for having been in here. You've made them feel up-to-the-minute, in-the-swim, with it, as they say.'

'That's our aim.'

'This meeting. About the council and their crackpot ideas for modernising us. What do you think?'

'Something needs doing, but quite what I don't know. It is chaotic.'

'Yes, but only for about ten minutes, then we're back to the peace and quiet. Is it worth spoiling the village for the sake of ten minutes twice a day, for three-quarters of the year?'

Jimbo took off his boater and smoothed his bald head. 'You have a point. But you haven't a small child going to school. We have and we worry.'

'Easy to take her across Shepherds Hill and pop her into school. Better than traffic signs everywhere. How about a voluntary code?'

'That would work for about a week and then . . .'

'You're right. This coffee's good. Could we get by with the bare minimum?'

'Who defines the bare minimum? Wasn't too bad when we had two minibuses picking up the children from outside the village. The council claim they can't afford it any longer, so now we've more cars than ever.'

'Even Nightingale Farm's tractor and trailer.'

'Exactly. Well, there you go, the Nightingale children were picked up, you see, by one of the minibuses, so that made life a lot easier all round. Two vehicles but twenty or more children, now it's perhaps the same number of children but it takes at least ten or twelve cars to get them here. However, I'll be at the meeting tonight.'

'So will I, Jimbo. I'm not having this village ruined by any damn council. They claim they can't afford the minibuses, yet they've money for all this traffic control nonsense. It doesn't add up.'

'Must press on. See you tonight.'

Mr Fitch placed his empty cup in the waste bin by the coffee machine, wandered around the Store looking in the freezers, assessing the quality of the goods on display, fingering the ripe plums, the glowing peaches, the bright, super-fresh vegetables and eventually left when he heard the children out playing in the schoolyard.

Miss Pascoe's class were out in the yard and Miss Pascoe herself was in her room opening her post. She heard the light knock at her door and called out, 'Come!'

So he did.

'Why, Mr Fitch! How nice of you to call. Please take a chair.'

'Good morning, Miss Pascoe.'

'And a very good morning to you. How can I help?'

'About this traffic business.'

Miss Pascoe's hackles rose. 'Yes.'

'I've been watching.'

'I saw.'

'It's the number of vehicles that is the problem.'

'Exactly.'

'But it's only for three-quarters of the year and only for about ten minutes twice a day.'

She sat in her chair, braced herself against the back, put her fingertips together and said, 'It only takes a split second for a child to be killed. A split second. A nano-second.'

There'd been an alteration in the tone of her voice. A stiffening of her attitude. A summoning of her resources. Mr Fitch realised she was one of these new women who were the bane of his life in business. They got things done but did they need to be so aggressive? Why couldn't they acquiesce as women used to do? 'I agree, but . . .'

'No, Mr Fitch, I'm having the one-way signs and the yellow lines and the lights.'

'Who says?'

'I do.'

'What if we oppose you?'

'Then the death of a child might well be laid at your door and if you want that kind of burden on your conscience then . . .'

'Eh?'

'Then I certainly don't. Something has to be done and quickly. The council have done the preliminary work and are all set for agreement.'

'Who says?'

'The county chairman of traffic planning.'

'It's county level, is it, already?'

Miss Pascoe nodded.

'I see. Well, I too have friends in high places. I shall see what can be done.' He stood up to leave. 'Don't think you've got the better of me. There's dozens in this village who don't want it ruined.'

'At what cost? A child's life? I have only the interests of my children at heart, Mr Fitch, and I can hardly be blamed for that when I'm the head teacher of the school. Can I?'

She fixed him with a stare which almost, but not quite, intimidated him. Standing up, she said, 'Excuse me, that's the bell and I have a class to teach. The children, you see, always come first with me.'

And she left him standing there! Alone, in her poky little office. She'd humiliated him. Yes, she had. Humiliated him. As he'd said to Bryn, women in authority. They didn't know how to use it. Well, she'd met her match.

He had to make an uncomfortable passage through the hall with the children springing about doing their Physical Education, climbing wall bars, balancing along an upturned bench, jumping over a horse. In his day they'd had half a dozen beanbags and some hoops, and been thankful. Indulged, that's what, indulged. He stormed across the playground, narrowly averting a disastrous stumble over a nursery child pedalling like fury on a little trike. They damn well weren't going to have their own way about this, not if he had anything to do with it.

He was one of the first to take a seat at the meeting that night, on the front row, determined to have his say. Unfortunately, unless he turned round frequently, he couldn't see who'd showed up, but judging from the babble of conversation there were plenty there, and most of the voices he didn't recognise so they must be parents from the school.

Bryn took his place, feeling exceptionally confident that

his arguments would sway general opinion. However, ten minutes before kick-off, when he saw the size of the crowd already gathered, he did wonder if it would be as easy as he'd first thought. It felt close tonight, the windows needed opening. But he had to succeed. His tourists wouldn't be half so enamoured of Turnham Malpas if all they could see were one-way signs and huge street lights. Three-quarters of the romance of the place would be gone. And Miss Pascoe confidently picking up a chair and placing it beside his own didn't help matters either. Honestly, you brought money to the village and what thanks did you get? None. Bryn loosened his tie a little, mopped his top lip and sipped some water, hoping to allay a touch of indigestion. That was better. He'd put a bright, confident face on the matter and he'd win through. Peter was there too, so he'd see nothing went wrong.

But the entire evening went disastrously awry. The parents were vociferous in their declaration that something must be done. Some even went the whole hog and demanded signs shoulder to shoulder along the roads, the green fenced off, yellow lines outside all the houses and around the green. By the time they'd finished the whole centre of the village was to be a no-go area for cars. No longer would you be able to pull up outside the Store while you shopped and any question of parking outside the school was completely ruled out, and you certainly couldn't park outside your own house, not even while you unloaded your shopping. As for lighting, Mr Fitch was convinced that Stocks Row would be akin to Piccadilly Circus if they had their way. He waited until they'd run out of further restrictions to impose, then he stood up, beating Miss Pascoe by a whisker.

'Mr Chairman, ladies and gentlemen. I wish Sir Ralph and Lady Templeton were here, but they're not. If they were, Sir Ralph would be appalled by your road safety ideas. But in that wonderfully gentlemanly way of his he would explain to you why they couldn't be allowed. He would talk about his village, a village with a Templeton at the head of it for more years than I know of. Certainly five or even six hundred years. Oh, yes, he has history and tradition at his very fingertips. Would that I had it too. We cannot, we must not, defile the village with such twenty-first-century trumpery as traffic lights and yellow lines. It would be sacrilege. We are here on this earth for only our allotted span, no more, and we must hand on to our children and our children's children a village fit for human beings to live in. Leave the trappings of modern society to the big cities. Here we have a haven . . .'

Someone at the back stood up and shouted, 'Haven! It won't be a haven if a kid gets killed. Never mind your poetic humbug, we're living in today's society, not blinking hundred years ago. Shut up and sit down, you old faggot.'

Bryn recognised the woman who'd tried to stuff his leaflets down his shirt neck. 'I think it would be better if . . .' But his voice didn't carry over the hubbub Mr Fitch's speech had caused.

While Peter had a word with Bryn, Miss Pascoe made up her mind to speak but Peter got to his feet while she was still thinking about it. His powerful voice carried right across the babble and he got the silence Bryn had tried for.

In reasonable tones he argued his case. 'Losing our tempers will achieve nothing. Mr Fitch is quite right. I would hate to lose our wonderful backwater; it would be

273

criminal to allow anyone to destroy it. There are all kinds of reasons for preserving our heritage and I'm quite sure that with a bit of common sense we can overcome this problem. A little give and take on both sides, a modification of plans, a certain subtlety, a large amount of good will and we would arrive at an amicable solution. I propose we form a committee . . .'

'Reverend! Please, not a committee. They cover a lot of ground but get nowhere, as you well know. We want action. Action! Action!'

A steady drumming of feet on the wooden floorboards and the shouting of 'Action! Action!' began, and there was nothing to be done about it. It was like some kind of primeval chant: a hate thing compounded by a wish for instant capitulation. Peter was appalled. Bryn was beginning to panic. Mr Fitch was on the verge of washing his hands of the whole matter.

Grandmama Charter-Plackett stood up at the back and stepped firmly to the front to take her stand beside Bryn. She banged on the table with the gavel Bryn had brought but never used. 'Silence!' If she'd been on board ship in a violent thunderstorm the very waves would have ceased their pounding. The noisy opposition, surprised by her reckless intervention, fell silent. You could have heard a pin drop. They expected that she would shout but she didn't. She spoke so softly they had to strain to hear.

'All this matter needs is some clear thinking. None of us is a fool, we all have brains, and I for one would like to have something done about the cars because I have a precious grandchild attending the school and believe me, your cause is mine.' She pressed a hand to her heart to emphasise her feelings. 'Precious to me here,' she said, patting her chest again, 'as I know all your children and grandchildren are precious to you. We all have their welfare at heart. The Rector is the man to chair the committee and have you ever known anyone more able? Level-headed, understanding, persuasive. What more can you ask? And he too has children at the school, don't forget, so who could have your interests at heart more than he? I propose Mr Fitch as another member, for his business brain. I propose Bryn because he found out what the council were up to and apparently has friends in high places . . .'

'Oh, yeh? Our Kev! High Places! Huh!' This from that uncouth woman Bryn had met after school down Shepherds Hill.

In her most superior tone Grandmama asked, 'And you, madam, your name is . . . ?'

'Angie Turner. Shepherds Hill.'

'You could be another member. Your forthrightness would be welcomed, I'm sure. We need people with plenty of get-up-and-go on a committee like this. After all, we're taking on the whole council.'

Miss Pascoe tried again to speak but Bryn overrode her. He objected to Angie Turner on the committee most violently. He stood up to put his point. 'I honestly feel that Mrs Turner wouldn't be quite . . .'

A man leapt to his feet, a big brute of a man with forearms built like ships' hawsers and a huge shaved head. 'Not out of the top drawer eh? Is that what you meant?'

'Well, no, of course not, far be it from me to . . .'

'Well, I'm Colin Turner, Angie's husband, and I'd like to know why she can't be?'

Unfortunately Bryn couldn't think of one possible

acceptable excuse for her not being on the committee. His hesitation was his undoing.

'Well, I'm waiting for the answer. You toad, we know you've not called this meeting because of the children's lives. It's because you want to retain the status quo for your own objectives; namely American tourists.'

Peter stood up again. 'Mr Turner . . .'

'With the very greatest respect, Reverend, this is not an argument for someone like you to be involved in. I'm well aware you'd have her on the committee without a second thought because you're not biased; you have respect for each and every one of us. I simply want an answer as to why he, *that toad*' – he stabbed a thick finger at Bryn – 'doesn't want *my wife* on his committee. It's as simple as that. Well?'

Bryn opened his mouth and nothing came out. Absolutely nothing. His mind went numb. He looked bleakly at Grandmama Charter-Plackett for inspiration. He opened his mouth again and still nothing came. He cleared his throat and uttered some fateful words. 'We'll be dealing with councillors and planning officers at the highest level and your wife . . . well . . . she has the children to think of . . . and it's not easy to find the time . . . and . . .'

Peter saw he was having difficulties, sensed he was totally flummoxed, but at the same time knew Bryn had to extricate himself or he'd lose face. But he didn't. Bryn looked wildly round the hall, searching for answers, saw Colin Turner leave his seat and begin to march purposefully towards the front. Bryn's eyes bulged, he ran a finger round his shirt neck, beads of sweat appeared all over his face. Grey-faced, he gripped the edge of the table, gasped

276

audibly and crashed to the floor before Colin Turner reached him.

There was an instant of total shocked silence, as though someone had pressed 'pause' on a video, before Peter leapt up and went to kneel beside Bryn. The moment he got close Peter sensed he was dead. There was such a pallid stillness about him: as though his soul had gone away.

'Give him some air,' someone shouted.

'Ring nine-nine-nine.'

'Glass of water. Quick.'

Peter pressed both hands on Bryn's chest and counted one, two, three, four, five presses. Paused, pinched Bryn's nose and breathed into his mouth. He did it again, and again, and again. Even before he'd begun he'd known it was too late, but he had to try. He tried once more but to no avail. Bryn had been stone dead the moment he touched the floor. Peter looked up at Grandmama Charter-Plackett and slowly shook his head. She went white, looked at Colin Turner and signalled the message to him with her eyes that it was too late: Bryn had gone.

Colin dropped to his knees and began the process all over again. 'He's got to live. He must. He must. He must.' Five times, five grunts, nip his nose. Breathe! Breathe! Breathe! Colin covered his face with his hands and wept. Grandmama put her arm round him. That was one sound she couldn't bear: a man weeping. Men's tears were so excruciatingly painful to listen to.

'I wasn't going to hit him. I wasn't, honest. I only wanted to address the meeting. I wouldn't have hit him. Not me.'

Peter took off his cassock and laid it over Bryn. 'Could someone go and get Georgie, please.'

Colin Turner said, 'Dr Harris! She'll help.'

Gently Peter told him, 'Bryn was dead when he hit the floor, Colin. It's too late.'

All Angie Turner could say was, 'Oh, Colin! Oh, Colin! Oh, Colin.'

Peter addressed the gathering. 'In the circumstances we'd better bring the meeting to a close. There's nothing anyone can do for now. Thank you for coming. Pray for Bryn before you sleep. It's a sad day. Goodnight. Goodnight. God bless you all.'

Bewildered and appalled, they all slowly departed, except for the key players in the drama. Angie was still saying 'Oh! Colin!' time and time again. She hadn't an ounce of fight left in her. Colin was rigid with distress. Willie had gone immediately Bryn had collapsed to alert Caroline, who had to push her way through the crowd that was leaving so sorrowfully.

'Give me some space.' Caroline knelt down, pulled back Peter's cassock, felt the pulse in Bryn's neck, which had been throbbing only moments before, placed her ear close to his mouth but could neither feel nor hear any breath whatsoever. She shook her head and looked up at Peter.

He whispered, 'He was dead before he fell.'

Colin groaned loudly, 'Oh, God!'

Caroline gently covered Bryn's body and stood up. Though not knowing the circumstances, she realised from his distress that Colin Turner must be involved. 'You weren't to know. There'll have to be a post-mortem; unexplained death, you know. Don't blame yourself.' She rubbed one of his powerful forearms in sympathy.

His eyes again filled with tears, his head shaking from

side to side in disbelief, Colin said, 'We tried, the Reverend and me. We did try.'

'I'm sure you did. Has anyone called an ambulance?' Peter nodded.

At this moment Georgie came in. They all made space for her. Caroline had straightened Bryn's limbs, closed his eyes and rested his forearms across his chest, so even before she saw that the whole of him was covered Georgie didn't need to ask. She drew back the cassock and stood gazing down at him. Without looking up she asked, 'I know you've a quick temper, Colin, did you hit him?'

'No.'

Peter expanded Colin's reply. 'No, Georgie, he didn't. Bryn couldn't find the answer he was searching for and suddenly he pulled at his collar and then dropped . . . dead. I'm so sorry.'

'You're sure he's dead?

Caroline answered, 'Yes, I am.'

'I shall want Beck and Beck from Culworth to bury him. They did my mother and were most considerate. Dicky, where's Dicky?'

Colin Turner said, 'I'm so sorry. So sorry. I never touched him. I never meant to.'

'Can't be helped. These things happen. Where's Dicky? I want Dicky.'

They'd heard the hall door open just after Georgie came in but hadn't noticed it was Dicky coming to look after her. He was standing alone at the back of the hall. 'I'm here, if you need me.'

'Dicky, ring Beck and Beck and tell them I want them. Straight away. I want him in their chapel of rest.'

Caroline interrupted her train of thought with a gentle

reminder. 'We'll have to wait for the ambulance. Sudden death, you know. There'll have to be a post-mortem.'

Georgie looked up at her, puzzled. 'Oh, of course. I didn't think. What do you reckon, Caroline? Heart attack?'

'Seems likely. But of course I can't say for sure.'

'At least he didn't know. Did he?'

'It was too sudden.'

'He'd have hated being ill. Not being all that brave. Dicky?'

Dicky went to stand beside her. He longed to hold her but knew instinctively it wouldn't be seemly. Georgie stood quite still, her arms held grimly to her sides.

'Would you like a chair, Georgie? Take the weight off your feet.'

The answer to Dicky's question was 'Go and close the bar. And the dining room. For tonight. Tell them why. Respect, you know.'

Dicky left without a word. So they stood there not knowing what to do next. None of them was heartbroken, except perhaps of them all it was Georgie who felt the worst. She'd left his face uncovered but no one had the courage to cover him up again. It seemed intrusive to take the initiative.

Peter asked, 'Has he family, besides you?'

'A couple of cousins. That's all. Distant. Card at Christmas, you know. There'll be no one to mourn. Except me.'

For long minutes they all stood silently apart, gazing fixedly at the dead face; despising themselves for thinking *there but for the Grace of God go I.*

Only the ambulance arriving spurred them into action.

Caroline went into a huddle with the ambulance crew, speaking softly out of respect for the dead and the bereaved. Peter began quietly praying. Grandmama and Colin and Angie stood mute, their eyes drawn, despite their resistance, to the ambulance men and the stretcher, and the blanket and the return of his cassock to Peter, the removal of the body.

Georgie, choked by the immediacy of Bryn's extinction, looked to Grandmama for help. A stalwart in adversity, Grandmama murmured gently, 'Come, my dear, I'll take you home.'

'Not to the . . .'

'No, no. To my home if you wish . . . you can have the same bedroom that you had before.'

'I thought of Dicky's . . .'

Firmly the reply came: 'No, my dear, that wouldn't be quite . . . right.'

'No, perhaps not.' Georgie allowed herself to be shepherded away.

Peter spoke to Colin and Angie. 'In no way at all were you to blame, Colin, remember. We were all witness to that.'

'Thank you, Reverend, thank you.'

'You're a star, Rector. A star. We're so sorry.' Angie dabbed her eyes with her tear-soaked tissue. 'We've got to go. Mum's sitting for us. She'll be cut up. She liked Bryn in the pub, you know.'

'So did we all. He'll be missed. Goodnight.'

'Goodnight.'

'Peter! Darling! Can we go home?'

Chapter 17

Dicky had gone straight back to the Royal Oak as Georgie had asked, but they already knew because some of the people who'd left when Peter had closed the meeting had gone straight to the bar for a stiffener and to spread the news. So when he walked back in, consternation was the order of the day.

Dicky was so stunned about Bryn dying that he hadn't given it a thought that his death freed Georgie to marry him. So when someone said with a nudge and a wink, 'Well, Dicky, he's played right into your hands,' he couldn't understand what they meant.

'Behave yourself,' someone else said angrily.

Dicky looked around, bewildered, his mind focused on closing up. 'Georgie, she's asked me to close early. In respect, you know. If you don't mind.'

There was a general mumble of agreement. A voice said, 'I propose a toast to Bryn. Raise your glasses! To Bryn, God rest his soul.'

'To Bryn!'

'To Bryn! The old dog!'

'To Bryn!'

Dicky didn't drink to him. Dicky wouldn't drink to him. Not on your life. The damned fellow couldn't possibly be dead. He'd be back, couldn't have had his life snuffed out as quickly as he had. Oh, no, he couldn't possibly have gone for ever. He'd be back if only to plague him. Dicky couldn't think what to do, so he went to find Bel.

She was taking an order for puddings in the dining room. Bel caught sight of him with his ashen face and stiff gait and her heart went out to him. She abandoned her customers and enveloped him in a bear hug. 'Don't worry! Don't worry!' She patted his back, smoothed his hair, held him close, whispered, 'He's gone now. Gone for good. He can't haunt you any more, love.' Out loud she said, 'I'm serving the puddings to this table and then I'll close up. You go and close the bar.'

Dicky found Jimbo clearing used glasses, urging the customers to leave, organising Alan and Trish. 'There you are, Dicky. It must have been a terrible shock. I came straight from the meeting; thought you might need a hand.'

'Oh, thanks.' Dicky had had one too many shocks of late, first Bryn coming back, then the incident of the cricket bat, then finding Bryn and Georgie in bed and now this. Dumbly he watched as Jimbo deftly rid the bar of its last customer, bolted the door, stacked the dishwasher with glasses, emptied the till, went to check the kitchen for Bel, carried the waste bin bag round emptying ashtrays, collecting empty nut packets, asking Trish to wipe out the ashtrays, did this, did that.

It slowly began to register in Dicky's overloaded mind that Bryn was out of the picture completely and absolutely. There'd be no more taunting from Bryn, no more heartache over him. He'd been blotted out. Georgie! How must she be feeling? He'd go and see. Fully expecting that she'd be back upstairs, he set off at a gallop to find her. But the rooms were empty. Abandoned almost. Deserted. Where was she? He ran all the way to the church hall to find Willie locking up. 'Where's Georgie?'

'I don't know, Dicky. Everyone's gone.'

'She can't have disappeared.'

Dicky, at a loss to know what to do, stood just inside the main door so Willie couldn't lock up. 'Is she at the Rectory do you think?'

Dicky looked at Willie. 'Do you think so?'

'Well, I don't know. Just a guess.'

'I see.' He couldn't face Peter, not tonight. No. Slowly Dicky wandered back to the Royal Oak, still badly in need of Georgie.

Jimbo was just saying goodnight to Bel. 'Mother's been on the phone, Dicky, in case you're wondering where Georgie is. She's sleeping at her cottage for tonight.'

Dicky turned tail and ran.

Bel said, 'He doesn't know whether he's coming or going. It's all been too much. And now this.'

Dicky hammered Grandmama's front door knocker. He pushed open the letter box and shouted through it, 'I need to speak to Georgie.'

The bolts on the door were pulled back and there was Grandmama beckoning him in.

'Where is she?'

'I'm just taking her a nightcap. You can take it up if you like, but don't stay long, she's exhausted. I want her to have a good night's sleep. Well, as good as she can get in the circumstances.'

Dicky started up the steep staircase.

Grandmama called after him, 'First door on the right.'

The door to her room stood open and Dicky could see her sitting up in bed in a voluminous white nightgown that certainly wasn't her own. The light from the bedside lamp drained all her colour; Georgie appeared to be white all over. He paused for a moment, thinking of what to say. Words didn't seem much good at present. 'I've brought you a nightcap. Don't know what it is.'

'Put it here.' Georgie moved the lamp a little to make room for the small tray.

'I don't know what to say.'

'Neither do I.'

Dicky laid a hand on the bed post and looked down at her, longing to give her a kiss. 'I'm here for you.'

'I know that.'

'It's not the time to be making promises.'

'No.'

'But I've been a fool.'

'No. You're the last of the great romantics, Dicky.'

'Am I?'

Georgie nodded. 'I've got to clear the old wood, so to speak, and then we can talk. I can't see beyond the next few days.'

'Neither can I.'

'Say goodnight, Dicky.'

'Goodnight.' He longed to hold her in his arms, feel her comfort, comfort her.

Georgie took hold of his hand and squeezed it. 'That's all for now. I've got to think. It's been so sudden. Whatever can have caused it? He seemed to be in good health. Never ailed a thing for years.'

'Heart gave out, I expect.' He held her hand in both

285

his. 'See you in the morning. Don't worry about the pub. Bel and I will keep things going. You can rely on us. Goodnight, love.'

Georgie picked up her drink and began to sip it as though he weren't even in the room. So Dicky left, numb with heartache.

He remained numb with heartache for what seemed like an age. They had to wait for the result of the post-mortem, yet keep the pub going as cheerfully as they could, order this, cancel that, pay wages, pay bills, this and that, that and this, all of it pointless or so it felt. The least that could be said for it was that it occupied his mind and, for a while, stopped him brooding. Dicky didn't dare talk about the future, nor the past come to that; in fact, he didn't dare talk about anything at all to anyone. Georgie stayed on at Grandmama's so they never got a chance to talk in depth. He couldn't, not with Grandmama's eagle eye on him. She didn't say it but he knew she was thinking that she wouldn't put up with any hanky panky under her roof. Not that he and Georgie ever got near it. There seemed to be something strange and alien keeping them from being close. Maybe it was the ghost of Bryn ever present between them. Perhaps after the funeral his ghost would go to rest.

Dicky was right. Bryn's funeral closed a chapter in his life, in all their lives and at last the way forward felt clear. As Georgie had said, the old wood had been done away with. Overnight Dicky got back his bouncy happiness and Georgie looked as though a huge weight had been lifted from her shoulders. She was more lively than she had been for a long time and regained a lot of her old sparkle. Two nights after the funeral Georgie moved back into the Royal Oak, and she and Bel and Dicky kept to the old routine: Bel sleeping at the pub and Dicky in number one Glebe Cottages.

There was plenty of nudging and winking going on behind the tinned soups in the Village Store as they had all fully expected that Dicky, now Georgie was a widow, would move in with her, but he didn't. Somehow Georgie wasn't ready for it, not yet. She'd explained to Dicky how she felt. 'I want to make a completely new start with you and I'm not quite ready yet. Bryn dying like he did, so suddenly, I didn't have time to get used to the idea and I haven't yet. I won't have you marrying half a person, because that's how I feel at the moment, only half a person.'

Dicky, being the romantic he was, could understand that and he didn't want half a person either.

'I've cleared his wardrobe and removed all his things from Liz and Neville's but I haven't quite got rid of *him*.'

Dicky, fearing his clothes might turn up at the Scout Jumble Sale, asked, 'Where have you taken his things?'

'To Oxfam. Where else?'

Dicky nodded. 'I see. It won't be long, though, will it? Before we marry?'

Georgie put her hands on his shoulders. 'No, it won't be long. But we'll have a very quiet wedding, very early in the morning, just us, and after we'll slip away for a few days' honeymoon. Then I shall have to get used to being Mrs Georgina Tutt.'

'Blessed day.'

'You see, if we marry too soon after Bryn, people will

287

think we were glad to see him go. Which I wasn't in a way, because he was doing everything we asked of him and you must admit he had changed a lot. He was much nicer to know, the divorce was going through and he was doing his best to make things right for you and me.'

'I admit he did seem to have discovered his heart.' Dicky grinned at her.

'He did discover it and all because of you. And he regretted so much that afternoon when, you know, we . . . he really was very cut up about how badly you felt about him and me . . .'

Dicky placed a finger on her lips to stop her going any further. He really couldn't take the wraps off that particular discovery, it still hurt. 'I don't want to hear about that. Let's put that behind us for ever, right now. There's only you and me to think about now, no one else.'

'You're right. Just you and me. But there is also Bel. Dicky, will she be all right, do you think, living back in Glebe Cottages on her own?'

Georgie saw a twinkle in Dicky's eyes. 'I've an idea she won't be living there on her own for very long.'

Surprised, Georgie asked, 'She won't?'

'Remember the chap called Trevor who used to deliver the bread and then got taken on in management? Well, Bel and he' – Dicky crossed two fingers – 'they're like that and I think there'll be wedding bells before long.'

Georgie was aghast. 'I'd no idea. She's kept that quiet. How's she going to fit in a husband as well as working at the Store, helping here and school caretaking? She'll never manage it.'

'No, I think you'll be looking for a new dining-room manager and the school a new caretaker.'

'Well I never. She never mentions him.'

'Made a mess of it first time round and it makes you cautious, doesn't it, I expect.'

'Give me a kiss.'

'What for?'

'For being such an understanding man.'

After the disastrous meeting about modernising the village no one had the heart to pursue the matter with the council, nor even to call another meeting, but Mr Fitch hadn't allowed the problem to disappear from his agenda. He knew the wheels of local government turned slowly but like an elephant they never forgot, and one day they would arrive with all the paraphernalia of modern city life on a couple of wagons, and he'd worried about it on and off ever since Bryn's sudden demise. Then all at once, in a flash of inspiration, he saw a part solution which might satisfy Miss Pascoe and also Angie Turner, and deter the council from going completely off the rails.

He set about the scheme the very next day. It involved, to begin with, getting Angie Turner on side. He debated whether or not to tackle our Kev too but decided he'd had enough backhanders recently and that he was getting far too greedy. No, he'd have to go direct, straight to the top with a generous plan, nothing to do with road safety at all on the face of it. But it would help the environment. After all, the main problem was the number of vehicles. Cut down on those and what possible reason could there be for large-scale capital investment in traffic control? Then he remembered Miss Pascoe. Drat the woman. She was a stumbling block and a half, and no mistake. He spent a distracted morning with the question of Miss Pascoe at the forefront of his mind. Then inspiration! Of course! Tactics.

So that lunchtime he arrived at the school and reorganised the supervisory duties so that Miss Pascoe was free to lunch with him at the Royal Oak. She brusquely refused alcohol of any kind as she was teaching in the afternoon, but she did listen to his plans. A complete refurbishing of the computer situation at the school, which he knew was dear to her heart, and also he, personally, would subsidise a reinstated minibus service to bring the children in from outlying villages and farms. 'One from the Little Derehams direction and the other from Penny Fawcett. How about that for an idea?'

'And the computers?'

'No more second-hand gear like that I gave you before. Up-to-the-minute technology. Cross my heart. Scanners, whatever you want.'

'All this is if I agree to the minibus idea?'

Mr Fitch had to smile. 'Well, fair's fair. This way everyone gets satisfaction.'

'You are a rogue. An absolute rogue. No minibus, no computers.' Her eyes twinkled, which took the sting out of her uncompromising statement.

'Something like that.' Mr Fitch grinned like a cheerful schoolboy caught out in a scam. 'Say yes!'

Miss Pascoe placed her knife and fork side by side, dabbed her lips with her napkin, then looked into those frosty light-blue eyes of his and said, 'I see nothing changes with you, you're always the same year in year out, nothing stops your scheming, evil mind from working overtime.'

'I take exception to that last remark. I'm only trying to do my best to help everyone. The village, the school, the children. Be fair.'

'If the staff agree, then yes. They feel just as strongly as I about the safety of the children, you know. They back me every step of the way.'

'Good! I've got to get the parents on my side. I'm sure they won't mind paying a small fixed sum to save them having to turn out twice every day to get the children to school and home again. That Angie Turner has a long walk, poor girl, having no car.'

'She's a firebrand, but nobody's fool. Been very upset by Bryn's death.'

'Haven't we all?'

Miss Pascoe looked at her watch. 'Got to get back.'

'No time for pudding?'

'Sorry. No. Must go. I think we can say yes to your diabolical scheme.'

He smiled to himself. 'I thought you would. I'm off to give Angie Turner a ride to school in my car.'

'Take her home too, it's only fair.'

Mr Fitch hesitated. 'You're a dragon, that's what you are. I'll be seeing you.'

'Thanks for lunch! An even bigger thank you for being so generous.'

'Not at all. My pleasure.'

Miss Pascoe got to her feet, picked up her bag and said mischievously, 'Just hope Angie's two-year-old twins haven't got sticky fingers.'

'Eh, what?'

Miss Pascoe laughed when she heard Mr Fitch groan as she left the dining room.

Jimbo stood tidying his souvenir display and thinking about poor Bryn. Such plans, cut down in a moment. Massive blood clot finding its way to his heart. Maybe he'd better start running again with Peter, but he'd begin slowly and build up. Jimbo recalled those early-morning winter runs, when the fields were covered with a light frost and the trees bathed in icy crystals, like a winter wonderland for fairies. He picked up one of the tins of sweets and studied the picture on the lid of the beck on the spare land and the little footbridge over it, and the huge beech trees in the background, and loved it. He smoothed his hand over a framed picture of the church with the words 'St Thomas à Becket, Turnham Malpas' on a small label attached to the mount. He chose a red pencil from the display and lovingly read the words on the side. 'All in such good taste,' Harriet had said with her tongue in her cheek, when she saw them for the first time. He chuckled. What would he do without her?

One of Vince Jones's doorstops caught his eye next and he stroked the decorative knob stuck to the end of it. He held it in his hand as though about to place it under a door when the thought struck him. Good grief! It was the third week in September! Third week! That rang bells. What on earth was it? He slapped his forehead with his open hand. Of course! My God! Bryn's tour. He checked the date on his watch. Four days and they'd be here.

But no one to meet them at Gatwick. No one to conduct the tour. 'Linda! Got to go. Won't be ten minutes. Hold the fort!'

'But the mothers will be in soon, I can't . . .'

She was too late. Jimbo had gone, running across the green as though the devil himself were in hot pursuit. He hammered on the back door of the pub. 'Georgie! Georgie!'

He heard the bolts being dragged back and the key being turned, and there in front of him stood Georgie still in her dressing gown. 'Sorry! Sorry! But I've just had a thought.'

Georgie stepped back to let him in. 'It'd better be good.'

Jimbo answered, 'Depends on how you look at it. Georgie, Bryn's tour, aren't they due in four days' time?'

Georgie looked at him as though he'd said the Martians were due any minute. 'Tour? Oh, good grief. Yes. You're right. They are. Never gave it a thought.'

'Paperwork. Was there any paperwork with his stuff at Neville's?'

Georgie tapped her head with her fingers. 'Can't think. If I find it what are we going to do? I can't conduct a tour.'

'I'll do it.'

'No, no, we'll have to cancel.'

'Too late. We've scarcely time to let the customers know, anyway. Meals, theatre tickets, no, it's easier to run the tour. The hotels will want paying in full, at such short notice, and they weren't cheap hotels, were they?'

'No. My God! They weren't. What are we to do?'

'First, find Bryn's paperwork, then we'll decide. Must fly, Linda's on her own.'

'Right.'

'When you've found his files give me a buzz.'

Jimbo fled back to the Store, his head whirling with ideas. If push came to shove he'd conduct the tour himself.

He would. Yes, he would. Could be fun. Give him a break.

Harriet, having delivered Fran to school, was already in the kitchens behind the Store making the icing for a wedding cake order. She turned to smile at him as she heard his footsteps. 'Where've you been, might I ask?'

Jimbo explained. Harriet listened open-mouthed. He concluded with, 'So I shall do the tour for him.'

'You will?'

'Yes. Can't be that difficult. Just need to read his files, get to grips with the itinerary, ring ahead and away you go.'

'Poor Bryn. Poor Bryn. He intended making his fortune with his tours. Probably would have done, too.' Harriet stood gazing out of the window on to the garden. 'Remember Stocks Day? Me saying I'd seen him? It was such a shock. Poor Bryn.'

'God rest his soul. He'd be delighted to know we were going ahead with it, though, wouldn't he?'

Harriet smiled. 'Yes, of course he would. Yes, that's the best thing to do. A kind of tribute to him, wouldn't it be?'

Jimbo nodded. 'Yes, he'd have liked the idea of that.' Jimbo dipped his finger into the icing. 'Yes, Bryn would be delighted.' He licked his finger clean. 'That's good.'